Award-winning Moroccan novelist and screenwriter **Youssef Fadel** was born in 1949 in Casablanca, where he lives today. During Morocco's Years of Lead he was imprisoned in the notorious Derb Moulay Chérif prison, from 1974 to 1975. *A Rare Blue Bird Flies with Me* is his ninth novel and part of his modern Morocco trilogy, along with *A Beautiful White Cat Walks with Me*.

Translator **Jonathan Smolin** is the author of the critically acclaimed *Moroccan Noir: Police, Crime, and Politics in Popular Culture* (2013). He lives in Hanover, NH.

A Rare Blue Bird Flies with Me

Youssef Fadel

Translated by
Jonathan Smolin

hoopoe

AN IMPRINT OF AUC PRESS

This paperback edition published in 2016 by
Hoopoe
113 Sharia Kasr el Aini, Cairo, Egypt
420 Fifth Avenue, New York, NY 10018
www.hoopoefiction.com

Hoopoe is an imprint of the American University in Cairo Press
www.aucpress.com

Exclusive distribution outside Egypt and North America by I.B.Tauris & Co Ltd.,
6 Salem Road, London, W4 2BU

Dar el Kutub No. 14340/15
ISBN 9789 77 416 754 6

Dar el Kutub Cataloging-in-Publication Data

Fadel, Youssef
        A Rare Blue Bird Flies with Me: A Novel / Youssef Fadel.—Cairo: The
    American University in Cairo Press, 2016.
        p.   cm.
        ISBN 978 977 416 754 6
        1. English fiction
        823

1 2 3 4 5   20 19 18 17 16

Designed by Adam el-Sehemy
Printed in the United States of America

To the martyrs of the extermination prison camps in Tazmamart, Agdz, Kalaat M'Gouna, Skoura, Moulay Chérif, Kourbis, the Complex, and Dar Moqri; those among them who are living and those who are dead.

Foreword

ON THE MORNING OF 10 July 1971, General Mohamed Medbouh and Lieutenant-Colonel M'hamed Ababou led a convey
of army cadets into the Skhirat Palace, located on the Atlan-
tic coast some twenty-five kilometers south of the Moroccan
capital Rabat. It was King Hassan II's forty-second birthday
and he was hosting hundreds of dignitaries, both Moroccan
and foreign, to celebrate. According to memoirs published
years later, the cadets began that day thinking that they were
participating in military exercises with live ammunition. As
they approached the palace, Medbouh and Ababou told the
cadets that the king's life was in danger and that they had
to shoot to kill in order to save the monarch. Following the
orders of their superiors, the soldiers entered the palace and
fired immediately, killing dozens in the ensuing chaos. According to the memoirs published later, the soldiers had no idea
that they were participating in a coup. Despite the high death
toll, Hassan II survived the attack and outmaneuvered Medbouh and Ababou, both of whom were killed during the coup
attempt. A number of captured soldiers were executed on live
television and hundreds of cadets were arrested and tortured.
After a farcical mass trial, seventy-four were given sentences
ranging from less than two years to life in prison.

Barely a year later, on 16 August 1972, pilots from the
Moroccan air force attacked Hassan II's Boeing as he was
returning to Rabat from a vacation in Europe. Even though

the royal plane was shot multiple times, its captain miraculously navigated through the attack and managed to land safely at the Rabat airport. Once on the ground, Hassan II gained the upper hand. The suspected mastermind of the second coup, General Mohamed Oufkir, reportedly committed suicide after meeting with the king later that day. Pilots and others suspected of participating in the coup were arrested, tortured, and put on trial. While most were acquitted or given light sentences, eleven were executed and five were sentenced to between ten and twenty years in jail.

The convicted soldiers from both coups were initially jailed in the Kénitra civil prison. But at 2 a.m. on 7 August 1973, fifty-eight of these men were blindfolded and put on an airplane. They believed that they were going to be thrown from the plane to their deaths, but instead, they were taken to Tazmamart, a prison built especially to house them. Today, Tazmamart is seen as the most infamous prison in the Arab world, a word synonymous with unimaginable suffering.

Located in southeast Morocco near the desert town Errachidia, not far from the Algerian border, Tazmamart consisted of two buildings, each with a central corridor around which twenty-nine cells were located. Each prisoner was kept in solitary confinement in a three by two and a half meter cell with a hole for a toilet and a cement slab as a bed. Because the prisoners only had the clothes they arrived in and two old blankets, they were almost defenseless against the freezing nights and blazing hot days of the desert, not to mention the scorpions, rats, and other vermin. Since the only light that entered the cells came from small cracks in the ceiling and doors, prisoners lived alone in near total darkness, almost never leaving their cells.

Fifty-eight soldiers entered Tazmamart and when they were released eighteen years later, only twenty-eight had survived the inhuman conditions. Tazmamart was a secret prison and the Moroccan public would not learn the full details of the suffering that took place there until the late 1990s. Nonetheless, for those who had heard of it in the 1970s and 1980s, the mention of the word Tazmamart provoked terror and the prison today symbolizes the cruelest excesses of authoritarian rule.

The soldiers at Tazmamart were not the only political prisoners in Morocco during the 1970s and 1980s. These decades, known in Morocco as the Years of Lead, were a period of widespread and flagrant human rights violations. Freedom of expression was stifled and fear spread through the country. Farcical mass trials and disappearances became the norm. During this time, thousands of student activists were arrested, tortured, and detained in notorious centers such as Derb Moulay Chérif. Youssef Fadel, author of *A Rare Blue Bird Flies with Me*, was among the young men and women who were held there during the 1970s.

Some political prisoners, however, were detained in locations that remained secret for years. Students Mohamed Nadrani, Abderrahman Kounsi, and Mohamed Errahoui, along with several of their peers, were abducted in Rabat on 12 to 13 April 1976 and accused of undermining state security. After nearly a year and a half of preliminary detention and intermittent torture, they were transferred to Agdz, a town in southeastern Morocco, without a trial. Instead of a prison, however, Nadrani and his fellow detainees were held for nine years in the old casbah of Pasha Thami El Glaoui and other sites in the region. Years later, when news spread that the Glaoui casbah had been used to hold political prisoners, the residents of Agdz were shocked and appalled.

Despite the horrors of the Years of Lead, political conditions began to improve in Morocco during the 1990s. With the arrival of the Alternance government, led by former political prisoner Abderrahmane Youssoufi, in February 1998, memoirs from political prisoners who had been tortured and detained during the Years of Lead began to emerge. While several daring novels and accounts had appeared earlier, they were confiscated and banned. Starting in 1998, however, dozens of memoirs, written in both Arabic and French, emerged, breaking the silence about the abuses of the Years of Lead.

Among these works were a number of high profile memoirs by prisoners who had survived Tazmamart, such as Ahmed Marzouki and Mohammed Raïss. Former detainees at torture centers like Derb Moulay Chérif published dozens of accounts and novels, testifying to their years of abuse. Mohamed Nadrani, Abderrahman Kounsi, and Mohammed Errahoui also published memoirs about their experiences of torture and imprisonment in the Glaoui casbah in Agdz.

Testimonies from the Years of Lead did not only appear in book form; a number of television documentaries and celebrated films were made about the period, some of them adaptations from, by then, well-known memoirs. And in late 2004, the sessions of the Equity and Reconciliation Commission, which focused on the abuse of citizens by state authorities between 1956 and 1999, were broadcast live on radio and television. While there is much to criticize about the lack of prosecutorial jurisdiction of the Commission and the interdiction on those testifying from naming torturers, it was an important step forward in the history of human rights in Morocco. For the first time, citizens spoke on live television about their abuses during the Years of Lead. Moreover, these sessions were conducted mostly in colloquial Arabic and not Modern Standard Arabic or French, the languages of the elite, ensuring that they reached a wide audience.

Youssef Fadel's *A Rare Blue Bird Flies with Me* should be read as part of this collective experience of human rights abuses, testimony, and reconciliation in Morocco. The novel, which was shortlisted for the International Prize for Arabic Fiction (also known as the Arabic Booker) in 2013, is the second part of Fadel's trilogy that explores Moroccan history and culture during the 1970s and 1980s. Like the dozens of memoirs about Tazmamart, Derb Moulay Chérif, Agdz, and other sites of torture and disappearance, *A Rare Blue Bird Flies with Me* recounts the incredible suffering endured. Unlike other works about the period, however, Fadel does not focus on a single real-world site of torture or the experience of one individual. Instead, he breaks new ground by weaving together details from dozens of accounts into a single novel. While traces of the real-life suffering at Tazmamart and Pasha Glaoui's casbah can be read on nearly every page, Youssef Fadel has transformed the Moroccan prison memoir into something entirely new. He has created a narrative that reflects the collective consciousness of the country during the Years of Lead. Even though Tazmamart has since been razed by state authorities and Pasha Glaoui's casbah in Agdz is closed to the public, works like *A Rare Blue Bird Flies with Me* ensure that Morocco's experience of torture, abuse, and political imprisonment during the Years of Lead cannot be forgotten.

Jonathan Smolin

1

Zina
Monday, 21 May 1990, 8 p.m.

1

A MAN I DON'T KNOW is standing in front of the bar. He acts as if he wants to tell me something, but I ignore him. I prefer to ignore what goes on in men's minds. As I approach he seems about to open his mouth, but he stops when I move away again. I avoid getting too close so I don't have to hear what he wants to say. I pass him from behind the counter, and whenever I open a bottle for a customer, I try not to get too near to him. Or to stay far enough away so I can't hear him. I look at the watch on my wrist. It's eight o'clock. I open a bottle and put it in front of another customer, though he hasn't asked for it.

But this won't change the words in the man's mouth into water. Or make his ravenous stares less insistent or decrease my caution. Finally, as I pass, the man I don't know leans on the counter, toying with his glass, and over the commotion of the bar, the loud music, and the noise of the pinball machine, he asks me whether I like flowers. I don't respond. I try to steer clear of problems. I've got enough problems of my own. I've learned how to hide my thoughts from people, to keep things to myself. For a day when the weather's clear. And besides, I don't know if I like flowers or not.

I move away again, uninterested in him and his question. I'm not someone who likes starting conversations for no reason. Customers are busy with their drinks and talking about the drought. His question doesn't interest anyone. No

1

one cares about flowers in a season without rain. Though it's May, the man is wearing a thick djellaba striped black and tan. It's as if he's sprouted up here in the middle of the bar at the wrong time and place. He's wearing black sunglasses that don't hide the traces of smallpox dug into his face. He follows my movements with his gaze and waits for me to come close so he can start talking again, but I don't pass in front of him. He plays with his glass, waiting for me to go by. I count the words he might say. It might be only four words, like the last time: "Do you like flowers?" It seems he isn't waiting for me to respond. He came to speak, not to listen. That's what I read in the movement of his fingers playing with his glass of water. And in the faint smile emerging on his lips.

Then I pass him. I hear: "There's a flower festival in the south this time every year. Single women go there to get married."

It takes me longer to pass this time, because I listen to all these words. As if the game's started to entice me. Will I go by a third or fourth or fifth time to listen to more of the man's prattle? I'm not single and I don't care if there's a time every year for single women to get married. I'm interested in the man's words like I'm interested in the drunken chatter every night in every bar. There's a gravedigger who only likes talking about the number of dead people he buried that day. And there's a carpenter who dreams every night of a wardrobe he escapes with, disappearing into the forests where the wood he uses comes from. When you stand behind the counter at Stork Bar, you're ready for every kind of chatter that pounds on the door of your head. My sister Khatima, on the other side of the counter in front of the register, talks and raises her hands, chuckling, not caring what this or that customer might say. She doesn't put a red rose in her hair like Madame Janeau, the former owner of the bar, but she gives customers a free drink or two from time to time. Maybe Madame Janeau used to get her flowers from the festival the man was talking about. I'm not like my sister. I'm wary of everyone who's interested in me in any way.

I approach him when I see him take a piece of paper out of his pocket and put it on the counter. I look at the paper and see it doesn't indicate anything. This time the man starts looking around like he's going to say something illicit. He looks like he wouldn't know how to laugh. I put a bottle in front of him. He looks around again and says, "Am I drinking it on your tab or are you drinking it on mine?"

Neither. Men like women who drink with them but I don't drink. My sister Khatima doesn't drink either.

I see now he's laughing. As if he's reading my mind. He has glimmering gold teeth, which make his presence here stranger. I see the piece of paper's still there. I open the bottle, but before I move away I hear him say: "At the top of the mountain overlooking the village that welcomes loud wedding parties, there's a casbah where widows and married women who lost their husbands in the coups go."

I remember an old dream. A memory lights up my mind. I understand. Before he whispers in my ear, I understand. All of a sudden, I'm disturbed. All of a sudden, I take the letter. All of a sudden, I turn to my sister Khatima at the other side of the bar. All of a sudden, the man whispers again in my ear: "You've got just enough time to catch the nine o'clock bus from Fez."

A man of around fifty who hasn't come here before. He doesn't stand at the bar longer than the time it takes for his compressed words to ignite inside me. He keeps standing, looking at me. As if he's waiting for me to jump over the bar to catch the nine o'clock bus. I disappear into the kitchen and open the letter. I know Aziz's handwriting. What am I going to do with his letter? Should I toss it in my mouth as if it's a seed of idle talk and chase it down with some water? I look at my watch.

I thought I'd forgotten. I was broken. I understood. I calmed down. I forgot. I thought the idea of looking for him again had died out, disappeared, and was extinguished.

I haven't left Stork Bar and the house above it for four years. Since Madame Janeau died and left the bar to my sister

Khatima. My sister took care of her more than Madame Janeau's family, which used to come every six months from France to see if the old lady had died yet. But instead of leaving the bar and the apartment on top to them, the old lady gave everything she had to Khatima, who took care of her and buried her in the grave they bought together in her final days. We threw ourselves into the harsh work that running the bar requires. And its daily problems with drunks, cops, secret police, and soldiers. From seven in the morning until the middle of the night.

How time has passed! All these years. And the idea of finding him hasn't left my head. The idea is still as fresh and insistent as it was when I began my long search for Aziz. I always thought he hadn't died, that the earth hadn't swallowed him up, that I'd find him one day. I began my search for him at sixteen. I'm now thirty-four and I'll keep at it until I'm sixty or seventy or older. I'll find him in the end. I love to imagine myself victorious one day. This feeling fills me with great happiness. I once went all the way to the Maamoura woods after a phone call from a man who said he knew where Aziz was. All I got was a fleecing to add to all the previous ones. I wasn't weak and I didn't despair. The false news gives time meaning. It keeps the flame burning. The false news spares the flame of memory, burning like the torch bearing it, and moves forward. I didn't hesitate for a moment before the Maamoura news, just as I don't hesitate now. I've got just enough time to catch the nine o'clock bus from Fez, as the man said. I go back to the counter without deciding whether I'll tell my sister Khatima or not. I don't have a good reason to tell her, or not tell her. I didn't tell her the previous times. Meanwhile, the man's left the bar without drinking his bottle.

2

At the station, the nine o'clock bus from Fez hasn't arrived. There are few travelers. They don't look like they're heading to a flower festival or a marriage festival. Three men are smoking and four women in ornate clothes sit on top of packs. There are some carts with thick sacks on them and dogs sleeping below. The ticket window is closed. One of the three men says it's been closed for years and points to a man standing under an electrical pole. The moment I see him, the man throws his djellaba hood over his head and turns his back to me. I think he's the same man, even if he's selling tickets. Black sunglasses, a pockmarked face, and the same black-and-tan-striped djellaba.

I approach him, and all of a sudden he takes out a ticket and hands it to me. Like any ticket seller, as though he wasn't just at Stork Bar. I look closely at him so he can recognize me. He seems confused when I tell him I just saw him at Stork Bar. My words annoy him. Yes, he was getting drunk, he says, but at another bar, and he begs me not to tell his boss so he doesn't get fired. There isn't the slightest hint of joking in his voice, even though the situation is almost a joke. Continuing to talk about it won't lead anywhere. So I ask him about the bus, when it'll come. He regains his confidence and energy and says: "It'll arrive at nine." I look at my watch. It's nine fifteen.

"The bus from Fez arrives at the station at nine," he says.

"Yes, it usually arrives at nine, but now, when'll it arrive now?"

"Nine, as always."

"But it's late."

"How's it late? It always comes on time."

"But it's past the scheduled time."

"What scheduled time? It's never past the scheduled time."

There's no way to come to an understanding with the ticket seller. There aren't a lot of travelers at the station, as I said. I ask one of them: "Has the nine o'clock bus come?" Just to be sure. I try to calm down. I sit on the curb and close my eyes to collect my thoughts and see more clearly. Did the news make me happy? Before, my heart would beat violently and my nerves would get upset whenever I heard news about Aziz. Simply imagining I'm getting news about him being somewhere, even if it's somewhere that doesn't exist at all, as happened a number of times. Just the idea would make me uncomfortable, whether I'm sitting or standing. My blood would pump wildly through my veins. As if it had lost its mind. Now, though, I have the feeling that my anxiety has subsided. That my previous energy has begun to dissipate. It's as if I'm sorry for Aziz. I was expecting a bigger flare-up in myself. Why didn't I take the news as I expected? It came to me just like that, in passing, without an effect, without a trace. Maybe it's the last four years I spent drowning in work, imprisoned in Stork Bar. Four years without a single piece of false news.

2

Aziz

10 p.m.

1

TIME PASSED WHILE I WAS having a lot of fun watching life in the corridor. When I was in good health, I could move to the door. Life's moving from side to side a few steps from me. Cockroaches play. They move behind each other like a drunken train. Their long wings move in every direction like finely made radars. Near them are scorpions with tails erect, waiting to ambush them. The cockroaches dance around them, indifferent to their threatening weapons. Rats surprise them and they flee. Some are saved in the cracks while others spread their wings to land on the highest point on the wall. The rats that think they're playing, they too attack them, pouncing on them, biting, sinking their teeth into the flesh of some, producing horrible noises, and eating others. Then the snakes appear, so the rats surviving the massacre are now forced to flee. After a while, you don't know who's running after who. Who's hunting who and who's eating who. A whole life near the cracks in the door.

I don't care about snakes. They've got plenty of provisions in the corridor. More than they need. It's the scorpions that concern me. Their poison, to be exact. They're peaceful creatures. I used to play with scorpions on my uncle's farm. They didn't sting me. I'd spread my palm out to them and let them crawl on it however they wanted. When a scorpion stung my uncle, I saw him make a wound at the site of the sting and let his blood flow. Scorpions sting when forced. The scorpion doesn't know my intentions, but

7

I have a clear plan. My idea is to surrender a finger to it, to spare myself from future stings and the stings of everything like it. If a scorpion stings you once you become immune to its poison. That's my intention. I won't waste my blood like my uncle. There's no blood left in me to shed. Forty-eight hours of delirium, then a week in bed. When I get up, my body will be immune to scorpion poison. And snake poison. And all poisons. My plan's clear to me. But the scorpion doesn't have the same idea.

There's a gap at the bottom of the door. Between the door and the ground, where dishes and a pitcher of water are pushed in. The scorpion peers out through the gap now, raising its tail and waiting for I don't know what. Then it moves, holding onto the wall, like something fleeing a trap, and stops. It looks at me and I look at it. It doesn't make any movement to betray ill will or a desire to cause me pain. I reach my palm out so it can stretch out on it, as I used to do in the countryside when I was a child. It skirts my palm with cunning generosity, avoiding me entirely. It doesn't pay me the least bit of attention. I can't say: Come here, scorpion, dig your stinger into my flesh so I can save myself from your coming poison. It has to understand this on its own without me explaining it. But it didn't do that before, when we were young, so why would it change its behavior now? It lowers its tail and begins climbing the wall.

I look at the scorpion on the wall. I know the hilarious conclusion to this expedition. It'll go up until it thinks it's reached the ceiling and then fall, because it's not a cockroach or a bat. What's the connection between scorpions and walls? I like the echo its fall makes. *Baf!* I then see it frozen in its spot, and it looks at me as if it's ashamed. That's another pleasure. It gathers itself, trying to guess what's going on in my head. I think that maybe it's finally understood my idea and it'll move to my palm. The scorpion keeps watching me. Instead of moving forward, it starts climbing again. When I hear the sound of it hitting the ground a second time, I let out a loud chuckle so it can hear me clearly. So it knows I don't need its poison. I hope its back is broken or its tail is smashed. I hope from my heart something horrible that happens to scorpions happens to this one. Its poison is enough for me.

My health is as good as could be, but my head doesn't have hair any more. Its surface is dug out like a pen where hungry pigs play.

2

The scorpion didn't sting my palm, as I'd hoped. As I was returning from my hopeless anticipations a rat bit a toe on my right foot.

Before the rat bite, I was passing time: enumerating the advance of time in different ways. These are some of the stages I passed through.

The first stage I imagine might have lasted for eight years. When it was difficult for me to remember the number of years I spent in this kitchen, when I lost count of how many, I found myself using a map to follow the escape of time. It became clear to me that time is a single expanse without day or night. Since that realization, my idea changed away from a sun rising or a day beginning or a night falling. All this is only present in the mind of human beings. Do you know when something begins and when it ends? Can you determine when something has ended and something else has taken its place? I understood that what human beings think about everything in existence is wrong. Nothing begins and nothing ends. Day doesn't follow night. And night doesn't follow day. Both exist at the same time as you embark on each consecutively. They're intertwined behind you, if it's night. Then raise your eyes a little, raise your eyes just enough so you can distinguish the rays of the day filtering between the cracks of the wall. It's not completely daytime. Maybe a sign indicates daytime is present somewhere. And memory is what you see before you.

The matter is simpler in this kitchen. A thick multilevel gloom, extending from darkness to darkness. There's no dawn for me, and no noon or late afternoon. A long line of nights of varying blackness. When I thought about it like this, I made a dawn and a dusk for myself, so after a while I could say this is the last bit of the day's light. My daytime. This is the beginning of nighttime light, my nighttime. I discovered that my days and nights in this respect have become full of all kinds of entertaining adventures. My new way of grasping time seems complicated and charged to me.

The second phase, when my activities were varied, might have lasted the same number of years. I spent part of it interpreting my dreams. I see myself in the bedroom with my mouth full of hair and I spend a long time trying to crack this riddle as if I were pulling apart a ball of tangled hair. There's another way to spend time: Counting the raindrops falling incessantly from the ceiling. They fall on my head even after the rain has stopped. There are days when I reach dizzying numbers, hundreds of thousands. When I think I've reached a state of delirium, I replace the number of raindrops with the total. Calculating for the purpose of calculating, without needing the raindrops. It takes about half an hour to count from zero to a thousand. I'd make a mistake deliberately so I'd have to count again from the beginning. Then I trace the number on my palm so I remember it. This is another link I use to bind time so it doesn't escape.

Then prayer. Not because of faith. Since I'm in this hole, I think I don't owe God anything. Why pray? Am I thanking Him? For what? Does the blind man thank the one who gouged out his eyes? Even if he does, I don't have the strength to fathom this kind of behavior. I pray as a kind of exercise in this narrow kitchen.

As for the rat bite, hunger is the reason. I'd given up thinking about eating a long time ago. Just as the rats and other annoying animals gave up hope of discovering a piece of stale bread among the heaps of my accumulated filth. Until the moment when I felt the rat gnawing on my toe. It started like that: With some idea in the rat's head about a piece of bread. Then the idea turned into a real rat bite. Before the rat bite, I'd been passing time in a number of inventive ways, as I said. But now I spend time counting the pulsating beats of my foot as it swells up. *Tak tak. Tak tak. Tak tak. Tak.* Three and a half beats during the night. A stench of rot rises up with the swelling. The stench doesn't spread all at once. Little by little. Followed by violent shaking in my foot and sharp stinging. A disconnected pain, but without the stench at first and then, little by little, with the stench as it starts rising from the toe that looks like a festering wound.

"What's this stench?" asks the cook from behind the door. I don't respond. I don't tell him it's me. The stench of my big toe that the rat bit because of stale bread he thought I was hiding from him. Then I don't smell any stench. I don't see the toe because my foot, which has swollen up too, is blocking it out. It's blown up completely and turned blue. A shining spot has appeared on the skin. It's hot to the touch. As if something's cooking inside it.

Since the stench began spreading in this disgraceful way, not a day has passed without me thinking about death because there isn't anything else for me to think about. I've gone through everything else. This is something new: I spend time thinking about death. My death in particular. And then death in general. About the disintegration of the body, its decomposition, and all the stenches it gives off during its life. These stenches erupt all at once, dragging an earthquake behind them. I don't see the cook's face. I hear his mumbling and his disgust. Sometimes his raving. Is he the same cook? Sometimes he pretends like there are many of them. Sometimes like he's the only cook. There's no way to know for sure.

Here's another idea: Does anything remain from the body after death except the stench?

Tak tak. Tak tak. Tak tak. Tak tak. Tak tak. Ta. Five and a quarter pulsating beats during the night.

Am I okay? I now have this new way to classify time. I wonder if I'm okay. I measure the stench of my inflamed toe, the stench of my pain, beat by beat. The lack of oxygen has begun to affect my nerves. I'm touching death. I'm moving alongside it. Hunger, bitter cold, germs, poisonous animals of all kinds. Disease in my leg, rising up. Death maturing. Pain throbbing with life. The body resisting. As if it lives upside down.

I cross the only possible path I have: From the door to the right corner. I limp. The line of life. My leg hurts. Or is it my thigh? I sit. I raise my thigh in the air to let the pain get its balance. Then I raise it up high so the pain will ease a little. My limbs fascinate me, so I raise my hand. I extend and raise my thighs together so I can see the difference. I repeat the motion seven times, but I count only three. I play with my hand a little. I raise my knee and press on my ankle. I know it's my knee and I say it's my ankle as I play with it in the air. Other than that, I don't know it. Daylight doesn't come into my kitchen. I listen to my body. I listen to its light beating. I seize the slightest vibration in it. I observe its continuous change. I don't smell the stench. It's mixed with other stenches anyway. The stenches of ten years. The cook smells it because he's on the other side of life.

The cook's the one who pointed out my raving when, from behind the door, he asked who I was talking to. I told him maybe I was talking in my sleep.

"No, two people were talking and making noise as they were moving around."

"Cook, maybe I was raving."

"No, two separate voices. The voices of two different people. The steps of two different people."

"What were we talking about, me and the person you think was visiting me, cook?"

His response doesn't clear up the mystery. He only insists someone else was visiting me at night to share the kitchen with me. I then hear what sounds like rattling. Rattling of anger? Or is the cook crying? I limp over to the door cracks and extend my neck. I can't see his face. A tear falls on the ground. Yes. He's crying. It's incredible. This hasn't happened in all the long years I've spent here, and they are many.

3

Baba Ali
10:15 p.m.

WE'RE PLAYING CHECKERS, BENGHAZI AND me, although my mind is busy and my ears are focused on the outside. We're playing in one of the two rooms on the other side of the casbah. It's an old casbah of Pasha Glaoui, or some other pasha, with a number of wings, like a small city. Every wing has its own courtyard, rooms, and kitchens. The commander lives in the wing where the pasha used to live. He's a soldier and doesn't like to appear without his military clothes. Benghazi and I occupy the slaves' wing. There are a lot of ruined rooms crammed into it, some of them on top of each other. If you see it from above, it looks like a well. Our two rooms are at the bottom. Two old and ravaged rooms where we eat, where we sleep and play checkers, Benghazi and me. We're not friends. Even though he tells me: You're my friend and my brother. His words are sometimes unintelligible, like he never learned to speak. His sentences are incomplete, and even when he finishes them they're meaningless. He says he speaks like this because he didn't go to school. I say that's not a reason. I'm also not educated but my speech is clear and understandable. That's why I don't trust him. That and other reasons. He'll come to a bad end in any case. He's a big gambler. He borrows money from everyone to bet on horses and dogs and to play the lottery. He borrows to pay back a debt and he doesn't pay it back. This won't end well. The people he owes money knock on his door and his wife has to tell them he's traveling. And on top of this, he's a salesman. He tells the commander everything that happens in the casbah, even though nothing happens. The commander barely leaves his office. He tells him what isn't happening so he can stay with him in his office. The commander listens to him because they're both from the same village.

We play checkers but my mind's busy with the sounds coming from outside. From time to time I hear what sounds like crying.

I turn to Benghazi: "You don't hear anything, Benghazi?"

Benghazi's absent. He's busy too. He has a black-and-white checker in his hand and instead of playing it, he tosses it in the air, catches it, and says if it's white side up, it'll be a boy. If it's black, it'll be a girl. The commander's dog, Hinda, comes in.

Benghazi calls the commander uncle to endear himself to him. Benghazi loves to be submissive and meek. The crying continues outside. I ask Benghazi if he hears it.

"You don't hear anything, Benghazi? Like someone crying?"

I listen closely again. But the crying has stopped. It's as if Benghazi hasn't heard what I said. He's busy with the checker he thinks will indicate the baby's sex. Instead of putting it on the board so we can keep playing, he tosses it in the air. The lamplight around the table dances back and forth. The features of Benghazi's face are also dancing. Busy with his wife, who's about to go into labor at home. He puts his hand on the dog's back, as if he's remembering his wife. And his son who hasn't arrived yet. The dog moves away. She flees from his hand, which was about to touch her back. She runs out.

This time, Benghazi looks at the checker, eying his future in its two colors. He puts it on the board.

"Benghazi, you don't hear someone crying?"

"Where?"

"In the courtyard."

"That Rifi, as they call him, who . . ."

"The crying's coming from the courtyard. The Rifi died last week."

"Or Aziz. Even he's got two cries left."

"It's coming from the courtyard, Benghazi."

"Or the owl."

What's the man saying? Owls don't cry.

"They sound like they're crying."

"Someone's crying, Benghazi. And it's not an owl."

We play for a while. The light dances between us. The face of Sergeant Benghazi dances. I wait for the sound to return. His features are dancing. I see some of them. I wait for the sound to come back to see if it was an owl, as Benghazi said. Or something else. The sergeant starts laughing, in an unexpected way. His face, half lit up, keeps laughing. I tell him to play as he laughs. I'm talking to the dark half of his face while the other half keeps chuckling. The dog comes in and sits down, looking at him. Benghazi laughs to disturb the game. I know him and his tricks. He keeps laughing to confuse me. In the end, he says: "I beat you." I tell Benghazi: "This time, whether you beat me or not, this time you're the one who's going to check out the prisoner, not me."

He doesn't hear me. We play for a few more minutes.

"You know my wife's about to . . ."

"Play."

"Tonight, I told myself. My wife's going to give birth. Today or tomorrow."

"Play, Benghazi. You're not going to confuse me.

We play for some time. I tell him he won't trick me by talking about his wife and he laughs again. "What's wrong with you, Benghazi?"

"I beat you."

I leave the room. Where's the sound coming from? From the kitchens? The courtyard? Behind the palm trees in the courtyard? The well to the south of the casbah? A big wing extends south of the casbah. The pasha's kitchens. The dog follows me. She doesn't like Sergeant Benghazi either. I don't hear a sound from the kitchens. Or from anywhere else. I say: *In the name of God the Merciful and the Compassionate*, and step forward. I don't like crossing the courtyard at night. It's full of the dead. I don't like the night here. I like the day. During the day, I see the sky. And the palm trees. I'm calm. But at night? You don't know what you're treading on. There isn't a spot you can put your feet without there being a dead body underneath. Or dead bodies. We've been burying them for twenty years. One on top of another. Dead on top of dead. For twenty years or more. No one knows how many. Because we don't bury them as they bury the dead in cemeteries. We toss them on top of each other. You can't be sure about this kind of dead. They can leave their holes at any moment. *Tfu!* May God curse them at night. This dog's following me. She slips between my thighs, almost throwing me on the ground. She's scared too. She also knows the dead leave their holes at night. They leave from every place, since they're everywhere. Under every palm tree. In every hole and in every crack. Without graves, as in the rest of the world.

I stand in the middle of the courtyard. As if someone put his hand on my shoulder, I stop. Something like a high-voltage current travels through my body. *I take refuge in God from Evil Satan.* I stop. The damned dog jumps back and forth and circles me. I don't know if she feels what I'm feeling. Did some of the current lighting up my blood and making the hair on my head stand on end hit her too? I try to grab her but she flees. If I'd grabbed hold of her, I'd feel safer. Me and the dog, it'd be two of us. But she took off. I kicked at her to make myself feel better, but only hit air. I left Sergeant Benghazi smoking his hash pipe and blowing smoke on his dreams. And here I am in the courtyard, kicking the darkness. Even the dog's disappeared. I turn in a circle and say: *I take refuge in God from Evil Satan*, and I step toward the kitchens.

This time, it's as if the ghost passes in front of me. The ghost's shadow passes before me. I stop again. It does the same thing and it stops too. What I see I don't see. I mean, I can't grasp its details. As if I see only its shadow. Something's shadow. The shadow of a body not of this world. The shadow of a person who died but didn't die completely. There remained of him the essential. The important. The hair on my head stands up. The blood freezes in my veins. Every thought disappears from my head. Should I run toward the kitchens or go back to the room? The kitchens are safer and closer. My legs abandon me at that moment. They refuse to move from their spot. Should I ask for forgiveness from the dead man? Even if I don't know if I was the one who buried him. Should I ask forgiveness from them all? The ones I tossed into their holes as well as those I didn't? For twenty years. Benghazi and me. Benghazi in the room, lighting up hash pipe after hash pipe. The dead don't scare Benghazi. He's not interested in anyone's forgiveness. And the noise that sounds like crying? Is it the crying of the shadow? Do shadows cry? Am I crying? Tears swell in the corners of my eyes. Instead of crying, I call the dog. Hinda? Hinda?

My tongue's heavy. I don't know how the sound came out. Did I really call out as you would call to a dog? I don't think so. I didn't hear my voice clearly enough to say the call was convincing. And the dog doesn't come. Hinda! Hinda! I'm not hoping she comes. I'm thinking about the shadow. My voice might scare it and it might disappear. I keep shouting as I run toward the building. Hinda! Hinda! As I run.

Aziz is still on the bench, just as I left him. The bench is a cement slab that in the past was a basin for washing dishes and utensils before the kitchen was turned into a cell, before the casbah kitchens were all turned into cells. The door is narrow. There are lots of cracks in it. I look at the prisoner through them. He looks more emaciated than before but he isn't crying. It's as if he's shrunk a bit. He's less than what he was yesterday. A child not yet ten years old. He was bigger yesterday. He was moving. Spread out on the bench, his body was moving. Today he's shrunk even more. And his movements

17

have disappeared. The little energy and the good intentions his body showed yesterday have disappeared. His eyes are open. But they're frozen. Like the eyes of the dead. Should I go in and touch his hand to see if he still has a pulse? For twenty years, it's been enough for us to look at him through the cracks. And at the others when they were alive. His eyes are open but is his jugular throbbing and pulsing with blood? He's the last prisoner. Relief will come to him soon. We'll all relax after he's buried.

I look for the key as if I was meaning to go in. I don't find it so I don't go in.

4

Benghazi
10:30 p.m.

1

WE'RE CASBAH GUARDS. WE DON'T have anything to be jealous about. We're not like ordinary people, as they say. And that's inevitable. Our job gets us appreciation and respect. Not to mention, as Baba Ali says, we eat food and we wait for death. No one will say I don't do my duty completely, either at work or at home. Food, drink, clothes, and other things. But when you have seven girls, and the oldest has vanished into one of the houses of Tighassaline or El Hajib or some other city to do those disgusting things with men, you say in the end there's nothing you can do, brother, when it comes to fate. Boys, at worst, they'll just be unemployed. But girls are born from a crooked rib. The best you can expect is she brings you a swollen belly. And that's if she didn't take off with the first freethinker who talks to her about getting married, the wedding and the ring, and then dumps her on the side of the first road. Everything I say is the truth. May God reward everyone for what they do.

I heard she'd settled down in Tighassaline so I sent someone to bring her back, and all of a sudden she disappeared. Then I heard things about her in Tangier or Marrakech. Only He, God the Sublime be praised, knows all I did to bring her home, to ignore all the gossip. I swear to God, if He wants to punish a living being and deprive him of sleep, He inflicts a series of girls on him. One after the other. But no one can say I didn't do my duty completely for them.

Baba Ali went to check out the prisoner because I beat him. I always beat him, in checkers and in other things. When I hear my uncle calling from his office, I say I'll beat him at other things too. My uncle is the commander, that's what they call him. He's in his office chewing tobacco or smoking. In his light khaki clothes, he's like an athlete without a sport. He fiddles with his black sunglasses or puts them on because it's nighttime. I always know what's going on in my uncle's mind. Today he's thinking about my wife, who might be in labor by now. He hopes the baby will be a boy. So we don't fall further into this pothole of girls. My uncle doesn't have kids. God didn't bless him with offspring to hold on to his memory after his death, because you won't find anything to remember him by. I think he's actually thinking about my wife, not about the baby that'll come out with his penis and his little testicles with which he'll compete with other men. But there he is putting on his sunglasses and walking toward me, asking: "How many are left?" I go back to thinking about my wife in labor. She'll have her eighth baby. After seven girls, I hope it's a boy. After this series of girls. In the end, he wasn't thinking about my wife and I hear him ask again: "How many prisoners are left?"

I call him my uncle, but he's not actually my uncle. I call him that so I seem like someone who likes him. But I don't like him. I pretend to respect him. Do you respect a man who's seventy, gets drunk, and doesn't pray? *There is no power and no strength save in God.* He doesn't visit the prisoners either. He only asks: "How many are left?" Baba Ali and I tell him: "Two hundred." He counts on his fingertips but that doesn't help him so he asks again: "How many?" The amount of money he'll get if the number of dead goes up is turning in his mind. And if the number goes down . . . He doesn't know which is better: That they die so his income goes up or that they stay alive so his job continues. *There is no power and no strength save in God.* My uncle doesn't know arithmetic, because he was in the military. He doesn't know the difference between sixty and a

20

hundred and sixty, because he didn't go to school. He became a commander like someone becomes the leader of a union or a minister. Or like I became a guide who doesn't guide anyone, or like Baba Ali became a cook who doesn't cook anything. Through connections, through people you know. Sometimes we tell him one hundred sixty-seven for fun, to laugh at his confusion. So they stay alive in his mind. As long as they stay alive, he's happy. And we're happy. They don't eat, they don't wear clothes, and they don't bathe. My uncle believes they'll stay alive thanks to the All-hearing and All-knowing. It doesn't dawn on him that they need the least bit of food or cleanliness to stay alive. I also don't want them to die out entirely. At least one of them has to be left for us to keep our jobs.

What can someone do if God has decreed that he should die in a particular way? It's God who gives life and death. So what's the use of asking questions about it? What can I or Baba Ali or anyone else do? We're only a guide and a cook, and my uncle told us to come here to Glaoui's casbah. That's what we did. Are we accountable for this? Both of us will die anyway. Before God the Almighty and Sublime, we'll be held to account, tomorrow, on the Day of Judgment.

I tell my uncle the number's still the same. How many? One hundred seventy-five. I think he'll bow his head as if a big rock fell on him at this news. But he just shakes it.

2

My uncle didn't go to school, but he's got experience. He learned everything in the military. He became a commander thanks to his intelligence. He learned, thanks to his intelligence, that the Makhzen is the most important thing in the world. I call him my uncle because he's the boss. And we always need the boss. Yes, my uncle's lucky, he's got a mind to think with. Even without school. Without the intelligence God Almighty on high granted him, the intelligence with which humankind thinks, there's no luck. That's what I always say.

My uncle's mind is full of tricks. Women. Money. Is there anything more important in the world? His fortune began when his luck called him. Not before, not after. When God granted him the good fortune to become a commander. A commander and a dealmaker at the same time. There isn't a commander without a deal. There isn't a deal without a commander. He's about seventy and he's building his houses on the outskirts of Meknès, with the money allocated for the prisoners. *There is no power and no strength save in God*.

My uncle's office is cold because of the air conditioner. Wide and cold. The curtains are drawn day and night. The breeze from the air conditioner plays with the hem of the curtain, so you know the breeze is real. It's always nighttime in my uncle's house. My uncle loves the night. He doesn't want it to end. During the daytime, when he looks outside, he covers his eyes with thick black sunglasses. When he goes back to the office, he lowers the curtains. So night doesn't leave his mind. This is the life he likes. He'd like it if the entire world were night. My uncle comes to life at night. Like a bat, as he says. The color of his pupils at night is yellow, like the eyes of cats. His teeth are an odd yellow, from his chewing tobacco.

The glass is in his hand as he looks away from the girl. The girl's beautiful. Her wide eyes and her voluptuous mouth would entice him, you, me, or any other man. But he thinks she's ugly. My uncle asks for beautiful girls but he always thinks they're ugly. I traveled seventy kilometers to bring him the most beautiful girl in the region. But he always thinks the girls are ugly. Instead of checking her out, he checks out the wall, and instead of smelling her, he smells the wall. *There is no power and no strength save in God*. My wife's in labor and I don't know what her giving birth will bring us. I hope it's a boy. Before I leave the office, I hear him tell me to take the girl back tomorrow to where I brought her from. *There is no power and no strength save in God*.

When I return, I find Baba Ali's just come back. I ask him, "Did he die?"

He says, "He's dead."

Then I ask him if he's still breathing, and he says, "He's still breathing."

I say, "Sit down and play."

"I'm not playing."

"I'll let you win next time."

"Next time, we'll both go."

"Play now."

"Don't talk to me about your uncle."

"Play."

"Or about your wife who's going to give birth."

5

Zina

11 p.m.

HERE I AM ON THE road again, on the nine o'clock bus from Fez that arrived after ten. I think about all the times I went looking for Aziz. Will this be my last? At the end, at the end of this night, will I see him? It's dark outside and inside the bus. I see shadows moving in the aisle between the rows of seats and from time to time I hear the muttering of a passenger dreaming. The travelers are sleeping, certain that their trip isn't so important as to be the first or the last, relaxed in the knowledge they're just coming from one place and heading to another. They aren't bothered by the heat inside the bus or the weather outside. Most are traveling to obtain some official document or to visit family or take a vacation. Their faces show signs of the calm future waiting for them. They aren't rushed or anxious. However I try, I won't be like them. But they don't know that, which is for the best.

What are the passengers dreaming of? Would I dream if I fell asleep? I wonder where they're going. Nothing indicates they're heading to the wedding festival. No singing, no scent of henna, no girls laughing, no women crying. Could any of them be so eager to make it to the festival that they took the night bus that came late? I wonder what my sister Khatima is doing right now. It's closing time. No doubt there are one or two asking for one more drink. They become like children, those drunks, at the end of the night. Then I wonder if there's someone on this bus, a man or a woman, heading to the same place I'm going. Someone like me, looking for a husband, a father, a son, who disappeared twenty years ago. The man who came to the bar might be knocking on other doors. If he's gone to all this trouble and taken all this risk, it must be for all the abductees. Or at least for more than one. I'm sure this person's on the bus. Maybe he's sleeping now in one of these seats. What's he dreaming of? I look around to find this person who'll lead me to the casbah, but I don't see anyone. I then turn a little to see the driver but I can't see him either. I watch the night through the glass. The humming of the engine is evidence we're moving. I see the wheels in my mind as they turn and swallow up the road and the night, swallowing up everything in front of them. We pass the time minute by minute. I relax at its rocking. A small moon is suspended in the empty space ahead of the bus. The small moon and I are going in the same direction. Sometimes a cloud comes between us but it doesn't cover it. The moon is ahead of us and sometimes we're ahead of it. It's also busy with the road and the hours that pass slowly. It also wonders how many hours are left until day breaks and it sleeps.

I imagine scents I don't smell. Scents of soil, plants, and different animals the night attracts. I feel a lot better after the anxiety of the past hours. I don't know why but I'm relaxing inside my skin in a strange way. Then, as in a dream, Aziz appears before me, in the pilot's uniform I kept seeing him in. A young man, as he was. Or an old man, as he's become. Always in the new pilot's uniform with the gold buttons.

I might have dozed off because, when I turn to the other side, I find the seat is now occupied. I don't dare turn to see who's occupying it. I can see out of the corner of my eye that it's a man. And that there's a plastic bag on his knee. And that his knee doesn't stop moving. The plastic bag is making an annoying rattle because his knee is shaking. I put my forehead on the window and stare at the night passing by outside to forget him. And to forget his knee and the rattle of the bag, but they're moving nonstop. As if there's something in him seizing the rhythm of his trip. The glass of the window is cold. Through it I watch the darkness outside and I think, here I am traveling again. If the bus keeps going at this pace, I'll get there at dawn. If I'd imagined myself a month ago hitting the road alone, again, traveling like this at night on a bus where I don't know anyone, to a place where I don't know anyone, I wouldn't have believed it. I had forgotten this custom. It's been at least four years since I left Azrou. I think about all this to forget the man and his plastic bag. But I can't forget either. A man like him can't be heading to a marriage festival. A disturbed man, carrying only a plastic bag because some news surprised him, as it surprised me. He took the first thing he got his hands on so he didn't miss the bus. Maybe he's the person I'm looking for. He might be the same man who came to the bar, but without the sunglasses, djellaba, or pockmarks. Or he might be someone like him. I imagine him as a shadow running behind his lost son. I imagine the doors he knocked on and the forests he crossed. And the hands he kissed.

I hear him let out a deep sigh so I turn to him. As if I'd been waiting for his sigh to turn around. The man realizes I'm looking at his knee, which shakes faster, and he says that it'll calm down after a bit and that he forgot to take his medicine when he should have. He grabs his knee and presses down firmly on it and it stops. It stops completely. As if he too feels the sense of comfort, he lets out another long sigh. I then hear him say he's been on bus after bus since the morning because he's come from Salé. He stops talking for a moment and then asks me why I didn't ask him what he was doing in Salé. He answers his own question, saying he's coming from Razi Hospital, a hospital for mental illnesses. He pulls a bottle of water from under his seat and empties half of it. I see only the shadows of his features, nothing to indicate who he is or where he's going. This morning he was in the hospital. He turns to me this time, but I don't know if he's looking at me or outside, and says, "You can't see my face in the darkness but I'm a senile man, very old, more than eighty."

I really can't see his face, but his eyes are sparkling in the darkness. The neighbors who took care of him in the past got tired of him. He has thirteen children, and not one of them agreed to take him in. Children! They forgot him. They ignored him. Do I know why? "Because children are always following their mother. Appearances are deceiving. There are no fathers. Only mothers. That's reality, the end. Family, it's a lie from beginning to end," he says sighing. "There's no family, nothing. Family, they're who you keep passing on the street without saying hello. You meet them on the stairs without saying hello. People you never saw before or you saw them once or twice. Everyone else except for children."

Why did he go to the hospital? It was just an idea. To get food and shelter. Or to find family. But they didn't let him in.

Does that mean he isn't going anywhere in particular? Does that mean he hasn't lost anyone in his life? Except for his kids who kicked him out? He might be looking for a brother or a relative. As if still holding out hope, I ask him where he's going. At that moment, some lights start coming through the windows. The travelers begin moving, making a lot of noise around me. A baby's crying grows louder. The lights come on inside the bus. People become more agitated and start pushing each other in the aisle, heading to the door. All this happens at once, and takes me by surprise. I think that if I look closely at their faces I'll seize traces of dreams still floating on their skin. No, their faces don't express anything in particular, just tiredness or hunger. Even the passenger coming from Razi Hospital seems in a rush. He leaves his seat without saying anything. I notice he's wearing a thick, worn coat and a wool hat. The driver says: "Half-hour break." The restaurant and square in front of him are lit up with many colored lights. Young girls, I don't know where they come from, appear around the bus. Skinny, half-naked girls, begging for water from those getting off the bus. "Water. Water." They wave their hands holding empty plastic bottles. From the other side, on the curb, other girls run up to the passing cars and buses, yelling like hungry birds. Then they hurry toward us too, shouting out: "Water. Water." In Shilha Berber and in other languages, thinking we're foreign tourists.

I don't leave my spot. On the back of the seat in front of me there are marks, names, and dates. All the concerns of the travelers in the same place. Scratches or deep carvings. Marks or strange letters. Who wrote them? Men or women? Or both? And for what? A mother or a child mocking his new world? Or an old man whose kids hate him and before leaving the bus to die in the middle of the road, he writes his last will and testament with these obscure letters so no one could penetrate their secret?

The passengers look over at the restaurant and go back to the bus disappointed. The ones who know the place are annoyed, saying the driver always stops at this restaurant, which serves terrible and expensive food, because he knows the owner. Others say something suspicious links the two. They sit silently frowning, like students in the classroom. Waiting for the driver, who comes back tottering after fifteen minutes, sits behind the wheel calmly, and turns on the engine with one hand while, with the other, he holds the snack he's eating.

6

Aziz
11:30 p.m.

1

I BEGAN MY MOVEMENTS EARLY this morning, looking for a piece of paper or cardboard or wood, anything hard I can write on, because I'm not doing well. A bunch of years have passed during which my mind hasn't, for a single moment, stopped repeating: I'm not well. I'm not doing well. I began this morning looking for something hard, as soon as the bird let out two tweets. I got up as soon as it let out its first cries wishing me good morning, without me responding. I don't respond to morning greetings, I replied to him. I don't talk to anyone in the morning. Even if it's a nightingale. I lost my confidence a long time ago. And what's more, I don't wish any living thing good morning.

I woke up strangely ready for work. I stopped and thought about the matter seriously, forgetting the bird and his morning twitters. It seemed clear to me: Today, I'll find something valuable. More valuable than anything I spread my complaints on. I don't know what this thing is. Its kind, nature, or value. I'll recognize it when I see it. I'm sure of it. Fundamentally, I'll know this is what I've been looking for when my eyes fall on it. Or my hands. I'm sure of this, two hundred percent.

It's not the first time I find myself on these kinds of solitary adventures. In my previous explorations, I've found a nail that looks like a needle and a rare butterfly. Back then, I was at the beginning of my time in this kitchen and I knew nothing about it. On that distant morning, I didn't mean to look for

31

anything at all. It wasn't one of my hobbies yet. I didn't know there were valuable treasures abandoned here, waiting to be uncovered. I was sitting, that morning, recently arrived in this place with its long nights that daylight doesn't differentiate, staring at the strange world around me: The blackened clay on the walls and the black wooden supports under the ceiling, with the stenches of people and cattle that have passed through here, stenches of never-ending suffering. I was listening to them. All of a sudden, I saw something moving on the wall. I went up to it. I thought, that's a butterfly. I tried to remember the shapes of the butterflies I had seen before, to remember all the butterflies I knew in my previous life. I got closer. It wasn't a butterfly. It was two drops of blackened blood on the wall. Old blood. It didn't have the shape of a butterfly or its joy. It didn't have the butterfly's scent. I put my nose on the wall and inhaled deeply. No, it didn't have a butterfly's scent, not an old one, not a new one. I sat back down, frustrated, almost hopeless. The dear solitary butterflies that my mind rejuvenated, all of a sudden their wings were fluttering again. Fluttering gently, as if they knew how hopeless and confused I was. Whenever I looked at the two of them closely, life flowed from them as if they were about to fly. I felt that life was pulsating on the wall. I said, as the northerners say: "Good is this life I see on the wall." A little life, in this kitchen that's like a forgotten archaeological site. But it's a life nonetheless and it deserves consideration.

I went up to it, sure I could read its mind. I don't like talking in the morning, as I said, but more than that, I'm not good at arguing with people. But I can read the mind of every flying being and I'm good at listening to them. All living things that fly: butterflies, cockroaches, and bats. But not human beings, because they don't fly. I don't know how to have a conversation with someone, I don't know how to respond to his questions, as he's naked without wings. But it's something different with a butterfly or a bird greeting me in the morning, even though I always mean to ignore its greet-ings. I have a special relationship with the flying animals. I understand their language completely.

I got close to the wall again. Two drops of blood. There wasn't any doubt as I got closer and closer. If it was a butterfly, if there was one atom of a butterfly in it, it would have greeted me as the bird does every morning. But it doesn't. When I got back to my spot again, the two drops that knew they were only two drops of old blood stopped playing with my mind. Their wings weren't on my mind anymore. But afterward, I understood something essential: This place contains treasures, including what I'll discover today, even if I don't know what it is yet. I only have to keep going. I forget the piece of paper and keep going. I forget I'm not well and keep going. Setting out from the memory of the two drops that weren't a butterfly. But they're a beginning for something I'll understand at the right time.

2

As I said, there are things I discovered after that, after the butterfly that wasn't actually a butterfly. Once, we were in the middle of a winter so horrible it was like nothing we'd seen before. The rainy season had started a while before, turn-ing the kitchen into a pool of icy mud. The cold burned my joints. It stung my ears more than in years past. You could feel it whistling inside your brain. With the passing of time and the falling temperature, it seemed that what I was searching for had some connection with the cold, with winter in gen-eral. With this exceptionally cold season in particular. That's extremely important. When I found this thing whose shape I didn't know and that wouldn't be a snail or lizard or butterfly, but had some connection to the rain or the cold, I'd be able to make it through this season, however harsh it became, with less damage than previous seasons.

Then this terrifying question, which I'd been avoiding until then, brought me to a halt: If I don't find this thing, how will I pass the winter? I'd already tied my jaw with a cord so my teeth didn't crack from the intense chattering. Worse, my eyes had already cried from the bitter cold. This is something shameful I haven't mentioned before. It hadn't occurred to me a human being could cry from the cold. A cold piercing the skin like a sharp needle that breaks bones. A cold like sharp daggers. I didn't cry from pain or injustice or frustration. I cried from the cold. Yes, it's possible. I don't want to squeeze myself again into this disgraceful position. That's why I did everything possible to search. And after one attempt, my hands fell upon something hard. And sharp. And cold. I pulled it out and laid it down again on the edge of the washbasin so I could catch my breath a little. An oddly shaped nail. I didn't know who put this nail in the hole in the wall or when. A nail like a needle. I didn't know it was there before my hand came down on it. The hand didn't know. Nor did the fingers or forearm. The hand didn't move forward at this exciting moment, with fingers trembling slightly, knowing they were on the verge of a new sensation. It was as if hidden hands filed it, sharpened it, and made a hole in the right end.

I put it aside for when I'd need it the most. I went back to the basin, looking closely at this unusual piece of iron, not noticing that my hands were pulling a string out of the blanket and putting the end through the hole of the needle, sewing something without knowing what. The hands didn't know what the string was making and neither did I. Then, without any sense of surprise, I saw a hat in my hands. At that moment, I realized I needed it. Needed this kind of hat designed in my hand's mind before its memory recognizes it. I thought, my teeth won't chatter this winter. I won't cry this winter. I won't need a string to tie my jaw so my teeth don't crash against each other, causing a catastrophe I can avoid now.

I knew once again that this place was full of things more valuable than the spots of blood of the people who'd died before me in this kitchen. More than a butterfly, which is invaluable.

3

I sit counting the pulses of my toe, as I'd counted the rain-drops falling from the ceiling before. *Tak tak. Tak tak. Tak tak. Tak tak. Tak tak. Tak.* Eleven and a half pulses during the night. Pain weaves its net. *Tak tak. Tak tak. Tak tak. Tak tak. Tak tak. Tak.* Eleven and a half pulses during the night. How many pulses until the cycle of pain is completed? But it's a pain that doesn't deviate from the circle of habit. I keep being amazed, asking myself how all this wonder happens in a kitchen of six square meters. Is it really a kitchen? The wooden rafters are black. The smell of burning lingers. And the clay gives the impression it's part of a wing of an old casbah. Abandoned. The ground is dug up with furrows and gives out the stench of human feces. After a series of pulses I didn't count entirely, I realize I haven't moved past my desire to get a piece of paper, which has occupied me this morning. I think about resuming the search and say to myself, where am I going to begin? The east side, where the door is? Or the other sides, where there are walls with this strange geography and curious history?

This experience is always new for me. With a kind of apprehension, I begin. As if in the woods, I have a kind of doubt. There'll always be a place my hands won't reach, as in any forest. There'll always be a strange place your eyes won't see as long as you can't go in all directions at the same time. Condemned by the single line. By the single path. And you have to choose, to take a risk. Either this direction or that. You might gain things and you might lose others. You might lose everything. Waste your energy and return empty-handed. You're not a chameleon so you can't see every angle at the same time. You're not the snake of legends so you can't stretch your seven heads to move forward in all directions. The darkness is intense around me, above all this. I'm only strengthened by my previous experiences. The butterfly. Then the nail. Then the hat. All my experiences are crowned by unexpected suc-cess. I begin with the closest place I know. The wall connected to the washbasin where I sleep. The wall connected to the basin doesn't require a lot of effort. I can cover its twists and turns even if I'm sitting on my knees. I won't need more than a half hour for my fingers to cover it all. I don't find anything in this direction. Hope always begins like that, with a little dashed hope giving you the necessary optimism to go further.

As for the other directions, they're still untouched. My ignorance of them hasn't diminished since I discovered the butterfly, the nail, and the hat years ago. I still don't know much about them. I often fell into this trap. The trap of moving away from the basin. Whenever I moved away from it, I'd delve into the topography of the kitchen and feel a deep frustration. But I'm calm tonight. Optimistic. I'm a step away from some kind of end. The place is full of ends. I come across copper hidden inside the clay. I'm not interested in it. I don't wonder at that moment what a piece of copper was doing in the clay. But it's a good beginning. Encouraging. I keep going. My hand falls on something small, round, nice to touch. It's a snail. Yes, we're in a warm month, maybe the darkest moment in it, but the snail is a winter animal. Does its presence here at this time have some meaning? I only pause at this question long enough to understand something else. After two hours of searching, I wonder: Does what I'm looking for require all this trouble? Should I retreat and go back near the washbasin so as not to use up all my strength in the exhausting process of searching? But what if what I'm looking for has a connection with the rat bite and the ruin it produced in my foot? This question encourages me to keep going.

I stop again after the effort I made to find the appropriate question. That's because I heard the bird again. Three tweets. This means in bird language that the cook is coming. I hear the sound of his shoes. I stop searching. As if giving myself an additional moment to think, waiting for him to pass. I don't know his face but I know his eye, which he looks through the door crack with. Not all eyes look alike. I don't know if it's his right or left eye, just as I don't know it he's white or black. Is he a soldier or a cook in the casbah or a night guard with no rank? This is the second time he's come today. After the third, I'll know it's past midnight. I'm getting ready now to stop him behind the door. Ten pulses. His eye doesn't blink. I count how long it'll stay behind the door looking into the kitchen without blinking. The eye stares at the darkness I'm swimming in. The man coming at this time and his eye still doing its gratuitous investigation gives me a chance to go over the difficulty of my search. To think about the possibility of backtracking. It's not too late yet. I hear his eye breathing behind the door and my hesitation increases. Should I keep going or stop? With the same heavy steps, as if trudging through mud, the man's eye leaves the hole in the door without blinking.

I go back to my search. I've gone far away from the basin, with no place to backtrack. My goal seems clear to me after the cook's visit, in a strange way and for the first time since I woke up. Suddenly I begin to see, as if a lamp was lit. I can't explain what was happening. It's nothing to do with lamp light, but it's another kind of illumination. If I wanted to express it in a different way, I might say it's internal. Like what happens when you close your eyes and see an entire life pulsating under your eyelids, not knowing where it is exactly. But there are glowing lamps, making an uproar with what looks like black light. I see now the bulges of the walls. And the holes. An endless stream of water. And endless spots of humidity. Green as in the spring. We are at the beginning of a heat that's announced its severity prematurely. Or the end of a winter. The scent of the walls is strong. A scent of clay, chaff, sweat, urine, and feces. I touch a long shape that feels like a thighbone. It's not the first time I've discovered the bones of people buried in the wall. That's why my fingers touch the bones without getting too excited, and keep going. Small streams, mountains, and rivers. Uncovering the clay on this side. More bones of someone buried in the wall emerge. I'm not on the wrong path.

The path to what? I don't know yet. Despite the bones that the water falling from the ceiling uncovered. Many people passed through here. They formed part of the structure's clay. I know I'm nearing my goal when sweat begins pouring from my entire body. I don't feel the passing of time. So I begin to listen to my panting. A strange sound coming from me like a whistle, as if I'm climbing a tall mountain. My heart beating. My toe ringing, *tak tak tak*.

My index finger heads to another hole. A piece of cloth. The clothes of the buried man were tattered. They became the color of clay. Very carefully, I pull on their ends. So they don't fall apart. I think about all the men buried next to me. In the walls. In the clay. How much time has passed since they were here? Did they spend their time counting raindrops? Or pulses of pain? Did they put on hats like the one I put on when the cold of the southern nights ate away at their bones? I'll think about them in due course. As for now, I wonder whether I should stop at this point or keep going. Is what I found enough for today? My hand doesn't care about these questions. Speech isn't among its customs. It doesn't concern it. My hand plays with the piece of cloth. I don't want to intervene in what it's doing. As if I've released a hunting dog in the woods. It won't go farther than the prey. Without surprising me, it comes back with a gold ring. I didn't know I was holding gold at first. I didn't know I was on the verge of unprecedented wealth. I go near the door cracks to inspect the piece of gold and I think about it in light of this last observation.

I'm thinking about my wife, Zina. Time passed without my mind stopping for a single moment, repeating what I couldn't tell her during our short time together. This morning I began looking for a piece of paper to write to her that I haven't been as well as could be for a while. All of a sudden, I find a ring instead of paper. All of a sudden, I see her image. Unclear because of all the time that's passed. But it's her. As I knew her at a time that disappeared long ago. The optimism that had dwindled returned. Did the man buried in the wall have a wife and was this her ring? Was her name Zina too? Did he used to put the ring on his heart so he wouldn't forget as I forgot? I forgot how to think about complicated matters. But now I understand all that I'll gain after this discovery. It appears to me with a mysterious clarity and I realize for the first time I'm on the verge of relief. For the first time too, as I turn the ring over in my hand, I realize that, after the many years I've spent here, year after year, pulse after pulse, I'll leave this place alive. I don't know when or how. I'll recognize this too in due time. Just as I recognized the nail and the hat. And just as I recognized the butterfly that wasn't a butterfly.

It's hard to remember Zina's address. More than that, it's hard to know why it's important. Some letters and numbers. Why is it so important? I didn't care about it before and I didn't see why it was necessary. It's as if I were looking for the way to our house, not recognizing it or the neighborhood or the city. The more I try to stop myself from thinking about it, the more I find myself occupied with it. Attracted to it. The more I'm preoccupied with it, the farther away it seems to be. As if it's playing with me. Is this the time for entertainment? It's as if, at this point, everything depends on finding it. Two numbers and some letters: A matter of life or death. I didn't know remembering some numbers and letters would be so hard. A cold sweat wets my forehead. I don't know why I let myself be pulled into this frivolous and exhausting search.

My attacks have become frequent and usually begin with a cold sweat covering my face and limbs, little by little. I won't get anything from my search. But who said I won't get anything? And how do you want me to leave this place without an address?

A feeling like sleepiness, heavy in my eyes, pressing on my forehead, like the effects of a drug. I put the piece of cloth on my knees. I won't relax unless I see in it the address of our house. I can't return to it unless I find it. All the effort I expended this morning stops at this. I'm in front of a final impediment that I've got to get through. I try to find a letter or a number or a picture of the house that brought us together among the ashes of faded memories. If I can only discover the first letter. The address starts to spin itself through the spider's web of nightmares, pulling itself out from among my memories. But it's little more than a fine thread, barely visible in the middle of the web. I can sometimes almost grab it. Letter or number? I see it getting longer. Longer. As I pull. I tug on the thread but it doesn't move a hair's breadth. Then it moves with a dizzying quickness, and all of a sudden the end of a letter appears in front of me. Or is it a number split open and not the beginning of an address? Or a letter taking the shape of a number, or a number that looks like a letter?

The letters finally come together. As if they're playing, they gather and start to roll down like balls, one after the other. Different numbers and letters, some of them with others in funny shapes, falling onto my head. They tumble down very quickly into the basin and then onto the dug-up ground. It's as if they've opened up a waterfall on top of me, and now they swim in pools of mud. Then the letter emits a sound that's sometimes like a roar, sometimes like barking, and sometimes like the meow of a hungry cat. As if I was on the verge of another one of my deadly crises. Does all this happen outside my head? There's no way to be sure. No, it gives that impression, so when the sickness strikes it is more deadly. I don't move a single step forward as the illness threatens me. My thigh keeps swelling up. The threat of pain arrives, stronger than before. Little by little, the speed decreases and the roar lightens and the waterfall becomes a river flowing gently, with letters and numbers spread out on the ring of the man buried in the wall. They spread out on the basin. My clothes are wet, as if I'd plunged them into a pool of water.

When the cook appears behind the door crack, I lift my finger with the ring on it as I imagine his eye wondering what's sparkling at the end of my hand. The eye disappears when I turn. I think it must have backtracked to see me better and figure out what it has to do. I hear its hesitation. Will it come in or not? I wave the ring on the end of my finger and the eye appears in the crack again. Then the door rattles violently. A long silence follows. The cook's voice is delicate, sharp. A feminine voice. Is he really a cook?

"What do you have there?"

"A gold ring."

Silence longer than the first, as if to think about the meaning of the words. He repeats them to himself: "A ring . . . a gold ring?" I think he's still listening to the sound of the words inside himself. Then his sharp voice comes again: "Where'd you get it?"

"You want it? Take it."

"Me take it? Why?"

"I don't have anything to do with it."

Why did I raise the ring before him and why did I tell him to take it? It seemed to me it was what anyone who found a ring that wasn't his should do. The ring disappears into his hands for a while, until I tell him I was lucky. I imagine him putting the ring on his wife's finger first thing tomorrow.

Then the ring comes back in his hands like a hot piece of iron. Silence comes back with it, different, rough, as if he's turned pale from extreme anger and the coarseness of fear.

"No, I won't take it."

"Why?"

"My uncle will kill me if he sees it on me."

"He's not going to see it."

"You want to get me in trouble?"

He tosses the ring onto the basin and retreats, fleeing toward the door. No, my silent pleas don't convince him. Maybe he thinks he'll have to do something for me in exchange for the gold. He pushes the door violently and his steps cross the corridor heavily, nervously, frustrated, and hopeless too.

7

Khatima
11:30 p.m.

1

I AM SITTING BEHIND THE bar in the same position Zina left me
in before she took off. I watch Abdesalam collect the chairs in
the corner and put them on top of each other or on top of the
tables. Abdesalam's hearing has become weak and he's gotten
old to the point where he scrapes the ground as he drags his
sandals over the tiles. I don't remember when he started doing
that. The bar's empty now. I'm waiting for the man to come
back. Zina doesn't know that the man in the djellaba spoke
with me before going to her. I told him I'm not stupid enough
to give him two thousand dirhams for a piece of information we've been trying to get for eighteen years. He told me
he didn't have any intention of taking money. His appearance didn't inspire trust or confidence. I asked him why he
would put his life in danger for some people he doesn't know.
I opened a bottle and put it in front of him. Then I whispered
to him, "Go to her and tell her."

I can't leave the bar unattended and go looking for someone who disappeared eighteen years ago or more. He left the
open bottle and went to Zina at the other end of the bar.

And that's all there was to it. I'm almost forty and I say
thank God I've made it to the other side with the least amount
of damage. Daily bread comes to everyone effortlessly, but if
they don't grab it, it goes to someone else. I can say too without
shame that Abdesalam's the one who opened my mind to this.

43

He told me: "This is your chance." Madame Janeau became old and needed a woman to take care of her. She hated her kids and grandkids because they visited her every six months to see if she was dead or not. They stayed at her house to fight over the inheritance. When she protested, they insulted her and left her swimming in her filth. So I took care of her for the last five years of her life. I wondered every day if the old woman understood why I added this trouble to my life. I was making her food and taking her out for short strolls in the woods when she was strong enough to walk. Then, when she couldn't get up, I washed her and scrubbed her body as if she was a spoiled little girl, as I thought to myself: when will she make her decision? I'd block my nose and try not to show my disgust. I swear to God I thought I was going to vomit on her once from the putrid stench coming up from her. But it was my chance, as Abdesalam said. And chances don't come along every day. In front of her, I tried to seem happy, like I was just knitting socks or boiling eggs. But inside, I'd say: when will this torture end? Time passed. Her French family disappeared. They were in France and from there, they kept watch and waited. We'd hear their voices on the phone every four or five months. Did the old lady die? No, not yet. I was also watching and waiting.

What happened to the beautiful Madame Janeau who used to welcome her customers with laughter in her eyes and a red rose in her hair? She'd become a bag of bones. Her hair fell out, a disease struck her dreamy eyes, and her skin became wrinkled and hung down from every side. She was close to the end of the road, but nothing indicated my destiny would change. I kept up my work because it was my chance and I didn't want to regret ignoring her for a single day. So one morning, Madame Janeau asked me to dress her in the beautiful clothes she used to wear in the days of her bygone youth. A long white dress with lace and a blue shawl and a fan. She combed her hair herself and put on deep red lipstick. She sat listening to the songs of Georges Brassens, as if she'd recovered her vigor. At ten o'clock, the French notary came and wrote out her final will. She died a week later. Fate had knocked on my door at the right time. Not a moment too soon. Everyone is born with his or her chance. But most of the time a person doesn't recognize it or it doesn't recognize the person. That's all there is to it. Would I have recognized it if Abdesalam hadn't been there, dragging his feet in the bar, taking pleasure in his annoying chirping for forty years? As if his single role in life was to open my mind. Other than that, I don't see what his role has been.

Not a day passes without me thinking about the road my sister Zina and I have crossed to get here. Alone, without anyone's help. My only concern now is the bar. My entire life is focused on it. How I run it. How I avoid problems with the drunks and the soldiers. How I limit the capriciousness of the commissioners who want to take it over with this pretext or that. I've gotten it out of a lot of traps and I'm ready to fight any battle I can to keep it.

Abdesalam finishes stacking the chairs and tables. He sits on a chair near the door and takes out a box of snuff. He makes a line of powder on the back of his hand. He inhales deeply twice. He wipes his nose on a dirty cloth. Together we look at the night outside. The movement of the passersby has stopped. The man in the striped djellaba appears at the door and I remember Zina. He comes up to the counter. Abdesalam leaves his chair and I send him to the kitchen. The man says, as if continuing a dialogue we'd begun, that he met Aziz three years ago when they were together at the same casbah. Aziz gave him a letter as he saw him collecting his things, thinking he was leaving the prison. They only transferred him and his group to another prison in Skoura. The letter stayed with him. He then takes out from under his djellaba a medium-sized envelope and says he and two other prisoners escaped from jail tonight and he has the letters of some of his other fellow inmates. He asks me to send them to their families. I ask him if he needs food. No, he doesn't. I ask him if he needs money. He says he really does. I give him what I can from the day's take and he leaves. I go out behind him but the night swallows him up. I sit in front of the bar looking at the darkness extending into the distance, then at my shadow cast by the light from inside. I hear the kitchen door open behind me. Then Abdesalam's soles. I hear the broom as it passes over the bar floor to collect the cigarette butts, crumbs of food, snot, spit, and obscene words the drunks left behind. After a little, Abdesalam will sweep all that outside. Yes, Zina and I have come a long way since the first day we arrived in Azrou. More than twenty years ago.

2—Aqba Street, Wednesday, 3 April 1972
Azrou nights don't resemble other nights. The scents of the cedar trees, the sprouts of wormwood, and the wild mint, coming from the surrounding mountains and from Ifrane and Ras El Ma. They penetrate even the lowest parts of the houses. You can almost see them entering, then playing in the courtyards of the houses. Especially at this time of year. Stork Bar is the name of the place I'm sitting in. It's a well-known bar. The only bar in all of Azrou. From it, I look out over the night. Leaning on the counter with my eyes outside the bar. My eyes following the secrets of night that descended a while ago. They don't see the big boulder at the city's entrance, put there as if to welcome those coming and wave goodbye to those leaving. My eyes imagine the boulder and the Meknès road in the other direction, rising toward the forest, on Aqba Street, where Zina and I live, between the boulder and the road. It's not a neighborhood, but a steep street, rising sharply, toward the sky, as if it'll fall back on you as you climb it. It's the most famous street in Azrou.

I don't like the summer and I don't like the spring in Azrou. The spring came weeks ago. The night descends from the forest with all its spring scents. There are still lights on. Spread out, in a few windows and behind some doors. Songs play behind the window blinds. Three women sit at the entrance of their house, smoking Casa Sports cigarettes and talking about what happened with the day's customers. Three drunk soldiers head up to the top of the hill and come back. They smell the scent of another woman. Of more prey. The game animals have returned to their lairs. And life on Aqba Street has been calm for a while. There's a girl at the door of her house chewing tobacco. She's waiting, looking for another customer. Three soldiers pass by without seeing her because she disappeared behind the door when she heard the sound of enemy shoes. The brisk evening business disappeared a while ago. The women of Aqba Street rely on their disturbed dreams.

I think about all this as I lean on the surface of the bar, waiting for Joujou to end negotiations with one of the café customers. A last client. He's a teacher. He appears in the bar at the beginning of every month. When he gets his salary, he comes to the bar to drink two beers. Always two. This is the first time he's asked for more than two beers. Because he's talking with Joujou and he's looking at me. Madame Janeau, the owner of the bar, is sitting behind the cash register count- ing the day's take. Her husband died about two years ago. He used to love hunting wild boar in the Ifrane woods. One of them took him by surprise on a hunting trip and killed him, so around her neck hangs his picture, which is all that's left of him. Abdesalam finished his work in the hall fifteen minutes ago. He's sitting now in front of the door to snort a bit of snuff. The bar is almost empty. Two last drunks lick the bottoms of their glasses so they don't have to leave. There are two soldiers too. Still wanting a last glass. The soldiers are sitting on the right side of the bar and on the other side is Joujou, going back and forth with the teacher as he passes his hand through his hair. Joujou passes his hand through his hair whenever he's negotiating with a client. So they respect him, he says. His hand reaches out to his hair spontaneously because it gnaws at him when he negotiates—this is what I say. His hair is always combed back. His hand's job is to keep his hair combed back, so he resembles the pimp he really is. That's everything. I haven't finished the day's work. I'm not like Abdesalam, who swept the bar, washed the glasses, took out his box of snuff, and sat at the door waiting for Madame Janeau to finish counting her money. The night still waits for me, in all its length. Only God knows how I'll make it to the end. I'm not as well as could be. I'm prematurely aged. I'm not even twenty and I'm finished. There's another life after twenty but I won't get there, I can't see it. As I can't see the boulder, because of the night. Or I can't see it clearly. It's as if I've reached the point where I see with only one eye. Joujou's negotiating with the teacher. Can you know in advance how your night will end with someone like him? Or with someone else? There's no way to know. Or you'll know when it's too late. I look at him and I see he's not wearing a military uniform. There's nothing to say he's a soldier hiding in the clothes of a teacher, not showing his military colors or his fangs until he's sure he's inside the house. That's what I tell myself to stay calm. I wait for Joujou to finish negotiations. He's been negotiating for half an hour. Joujou doesn't like spending the night without work. Even if it's with a repeat customer, recoiling, not knowing what he wants, like this teacher.

Joujou says the sweet money comes at night, especially when the customer's a civilian.

Madame Janeau gets down from her high chair. She moves her thighs to get the blood flowing in them. Her face has lost the freshness of the morning but the rose in her hair hasn't faded. She wishes Abdesalam and me a good night and leaves for her house above the bar. Abdesalam gets up and brings down the first shade: "Everyone, let's go, we're done." He heads over to the light switch.

"Give us another beer," one of the soldiers says.

"You know the rules, brother Laarbi."

"Last one, Abdesalam."

Abdesalam doesn't pay attention to his reply. He turns out the lights and begins to bring down the second blind. He leaves an opening of half a meter.

3

Yes, I'm Khatima and I like laughing when I'm having a bad time. I'm nineteen. Zina and I have been living with Joujou for two years, waiting for God to grant us relief. Zina's fifteen. I don't like life here with Joujou the pimp. I don't know how life would be somewhere else. I don't have the slightest idea. It might be better somewhere else. I always say: Life will be better somewhere else. In Casablanca, for example. Casa is the only city I know. I haven't ever gone there. But when my aunt Taja visits us, she tells us about Casa. Zina and I imagine it. We can almost see it. I like it. I imagine Zina will like it too. Aunt Taja tells us it's a city where you can still take advantage of people's naïveté. We imagine a lot of things, but haven't tried living there to know for sure. What's important is that life here is hell, but I thank God. I've been putting money away for a while so I can send Zina to Casa. She's got to take care of herself far from Azrou. I don't want her to stay here. In hell. She'll escape with her skin, I say.

Zina's everything I have in this world. We disowned our father. We fled from him. We don't like our father, and I'll explain why. Our mother, when she noticed she'd started to get old, suggested to him that he get married again. And she's the one who got him engaged. She's the one who set up his second marriage, so he wouldn't leave her. But on the wedding day, he left her. On his wedding day, she went into the kitchen and stayed there. She went into the kitchen and toiled there until she died. I was afraid he'd abandon us. But I didn't leave the house because of my father's marriage. No. Let him marry even twenty women. I left because of Zina. Zina's the dearest thing in my life. Dearer to me than my father and my mother, who gave birth to me.

I don't want her to follow my path. I'll wait another year or so. I'll wait until she's seventeen and I'll send her to Casa to live with Aunt Taja. That's better for her. Maybe we'll go together. It'll be better for us. I don't know what she might do in Casa. Learn a trade. Or meet a nice guy. What's important is that she doesn't follow the same path I took. And fall into the same trap. I was fourteen when Zina and I fled. What can a fourteen-year-old girl who's never left her village do? One who's dragging a ten-year-old girl behind her? I die of laughter when I go over the story in my head and imagine the scene. A ten-year-old jumping ahead of me and singing as if she's going to the wedding of one of the neighbors. It wasn't the first time I'd thought about fleeing. But I never thought I'd take my sister with me. Where would I take her? Whatever life was like in our village, it'd be better in the labyrinth of the city. I myself didn't know exactly where I was going.

Our father was the reason. I've never seen a creature like him in my life. Nice to everyone, except us. Me, Zina, and my brother Mohamed, who was in the mountains with his three goats from dawn until dusk. And my mother, when she was alive. Nothing we did pleased him. We gathered wood, kneaded bread, fetched water, and prepared food, but he wasn't impressed by any of it. Nothing satisfied him. When we finished all the housework, which would last until late afternoon, he'd send us to collect wood for the neighbors. Yes, for the neighbors. He'd say he was doing a good deed with this, but he wasn't the one who was miserable. Or whose hands and feet were made bloody. The neighbors invoked him in their prayers. They'd say: "Si Salih, Mr. Virtuous, is a virtuous man." There isn't anyone who can match his good deeds. May God preserve his house, they'd say. Zina and I would come back from the forest, our clothes torn, our forearms bloodied, with thorns stuck all over our clothes and skin, stabbing us like sharp spurs with every step. And they'd say: "Si Salih is a virtuous man."

It didn't stop there. At night, at three in the morning, we'd hear him calling out from the other room, from deep in the darkness of his room: "Khatima, you closed the door?"

"Yes, Father, I closed it."

Then, fifteen minutes later: "Khatima, you gave the donkeys something to drink?"

"Yes, Father, I gave them something to drink."

It's like that until dawn. You'd think he doesn't sleep. Or that he's determined not to sleep so he can disturb us for the little time we have to relax before beginning the toils of another day. But regardless, they say Si Salih is a virtuous man. There's no one like him when it comes to good deeds.

One night, we got together the little we had and we left.

4

That night, when we entered the room, the teacher began taking off his clothes. I asked him about a condom. I said, "You got a condom, nice guy?"

He said, "I don't."

"I'm not sleeping with you without a condom."

I handed him one. He said he doesn't use them and tossed it away without looking at it. I asked him why he doesn't use them. "It's the same," I said.

"It's not the same. I tried it before. I didn't feel anything."

What're you going to feel? Am I your wife or girlfriend? I'm just a whore. But I'm not crazy enough to sleep with you without a condom. I told him, "If you don't use the rubber, I'm not going to sleep with you, nice guy, even if you give me your whole paycheck."

"Why?"

"It's like that. I'm not a cat. I don't have sex without a condom."

When I realized he was insisting, I lied to him. I told him I was menstruating. I took the condom, tossed it on the bed, and told him, "It's better for you to use this."

Lying is the key to getting through to this kind of person. I lied to him so God would show him the way and he'd use the condom. But he kept quiet, holding on to his twisted idea. I said it to him nicely. I didn't address him as if he were a goat herder or a sausage seller. I talked to him like an English teacher.

When I saw he was putting on his shirt, I asked what he was doing. I told him I was only joking with him. I don't have my period or anything. I was thinking about Joujou. What would he say if he sees him leaving a few minutes after going into the room? He was sitting at the reception, getting drunk, playing cards with Zina, and counting the cash he'd get after the teacher leaves. I tell myself Joujou's going to break my face. I shouldn't have joked with the teacher.

"What're you doing, teacher?"

"I'm getting dressed. I'm leaving."

"And Joujou? What'll I tell him, teacher? Joujou's waiting for his take from your pay."

As if he hadn't heard what I said, he opened the door and left.

Joujou didn't say anything when I came back. He was still playing cards with Zina. He was drunk. He opened his mouth and closed it immediately. He remembered his dentures as he looked up at me. As if there was a connection between the disappointment of my night and his dentures, which he'd put in a dish of water. Joujou doesn't like talking without his dentures. Even if he's drunk. Joujou didn't say anything at that point. He kept playing.

5

I got up that morning not doing well, feeling dizzy. My knees were weak. My body was shaking. But I made breakfast for him and sat down in front of him. Joujou was wearing jeans and a red shirt, his hair shone as if he'd already started work. Joujou loves red. Maybe it's the color of pimps. He loves to brush his hair back. He loves to grease it with Brilliantine.

His name is Jilali but on the street, at the bar, and at the market, everyone calls him Joujou. He's always been a pimp. From the day I saw him at Lalla Zahra's house. The first house Zina and I stayed at. She's a good woman. Fat, old, and kind, her hair white and red from all the henna she puts in it. She has a wart on her nose the size of a chickpea. But she has a repulsive side to her. She loves whiskey. And she loves Joujou. I spent about three years in her house before meeting him. One night they came home drunk. Drunk, embracing each other, and singing. Joujou, as now, was wearing the same jeans and red shirt. He was propping her up so she didn't fall. He moved away from her and she fell in the middle of the house like a bale of chaff. Joujou's been to prison twice because of hashish. He's thin, with a long nose and a deep scar dividing his cheek in two. He's evil and malicious. Everyone stays away from his kind, even the police. Lalla Zahra said proudly: "Once, they brought a van full of cops but they couldn't arrest him. Not because he's strong. But because he vanishes into thin air. They couldn't grab him." Maybe that's why the old lady fell in love with him. And for the additional and understandable reasons that he warms up her bed at night and protects her during the day. She bought him a gold chain and a gold ring and a bottle of Brilliantine. When she's drunk, she tells him he should be careful with the bottle since it's expensive. But Joujou empties it in one week.

One night she bought two roosters. She slaughtered one of them and told him: "Come eat, my love." Joujou went up to the plate and kicked it so hard the breast of the rooster stuck to the ceiling. He spewed insults at her. He vomited onto her all the malice and hatred he'd collected in his heart while living with her. The old lady started laughing. Joujou insulted her while she laughed. Her eyes were shut and the two gold teeth in her mouth glimmered. She became uglier. She raised her hands at him and in her laughing, perverse manner told him: "Come to me, my love, embrace me."

I saw him hit her a bunch of times. I saw her face bloodied. Red spit running from her mouth as she laughed, telling him: "Come here, my love, hit me, kill me, but embrace me afterward." She'd turn to me, wiping the blood away, and say, "Joujou loves me."

One day Joujou asked me: "What're you doing with Lalla Zahra? She's exploiting you."

Zina and I had been at Lalla Zahra's house long enough for me to know the time had come to try somewhere else. I was thinking seriously about moving from her house to the house of a widow whose husband had died in the Indochina War. From the beginning, I understood Joujou's intentions. A pimp's always a pimp. I thought, Joujou exploiting me is better than Lalla Zahra exploiting me on the pretext that she opened the door of her house to me the day I came to Azrou without knowing anyone. And besides, Joujou's a man. He'll give me my livelihood. He won't eat me up. He's not going to leave me without a penny like that pimp Lalla Zahra. But on one condition: My sister stays with me. And playing around with her is forbidden. Got it? At that time, Zina went to a school to learn to type. But the school, instead of typing, was teaching girls how to whore. I thought it's better she stays home so I can send her later to Aunt Taja's. Or we'll go together.

It was a Friday the day we left Lalla Zahra's house. We got our bags together at night and waited for the sun to come up. As if the old lady had guessed something was being done in secret, she spent the whole night drinking whiskey. The old lady loved drinking Black & White whiskey. There was a picture of two dogs on the bottle. She always thought they were two cats. Whenever one of her customers came to see her, she hit them with the same question: "Did you bring the whiskey with the two cats?" As we were about to leave, she stood in front of the door. Her fat body blocked it completely. Her body was the size of the door. Joujou didn't say a word. He went up to her and punched her in the face so hard I heard her teeth break. We went out the door and left her looking for her teeth. We heard her saying to him she'd be waiting for him at dinnertime since she'd be slaughtering the second rooster. She was laughing, but without teeth this time.

6

So I make him his breakfast and sit down in front of him. He's silent. Maybe he's waiting for me to throw myself on his hand and kiss it. Maybe he's thinking I'd sit between his knees crying. He looks at me, always expecting something from me. His malice is fixed on me. I'm not expecting anything good. He brushes his hair again, oils it a second time, puts his dentures in his empty mouth, and then sits eating breakfast. He's waiting for me to say something he likes. What'll I say? I don't have anything to say. At this moment, in the state I'm in, there isn't anything to help me say something, even if I wanted to. The spinning in my head hasn't gone down. The trembling has spread to other parts of my body. I look at him and think: What am I doing with this pimp? Without the scar on his face, Joujou would look like a nice guy. The scar seems deeper than yesterday and this increases my hatred for him. My hatred for all pimps. As if Satan has kept digging it with an ax.

Not a word leaves his mouth, neither good nor bad. He lights a cigarette and starts playing with the pack of matches between his fingers. He doesn't reach for the cup of coffee I made for him. The stupidity of the situation hits me at this moment. What am I doing with this pimp? I've been in his house for two years with nothing to show for it. What did I expect? Maybe staying at Lalla Zahra's house would have been better. He looks like he's planning something, and hiding it by playing with a pack of matches. People are all the same. They're the same wherever they are. Nothing's changed since they appeared on the face of the earth. Why would he be different? Everyone's the same: my father, Lalla Zahra, Joujou. I'm not afraid of Joujou. Why would I be afraid of him or anyone else? Should I be afraid of him just because his scar is more threatening than it was yesterday? I'm ready for anything.

I've saved some money. Enough for Zina and me, as long as we're careful. For Casablanca or any other city. I'm not desperate, I'm always optimistic. I expect good things for me and my sister. I saved enough for this year, at least. At the end of it, we'll go together to Casablanca. My hand on hers, instead of me setting her loose alone in a big city like that. This might be the chance I've been waiting for. Maybe the time has come for us to change our fate. To go for what we want. Or in any direction that gets us away from Joujou. From Lalla Zahra. And Azrou. Whatever that direction might be. The important thing is that something changes in our life.

How many times did I stop myself from thinking about how I'll die young because of all the diseases I got from the soldiers? How did an idea like this come to me? I'm not afraid of death. I welcome it. I'm thinking about the fate of Zina after me. I'll welcome death when I've put Zina in a safer place. At Aunt Taja's, for example. I'm not doing well. Since I woke up, my head's been on fire. The fever isn't going away. It seems to me, from another perspective, that the time has come to expect good things. I don't know what I'm waiting for or what I expect.

Zina is sleeping in her room. When she wakes up, she comes out of the room stretching and yawning. Light, happy, careless. On her skin is the scent of a calm night. She crosses the room in a thin shirt and goes into the kitchen. Joujou's wandering eyes follow her. He doesn't utter a word. He takes a sip from his cup, slams it down on the table, and leaves. I don't pay attention to that moment. I don't think about the meaning of his look.

7

Normally the bar is empty at this time of the afternoon, with only a few horse bettors and Aziz, who works at the airbase.

56

The moment I step inside, I see Joujou playing pinball. The English teacher is sitting in the same place as yesterday. Aziz is leaning on the bar and drinking beer. Joujou avoids looking at me. He acts like he's busy with his hair. He's passing his hand through it and looking all around, but not at me. The teacher looks up at me then looks down as if ashamed. I say hello to Aziz, pull over a crooked stool, and sit down next to him. Aziz works at the airbase. In Kénitra. He flies airplanes. He loves to sit at the bar and talk with Madame Janeau. I don't care about what they're saying because they always talk in French. Aziz never moves from his seat until he leaves the bar. While there, he talks with Madame Janeau.

My head hurts. The veins have been beating at the base of my head since I woke up. The noise of the pinball machine increases my headache. Joujou brings his fist down on the machine's glass surface as if he's bringing it down on my scattered head. As if he's compensating for the words he didn't direct at my face this morning. Then, chewing tobacco, he leans over to the teacher and whispers something in his ear. He hits the pinball machine glass again, so hard you'd have thought it would smash into pieces. Madame Janeau doesn't say a thing. She's busy listening to Aziz. And Abdesalam is filling the horse-betting sheets. What's the pimp saying to the teacher? There's no way to know, even though I'm concentrating on it. I don't like the sight of the pimp this morning.

"What's wrong with this guy?" asks Abdesalam when he finally notices the pinball machine glass will be smashed if he doesn't stop. What's wrong with this guy? Then Madame Janeau asks me too.

I tell her: "I don't know, Madame."

Abdesalam gets up, saying: "I don't like this guy."

"Me neither," I say.

I haven't liked him since he slammed his cup of coffee onto the table and left agitated. I look at him and I say there's nothing to like in this pimp this morning. Then I see him move

57

away from the pinball machine and sit at the teacher's table. This pimp's devising something, I think. Even Abdesalam noticed the change. That's why he kept asking what was going on. Madame Janeau too. I replied: "I don't know, Madame. I swear I don't know what the pimp's looking for this morning."

As for Aziz, he turns to me and shakes his head apologetically, smiling. When I look back at the teacher's table, Joujou has disappeared. No trace of him in the whole bar. Not at the counter or the pinball machine. Aziz points at the door and says, "Your pimp's left, take it easy." But I can't. I won't take it easy just because Aziz said to.

Aziz works at the military base, as I said. For forty-eight hours at a time. After each shift, he drives his car, a Simca 1000, without stopping, all the way to Stork Bar. Forty-eight hours he works and forty-eight hours he gets drunk. That's the program. But he's quiet, mysterious. Silent all the time. When he isn't talking to Madame Janeau, he's silent. As if he's afraid of mixing with people. He looks like Abdel-Halim Hafez. He has signs of sadness on his face. The same signs that mark the face of Abdel-Halim. When you stare at him for a long time, you're sure this isn't the right place for him. You ask, what's this young guy doing here? You don't know why you ask yourself this question, especially when he comes in the pilot's uniform. A blue uniform with glimmering brass buttons. Although usually he comes in a tracksuit and sneakers, as today. How old is he? Not older than twenty-eight. Sometimes I sit watching him and I wonder what life a woman could have with him. No matter what, it wouldn't be like the hell we live in with this pimp.

After fifteen minutes, Joujou comes back. With who? Zina. When she sees me, she runs toward me. Joujou pulls her violently, drags her to the table, and pushes her down in front of the English teacher: "Here's your place."

He takes a step toward me, sticking his chest out, and says in what sounds like a victory song, "That's her place," and then he goes back to the table dancing and stroking his hair. I run toward him. What's my sister doing here? He pushes me toward the bar. With a roughness I wasn't expecting. A strange, surprising fear takes hold of me. The customers are watching. Frozen in their spots and looking at him. The same despair overwhelms them. And the teacher? He seems like he has no misgivings at all. With a bowed head, playing with his glass, waiting for it to end. I don't know what's going on in Madame Janeau's head at that moment. She's taken out her small mirror, put on deep-red lipstick, and begun doing her makeup for the coming half day.

Zina's started crying. I can't bear Zina's crying. I can't stand to see her tears. It's my fault. That's what I think at that moment. I'm the one who pushed her to this life. Everything's fallen apart. Everything I did for her isn't worth a thing anymore. God alone knows how much I fought for her to live a normal life. God alone knows how much I fought so she doesn't lack anything. I put her in school so she could have a profession. And here she is crying. The pimp grabs the teacher's hand and puts it on her knee and tells him to try out her freshness on the spot. Why doesn't the earth split open and swallow us all? Joujou's relaxed. He doesn't care what I'm thinking. He leans over Zina, grabs her by the chin, and begins nodding her head and laughing. He then sits at the table and puts his hand on her shoulder. The beer spills from the glass in his hand. No one knows how to deal with him.

Aziz gets off the stool and moves toward the table. Joujou notices him and gets up. He doesn't stand up all the way because Aziz hits him with a single blow that throws him to the ground. No one sees it coming. It comes quickly. Only the pimp sees it as he's falling. Then, laid out on his back, all his malice leaves him. His blood, like the blood of any pimp, flows out on the bar floor. You don't know where it's coming from. Abdesalam comes out from behind the bar and says to the horse bettors: "Get out of here before the police come."

The English teacher and the horse bettors, as if they've come back to life, grab the pimp and drag him outside. With excessive zeal, as if they were waiting for the chance to take revenge on him.

Aziz takes Zina's hand and leads her to the bar. He puts her on the stool. She's happy. High on the stool. For the first time, in all her femininity, Zina's suddenly become a woman. A young, beautiful, happy woman. With her whole life in front of her. I'm happy too. Happy for her happiness. The only thing I feel is tears coming down from my eyes.

After fifteen minutes, the horse bettors go back out to check on the pimp. He's disappeared. They find a drop of black blood where he'd been lying.

Until now, I don't know when the idea occurred to the pimp. Did it ferment in his mind little by little? Or did it come down in one fell swoop this morning while he was watching Zina cross the living room in her see-through shirt, nearly naked, strutting, with her bare white forearms, crossing the living room with childish indifference? Zina's grown up. She was always beautiful. She's grown more beautiful this morning. Her chest has filled out. I think her walking in front of him this morning, almost naked in her see-through shirt, with her breasts swaying languidly, that's what aroused Joujou's devilish ideas. At that moment, he didn't say anything. It was enough for him to take a sip from his cup, set it down hard, and leave. But the idea was there. I didn't notice it as it rang out in his head like a bell, but it was there. I go back to the bar counter. Aziz turns to Zina and asks her: "What are we doing now?"

She tells him: "Let's play."

Aziz gives Abdesalam two twenty-dirham bills and tells him to put a bet down on horse number seven. I've played the horses many times but no horse I ever bet on won. From this angle too, my luck's twisted. But who knows? Luck might be my ally this time. The number seven might be our lucky number, mine and Zina's.

8

Aziz

A Little after Midnight

1

LIKE A BELL THAT DOESN'T stop ringing, sores have crept over the sides of my body. I'm anxious about the catastrophe that will befall me if I fall off the slab tonight. This bell started going off in my head a while ago, with its ominous song: You'll fall. *Din din din.* You won't fall. *Din din din.* The path begins as usual with a round of pain attacking my body little by little until it's a cascade. I haven't fallen yet but my body tells me tonight it'll fall. If I fall on the ground, I'll spend the night there like an overturned cockroach. The ground is wet, with a thick crust of mud. When a stream of dim light comes in, I see bubbles gurgling on its surface. They appear and disappear in a persistent movement as if they're millions of small worms turning around by themselves. Maybe that's what they are, because they make a sound like a reptile under the ground. If my weak body falls on the ground, there'll be no morning, as death will have come and gone, taking with it what's left of me. That's why you see me starting to take some precautions before illness overtakes me. I tie my hand with a rope and hang it over a nail on the wall. I tie the other end of the rope to the toe the rat bit and stretch out. I look at the ground under me. Dampness. Water. Death.

In this phase, illness isn't connected to this foot or that anymore. It's passed them and entered the rest of the body. The illness usually begins with a kind of simple disturbance, like any other. Because of the bite, it began early tonight as if someone was pressing on my fingers one by one. The right hand first, then the left. Afterward, my fingers stiffened. As if I had a bunch of stiff rods instead of fingers. Or as if they'd been injected with a full dose of anesthetic. From there it made its way to the other limbs. What I feel in this stage of advancing illness is what wood feels as fire eats it up. A true burning in the veins inside the chest before the blaze engulfs the rest of the body. Stiffness replaces another kind of feeling, with doubled pain. The pain becomes universal, unbroken. It lessens and then grows in an internal, secret symphony, harmonious with its role, and you suffer because you listen to it with all your senses that become increasingly clear and aware, as if the pain stimulates them. Here too any movement becomes painful and awareness of it becomes harsh to the utmost degree. In this state of mine, I have to take every precaution to avoid falling from the slab. When any movement is impossible for me, my sick body falling on the wet ground with all kinds of filth means death. I cannot fall asleep. Sleeping is falling and falling is death. It's easy not to fall in times of waking, as in now, if you could call this being awake. Realizing exactly what's happening to my body, to every organ in it, to every cell, but incapable of moving. My body is a pile of screaming, noxious pain. But more than this, I must not sleep.

The best position is to lie down on your back. Sleeping on your side always tempts you to turn to the other side. As for sleeping on your back, nothing compares to it. It makes you feel that you're seeking refuge on the ground. You insist on staying there. Only the dead are buried on their sides. I'm still alive and I intend to stay alive. My hand is tied to the rope. And the rope is looped around a high nail on the wall, with the other end tied exactly to my toe. When sleep descends on me suddenly and my hand relaxes and falls, it'll pull the rope that'll pull my bitten toe up, doubling the pain that'll make me scream and I'll wake up despite myself. That's how, in this strange balance, I'll escape from falling.

The illness moves in the same way, and it got me used to it. It increases and increases until it becomes a burning mass. A flaming ball. Except the head. The head is submerged in another kind of pain: the sharp awareness of all the different degrees of the rising pain, like an overturned waterfall. My breathing only returns as a broken-up track of whistling. It too has its rising notes, according to the advance of the night and the penetration into the thickets of the illness. All my senses are aroused, vigorous, following the least movement and the least sound. The pain's rising now. I say at this advanced time of night, I might not fall tonight. I'm waiting to fall. That's the bell ringing again: You'll fall. *Din din din.* You won't fall. *Din din din.* Dawn is still far off but we, my body and me, we've made it through an important part. Sometimes it seems to me I'm tumbling, then I discover it's only my mind playing with me. Other times, I go easily into a short nap, lasting not more than two or three seconds (two or three pulses), when I see myself fall or see myself wondering if I fell. All this before the string on my right toe is pulled. I scream without knowing if it's the string pulling my toe or if I dreamed of the string pulling my toe. Or that none of this happened. That I didn't dream or I didn't scream, that nothing happened. All the torture's still in front of me. The falling. And then death. Then . . . And what is death? An eternal smell. A calm descending to the final resting place where there's nothing. I wait for dawn to be sure of all this.

I feel like I'm dozing off. I turn slowly toward the kingdom of unconsciousness and I expect the toe to rise up to make me scream but it doesn't rise up and I don't scream. *Din din din.* You won't fall. *Din din din.* You'll fall. Sleeping is falling and falling is death. I look at the ceiling. Has the bird come back? There are eyes looking out. Many eyes and mouths laughing. Faces changing shape, with long fingers piercing the holes and coming down and down. Then going back up and up. Nothing's clear and the faces mock my fear.

I lie on my back, as if I'm bound to the cement basin by a thick rope so I don't fall. Here cooks used to wash the dishes of the local governor without one of them knowing what it meant to fall. Or maybe they washed dead men in it.

The faces mock my fear. And my imaginary rope and the string attached to my toe. They mock my disgraceful trick as I threaten them with my tied toes. I'm not joking. It's a matter of life or death. But they keep laughing and mocking. I avert my face. I see a plastic can on the wet ground and thirst overwhelms me. The desire for water becomes so oppressive that I want to fall to get closer to the water. The water's there, underneath, in the plastic can, two liters at least. Oh, the day's passed to its last drop and my share of water hasn't run out? Do I break the rope and move to the edge? There are big rats trying to turn the can over so they can drink too. They pretend they're gnawing so I can see their fangs. They're used to waiting for me to fall, looking at me with red eyes and waiting for me to fall so they can bite my other foot. Then the ground shakes and turns me around as it does for a drunk, as I make a conscious effort to say that I'm finally falling.

2—January 1972

I'm sitting in the tower watching him at the door of the storehouse. His helmet under his arm. He's getting ready to get into the plane with everything he needs. He seems happy. Like anyone getting ready to fly in the sky. I watch the plane too—it's on the ground, about twenty meters away. As if it's waiting for him. I think: This plane knows me. We traveled together in the great sky. We danced above Kénitra as it was sleeping and then as it was waking. A plane with one seat. Green like the color of olives. Its front like the head of a hawk with its fine beak and two windows like wide eyes. It's my friend Captain Hammouda, who's standing at the storehouse door, stealing a glance at the tower, hesitating. Is he going to move toward the plane or not? Finally he moves. He circles around it. He looks at it, passing his hand over its surface, as if he's its new owner. Now and then he looks toward the observation tower where I'm sitting watching him. I hesitate too. Should I go down or not? In the end I go down. I go down and approach the plane. Hammouda has backtracked and disappeared into the storehouse. I follow him. The smell of kerosene and gas surprises me. The smell of burning oil. The smell of a world I know. A smell inhabiting my body. Igniting my blood. It's as if I went in to renew my connection with it and to fill my lungs with its scent. My fingers and my mind are on fire and every part in my body wants to pounce on this piece or that. Captain Hammouda is in his green uniform as if he's trying to hide between the piles of instruments and engine parts being repaired, but he doesn't succeed. His height doesn't help him disappear. I move behind him to surprise him. Confused, he says he's looking for his glasses. He doesn't mention where he put them. He tries to hide his confusion, or maybe he wants to apologize because he'll fly the plane I was flying. Maybe he wants to apologize but his tongue isn't helping him. I pretend I'm helping him look for his glasses. I ask him jokingly if he can fly without them. He doesn't respond. We look for a while. I hide behind the instruments. I leave the storehouse without him noticing me. Without him turning toward me. He knows I've left but he doesn't want to turn so he doesn't have to acknowledge it. I go back to the observation tower and the smell of burning oil and gasoline follows me, fills my head and my lungs, fills my blood. I watch the door of the storehouse again and wait for Hammouda to come out. I don't see him. I expect him to come out at any moment. I wonder what he's doing in there and what's going on in his head.

The ringing of the plane's engine fills my head even when I'm far from the airbase. When I leave the base, I'm still there really. I love planes and the sound of their engines. The noise fills my head day and night. By day I fly and by night I dream I'm the pilot and the plane. But this isn't what the colonel, the head of the airbase, thinks. My happiest times are when I find myself flying in the sky. But yesterday the colonel told me: "Aziz, forget the plane. Forget the sky. The ground is better for you."

I feel like dust is coming down on my face and covering my mind. The colonel, the person responsible for the airbase, is sitting behind his desk as I stand before him and listen to him and tell myself that, except for flying, I'm not good at anything. This is my profession. I only learned this one thing. Flying is my life. Since I came to the airbase seven months ago, I haven't been doing anything but this. I fly. When I don't fly, I'm in the storehouse, poring over the engine, examining its coils. The heat on the plane's surface scorches my face and I remember we've spent a lot of time in the sky, the plane and I. I give it a rest. I circle around it and wait for its engine to rest, not knowing, as time passes, if it's resting or not. Then I go up to it and see it's still emitting fumes and I tell it to calm down. I say I have to leave but I don't leave. I get up on the machine, clean it, and rub it bit by bit so it revives and its calmness and liveliness return to it. Its great love is the sky. I say I have to leave but I don't leave. I sit next to it, asking if it liked how we spent the day.

My friends make fun of me at the airbase: "What're you doing, Aziz? You're good at taking off but not at landing?"

It's before lunch and we're in the snack bar drinking after-noon beer and all of a sudden Captain Hammouda lets out a strange chuckle. Captain Hammouda's my friend and he likes talking about the same thing: "One day, Aziz, you'll fly off and you won't come back."

Sometimes the colonel intervenes too, joking, I think he's joking, when he asks me in front of the other pilots: "Didn't you learn how to land in school?"

But yesterday, when he called me into his office, he wasn't joking. He sat in his usual stern way, moving his papers, and not looking at me. It was hard to breathe, as if dust were blocking my nose and mouth. What was he doing? He was moving his papers between his fingers and pointing at the observation tower. As if he were telling me that's my place starting tomorrow.

Tomorrow comes quickly. Bringing with it disappointment. Captain Hammouda seems confused, standing in front of the storehouse door holding his helmet, moving one foot forward and holding back the other. Captain Hammouda isn't laughing as he pretends to look for his glasses. He doesn't want to embarrass me.

What are they doing now in the snack bar, all of them, including the colonel? I sit in the tower now, watching it. The plane I spent seventy-six hours on looks like an orphan on the ground without me. Without a friend. Without a captain. Without Aziz. Its new captain has disappeared into the storehouse looking for glasses that don't exist. From there, maybe he's watching me. As I'm watching him. I pretend I'm not watching him. Like he's pretending. Other planes took off a while ago but my plane was left waiting for the captain who'll give it back its glow. And I stayed behind, in the tower. I'm not doing anything. I don't touch any of the buttons. I watch the door of the storehouse and wait for Hammouda to come out in his green uniform with his helmet under his arm to take my place.

"It's forbidden for you to fly, said the colonel, "Because you don't know how to land. In the whole world, is there a captain who isn't good at landing?""

I do sometimes forget myself. The heights make me dizzy. I get lost in a delicious dream. The sound of the radio comes to me: "Aziz, come down." But I don't hear it. The unconfined space intoxicates me. Close to the sun, in a strange way, as if it rose for me alone. Sometimes I have the mountains under me on one side and the forests on the other, sometimes the vast expanse of the sea. But what takes me completely is the view of the river. When I cross the city, I see it: countryside in every direction and the river moving freely in it like a gigantic snake. I follow its zigzags. I twist where it twists. Sometimes it disappears behind a mountain so I bide my time. I give it enough time to disappear. To surprise it again. We both love this game. The river and me. Then I go up and up, to where it's small, a trickle of water embracing the hip of the mountain.

3

In front of the plane's yoke, I float again, I float in a calmness like the intoxication of the eternal. All the worries of the day, those that turn hair white without you noticing it and make your veins dry out, all of them are gone. Because of the pure oxygen filling my lungs. The earth stays large underneath. However far away, it stays large. But it doesn't fill me with delight. Being hidden in the heights is what obsesses me, nourishes me, nurses me. But not in the way a mother nurses her baby. I'm nourished from its hidden milk as I play. My two hands, which aren't good at anything on the ground, find here, high above, their hidden skill. I notice, and then realize that what used to terrify me doesn't anymore. It stopped. My body, things and their shadows don't terrify it. There are no shadows here. Nothing follows it. Or subdues it. Because it's outside my will. I hear it neigh. I see it tremble like a foal on the farm. I can't do anything to it. I can't control it if it occurs to it to pretend to be stupid. Its acrobatics, I can't control them. I can't keep it from flying without stopping. Will it hear me if I tell it to stop flying because the colonel asks me to? Will it hear the radio as it tells Aziz to come down? Where's Aziz? There's no trace of him on the ground. His body isn't his anymore. He can even become a bird, changing his clothes if he wanted. And I only hope for this. My body wants to go all the way to the small village where I was born. Why don't we take a little peek to see if my father's come back, pushing his ram in front of him? And I know my body won't wait for me to respond because it'll have changed directions, going up, always up. Toward the sun.

The ground isn't above or below. It's in one direction sometimes, then another, depending on the plane's intentions. Sometimes upright like a wall, sometimes level as if its good sense has come back to it. Sometimes the sky becomes an earth and the earth becomes a sky. Then it seems as if a sudden spring comes over it. A summer follows it more suddenly. The plane wants that. Despite the pilot. The sudden summer comes to the edge of the window, looking over the pilot, and then flees. Its scent stays long enough for the pilot to say: A nice summer's passed by me alone. The sky lights up little by little. It becomes golden. It ignites more, as if a universal flame is devouring it.

The plane comes back to earth, the sound of the radio having disappeared a while ago. But I haven't come back with it. Evening's here but I haven't returned to earth yet. I still carry the day in my blood. This is its color, and its calm is opening up even the arteries of my heart. Should I land? I wait a little. After a moment, people will be sleeping. Look, they're getting ready. We're up above, we're tending small animals walking on all fours below. After a little, they'll be sleeping. Lights come on here and there. Dense in one direction and sparse in another, few animals are dreaming of the next day. Their dreams shine interrupted and continue at the same time.

4

Strange ideas are filling my head this morning, since I got to the tower. Since before I got there. My place isn't here. I try to forget the plane. To forget Captain Hammouda. I leave the tower. I walk on the ground in the airbase. It's hard to breathe. I approach and touch the surface of the plane. Its touch eases my soul. I go back to the snack bar. I remember the pilots have returned. Mbarek, Qasim, and Siddik. The dizziness of the sky they just returned from envelops them. Its scent and its alchemy envelop them. Unseen envelopments of the sky they returned from laughing shroud them. I alone see it. I hear their happiness and I understand. They drink their beer and tell stories. They wait for me to appear, then drag out their stories longer than necessary.

"What're you doing, Aziz?"

"You're good at taking off but not landing?"

"One day, Aziz, you're going to take off and not come back."

I cross the snack bar. I don't turn toward them. I avoid looking over to where they are. I move away from them and their joy. I find myself in the parking lot and I throw myself inside my Simca 1000. I get moving and soon find myself outside the airbase, not knowing where I'm going. I let the car lead me without knowing where it'll take me. I don't care. Needing air, I move away from the tower. And from the plane and pilots. I think Captain Hammouda might have come out of his hiding place. After a little, I'll sense him flying above me. I raise my head but I don't see him. I hear a sound behind me and I raise my head, believing it's the plane's engine. I know the sound of its engine like I know my own voice. But it's all mixed up. I think its sound might have changed after it moved to another pilot.

I drive aimlessly, at the beginning at least. A few cars pass. I don't care about them. The sky's blue and there's no trace of a plane flying above. Captain Hammouda's my friend but I think I won't talk to him after today. I'll avoid him. When our eyes meet by accident, I'll pretend like I'm tying my shoes so I don't have to say hello. As for the colonel, I have to flatter him. Not for much longer, though, because maybe I won't go back to the base. I don't have to. I'm still young, twenty-seven. My whole future's in front of me. What'll I do in the observation tower at twenty-seven? Watch others fly? Set lanes for them to take off and land? My respect for him has run out. I'll still flatter the colonel, yes, but as for appreciation and respect, I won't ever respect him like I used to. Bad thoughts crowd my head. Thoughts that don't usually come to me as I don't like to find my head full of them. But despite that, they overwhelm me completely. I open the car windows. A cold, invigorating air hits my face but it doesn't take away my anxious ideas. I recognize the hills around me and I say to myself: "We'll cross Wadi Baht now." After a little, we cross it. I say out loud: "Here we've crossed it, the car and me." If I'd been flying in the plane, I wouldn't have said something like this. I now say the words of those moving on the ground. Here we've crossed the river. At this time of year, it's calm. It has eaten its share of people and animals and it sits relaxing. After two hours, I recognize the Azrou woods and I know I'm going toward Azrou.

I park the car next to the sidewalk and go into the Stork. The only bar I know. It's empty at this time of the afternoon. A few customers drink beer and play the horses. Joujou's playing pinball, hitting the flippers and chewing tobacco. I don't like this guy. I turn my back on him and share Madame Janeau's food. Bread, a piece of ham, and olives. Khatima comes in, says hi, and sits near me. Usually she sits far away. Maybe she sits near me to piss off the pimp. I think we're like each other, Khatima and me. We're both in a bad mood this morning. Joujou walks by behind us. She doesn't pay attention to him and he doesn't pay attention to her. He then goes back to the pinball machine and starts hitting it. Madame Janeau asks me why he's hitting the pinball machine so hard. Khatima's the one who responds to her.

The pimp passes behind us shaking his butt, and leaves the bar. I think about my fleeting luck and my situation seems miserable to me. Then I tell myself I'm exaggerating and that my situation isn't worse than the pimp's. Afternoon beer is a good thing, and I gulp from the bottle. Madame Janeau puts a beer in front of me and says it's from Khatima. She smiles at me and I thank her and go back to the anxious thoughts overwhelming me. I only come to when I hear the pimp next to me making threats. I turn toward him, where a fifteen- or sixteen-year-old girl is sitting. She's looking around, terrified. My anger at the pimp grows as I see him point at the girl menacingly. Her name's Zina. I learn her name when I hear him say: "Zina, from this moment, she'll enter the business." He then goes back to his table, shaking his butt. I think about the terrified girl, who hasn't become a woman yet and who looks around with eyes whose clarity makes their terror more intense. Her terrified eyes look at me. She begins crying and the clarity of her eyes disappears. All the anger I accumulated during the day courses through my hand. I knock the pimp to the ground. Unconscious. As if I'd hit him with a bomb. A lot of blood runs from his mouth. And from the back of his head, which hit the corner of the table as he was falling. I take Zina's hand and the fear disappears from her eyes. Tears disappear but their clarity hasn't come back yet. I turn toward her and say: "What're we doing now?" She says: "Let's play."

9

Zina

Around 1 a.m.

1

I WAKE UP FROM A nap confused, not knowing how long I was asleep. I look at my watch. It's a few minutes before one o'clock. There's complete silence on the bus. I amuse myself with the sound of the engine rumbling through the night. The seat next to me is empty again. The eighty-year-old man who hadn't found a family to take him didn't come back. Is he still on the bus or did he get off at the last stop? I try to find a comfortable position to fall asleep again. Clouds gather above us and the moon disappears from the part of the sky above me. Maybe it's lighting up the other side of the bus. I put my leg on the empty seat, not wondering anymore if there's a moon or clouds. My stomach feels like there's a big hole in it. I remember I haven't eaten anything since lunch with Khatima, and I try in vain to remember what I ate. I remember distant things but I don't remember what I ate.

The bus finally stops in front of a building whose walls rise up into the darkest part of the night. It looks abandoned, with a thick darkness enveloping the garden in front of it, except for rays of light escaping from the blinds. The travelers protest again and the driver says he's got to stop to ask about the condition of the river before crossing it. There isn't anywhere open right now except for this inn, the Chinese man's inn.

At that moment, the inner door opens and the light escaping from behind it casts thick shadows in the garden. There appears at the door the shadow of a man waving at us, gesturing that we should enter. He begins yelling not to pass by the pool since it's empty. At the door, the man welcomes us, saying storms have raged all week, with water flooding them from every side. We might find the road cut off at the bridge. The hall we enter is wide. The window blinds are drawn and the hall is crowded with different kinds of furniture: dilapidated couches, tables with cut-open chairs around them, glass cupboards with reliefs of wooden sailboats and huge oysters on them, mounted boar heads on the wall, datebooks blackened from all the dust covering them, and five big wall clocks, none of them working. Plants hang from the ceiling, many of them, different kinds. It's as if we've entered a kind of bazaar. The man who welcomed us seems a part of the place with his short stature, unshaven face, narrow eyes, and rotten teeth. He might be the Chinese man the driver told us about. He looks like he's from China. In the hall, he tells us that the day before yesterday, the river waters swept away the body of a man whose family was crossing with him to bury him on the other side and they haven't found a trace of him. He turns toward the corner where a man and woman are sitting. This man agrees with a shake of his head and the woman next to him laughs. The Chinese man says he's a judge who knows more about these things than we do. He's drunk, and so is the woman next to him. There's a big plate of grilled meat in front of them. The woman is excessively fat and, like a balloon, is sinking into the couch. She's wearing an embroidered caftan and eating without stopping, laughing in a loud voice at every word coming out of the judge's mouth and every movement he makes.

The travelers spread themselves out at the tables. I don't see the old man among them. A woman sitting by herself catches my attention and I sit down at her table. She doesn't notice me because she's busy with a small package, untying its knot and taking some chicken and bread out of it. She puts it on the table and breaks her bread into small pieces. She lifts her head and looks at me, smiling as she hands me a piece of bread and pushes chicken in front of me. I remember my mother, because this woman looks like what remains of her in my memory. She has the same excessive beauty, persisting despite the forty years she lived or because of them. Her face is white and round, her skin clear, her eyes big and lined with kohl, and her lips prominent and inviting in a way that stirs inside me a feeling I'm ashamed of. Like a strong, overwhelming desire you don't know where it comes from.

My mother might have had the same lips. She'd tell Khatima and me she was the most beautiful girl in her village. Her parents forbade her to go out. She stayed forgotten at home until no one remembered her beauty. After that, our father married her. He was, by chance, passing by, not knowing her story.

My confusion hasn't gone away since I woke up and it increases sharply after sitting at the woman's table. The painful images she inspires in me. I head to the toilets and wash my hands and face with soap and water. I sit eating, busy with her more than with anything else around me. Her hand nearly touching her face as she devours small pieces of chicken and chews them so slowly you'd think she wasn't eating. She finishes chewing. She wipes her fingers. Now she's peeling an orange distractedly. Her fingers are doing the work but her mind is roaming elsewhere. I fix my eyes on her face and my confusion increases. I try to imagine things. Time doesn't erase beauty like this. It'll watch over this beauty her entire life. Whenever I look closely, I become more certain she might be my mother's younger sister, as I don't know if my mother had a sister or not.

Without thinking, I touch the slip I'm wearing. I find it wet and remember the dream I had during my nap on the bus. Aziz was running in wide, barren land, heading toward the woods after climbing the tall walls of a casbah, fleeing from the cellar where they put him. He hears voices following him. He runs faster. He goes into the woods where I'm hiding behind a tree. I take his hand and open a door for him in the tree. We go into a wide place without a horizon, like a sky, perhaps. We find ourselves naked and sitting on clouds. He looks around him, out of breath, his penis erect like a shaft. I grab hold of his penis and begin playing with it. I massage it with my hand, up and down. I ask him if he likes how I'm playing with it. He closes his eyes and lies down on the cloud. He feels his penis go cold despite his erection, so he apologizes, saying: "It's the cloud." I ask him if he wants me to warm it up and I get on top of him and feel his cold penis moving up into me, up to my cervix, as I press down to push him farther inside, then I move up and down more forcefully. He too is moving under me, up and down, and we stay like that, rocking in the cloud as I wonder if I'm awake or asleep. I look at him to know. His eyes are closed and I don't know if he's awake and enjoying the moment in his own way or if he's sleeping. Then suddenly he turns me over on my back and his penis hits against my insides violently, with a delicious savagery, and I grab hold of him and pull him to me roughly as his sweat pours down on my face, like rain, and enters my eyes, my nose, and my mouth. It tastes sweet in my mouth. I feel his semen spray the sides of my vagina mercilessly, like a violent waterfall. I touch the liquid but realize what I'm touching is blood. I wake up confused, and my confusion has stayed with me.

In the tavern's hall, as I sit in front of the woman with the nice face, going over my dream, I think it's lucky the woman's oblivious to me, peeling an orange absentmindedly. Lucky for me they're all oblivious. The travelers are eating. The judge is getting drunk with the fat woman, who's laughing as she devours the grilled meat. The Chinese man's moving between the tables, putting down plates and picking up others.

This idea occurs to me: Is she going to the casbah too?

I ask where she's going and she asks me the same thing. I then ask her if she knows the casbah where I'm heading and I tell her my story, of our marriage, Aziz and me, and his disappearance and the years I've spent looking for him. It's as if I'm seeking her affection. Quickly, I ask God to let her stay with me. (Other unhealthy ideas occur to me. I hope, for example, that the trip will last longer than the hours that are left. I hope I'll put my hand on hers and keep holding it for the entire trip.)

On the bus, we sit pressed against the other to the right of the driver. Her shoulder against mine. I feel her warmth piercing my body like a delicious current making my saliva flow. She asks me if I have kids. "No," I tell her, taking the opportunity to turn and look at her face.

She's understood my bodily curiosity and maybe my exposed ideas so I tell her she reminds me of my mother and that she resembles her a lot. I tell her my mother was beautiful. She says she has eleven kids. That she used to be beautiful. The most beautiful girl in her village and in all the villages, near and far. Except for her beauty, there was nothing else to attract men. Young men went to great lengths to get engaged to her. They'd shoot at each other with rifles for her. There was the one who divorced his wife for her, the one who swore he'd renounce marriage if it wasn't with her, and the one who killed his neighbor, his friend. Before she got married to the man who'd be the father of her eleven children—he was a poor famer who could barely earn his daily bread—a hashish trafficker won her. On the day of the betrothal, he came in a white Mercedes, bringing with him polished words and a procession of luxury cars and carts carrying all sorts of gifts. Immediately after the marriage, in order to take revenge against her beauty, he started staying up all night with his girlfriends in their bedroom. Then he abandoned her and left her for years, neither married nor divorced. And if it hadn't been for people intervening to help her get a divorce, she would have remained like that.

Once again, the dream I had comes over me. I try to forget it but whenever I try, I remember its details and I feel more embarrassed. Do I remember the number of times we slept together, me and Aziz? Five? Six? Was it with the excitement and desire and harshness of the dream? I've had this dream a number of times before. Almost the same dream, and whenever I wake up from it, I shed blood. Thankfully for me, this didn't happen in the tavern hall or now, on the bus, as I cling to the beautiful woman.

2—Spring of 1972

I like being happy. I've never been happy like I am now. Sitting in the airbase, in the pilots' café, looking at Aziz. It's the fourth time we've met here. I look at the pilots coming and going in their blue uniforms, talking with nonchalant liveliness. Coming and going, as at home. Aziz isn't coming or going because he's sitting with me. He looks at the plane that's not there. The plane took off a while ago but his eyes are stuck on its spot, on the ground, behind the glass façade, near the storehouses. Under the ashen sky. His presence next to me is like calm music warming my heart. It's been two months since we met at Stork Bar. I think about him all the time. Night and day. Aziz is looking in the same direction. His mind is busy with the plane. I think he's waiting for his turn to fly. He didn't say it directly. He told me: "When I fly, I can't land anymore." He said it in front of the pilots, who laughed a lot. I laughed too.

The café is surrounded by glass. Wherever you turn, you see the airbase. The airport, then the storehouses, in one direction. It might rain even though we've made it through winter. The pilots' houses are in the other direction. Then the offices and the commissary. Aziz says he'll live in one of these houses soon, before he finishes his second year, since the colonel appreciates him. He says it looking in the same direction, in front of him, always in front of him, where the plane landed a moment ago. He turns to me and runs out. I see him now near the plane. He likes the sound of its engine. I don't like the noise because it splits my ears open, but Aziz likes it. He approaches it, until his face touches its face and he smells the scent of its metal. He talks with the pilot. The two disappear together into the storehouse. I wait for him to beam. Aziz. In his beautiful blue uniform. The pilots in the café come and go, laughing. Their voices are loud. His voice would have been loud if he was in the café like them. But he disappeared into the storehouse. He'll appear after a little. When Aziz emerges laughing, my heart will quiver.

For the third time, a plane lands and he leaves the café to stay near it and to talk with its pilot, and the two disappear together into the storehouse. Behind the glass façade, a bird lands. If there hadn't been glass, it would have landed on my heart. He tells me good morning and flies away. There on the ground, behind the façade, a big olive-colored plane appears under the ashen sky, the sky of the airbase. Big, awesome, and severe, like a big bird. That's how Aziz likes it. He hovers around it now, having left the storehouse. He looks at me. He's happy too because he's going to fly. Because I'll see him flying. For the third time, he hovers around the plane. Then he jumps into it and disappears. The engine churns, making the roar Aziz likes. The plane moves away, gets smaller little by little, until it becomes the size of a pomegranate, then vanishes from sight.

Khatima tells me to talk to him about marriage. I tell her I can't. I can only stay sitting next to him. I look where he looks. I see what he sees. When he's with me, my blood loses its balance. I'm incapable of talking, incapable of thinking. I'm incapable of standing when he's sitting, or of sitting when he's standing. Since the first day I saw him at the Stork. When he took my hand, led me to the bar, and asked me "What are we doing now?" and I told him, "Let's play." Since that moment, we've been playing. We don't deny ourselves any game, whatever it is. But Khatima tells me: "Marriage is marriage, you wretch." She wants to save me, she says. So I don't get lost, like she did. But I'm lost with Aziz. Because I'm weak before him. Whatever I do, I'll be lost.

We didn't go back to Joujou's house, after what happened at the Stork. After Aziz broke his jaw and the corner of the table smashed what was left of his head, we went to a hotel.

A miserable room in a miserable hotel like before. For two full months Khatima's been asking: Is this a life? The lice will eat us up in less than a week if we stay in this filthy room. As if she's afraid our miserable life will keep going like this, she tells me: "Talk to him about marriage, you rascal." She's changed too. She's started crying a lot. When she doesn't cry, she thinks about our new life. Far from Joujou and pimping. Far from the miserable room. A life we haven't seized yet. That's why she's exaggerating everything. As if she doesn't believe she might rid herself one day of her life of prostitution. As if this ghost from our past and present will threaten us forever. Not an hour passes without me hearing her voice: "Talk to him about marriage tomorrow." Khatima can't understand what I want. What I want is to stay with him. With marriage or without.

When he's finished flying, he comes back to the café, aglow. As if he's been in the hammam. Does flying produce this much change? He sits so close he's touching me this time, as he rubs his hands. The pilots look at us. They smile. They sip glasses of beer and smile. They seem happy. They seem carefree, in their spiffy uniforms. I'm happy because Aziz is like them, carefree, as he sits next to me. They're stealing glances at us. In the street, passersby look at us too, at me and Aziz. Under pouring rain sometimes, and other times when there's no rain. The girls stop on the boulevard, under the jacaranda trees, as Aziz holds my hand. They look at us, first at his carefully pressed blue uniform with its gold buttons, then at me, and wonder who's this young girl walking next to the pilot. And I walk next to him and feel my small hand sweating in his. I get embarrassed and pull it away. I wait for his hand to return, searching for mine. I say I don't want more than this light tremor running through my entire body as I see my hand waiting for his. Khatima herself imagines other things and when I come back home one Sunday morning, she asks me: "Did you talk to him about marriage?" No, I've got another idea in my head. I won't tell her. I won't tell anyone.

On that day, at that moment, when he hit Joujou in the face, I wasn't expecting anything. The idea wasn't there. It didn't enter my mind, the change that would happen in me. I couldn't have imagined it. If I saw myself at that moment, I wouldn't have recognized it. Even when he asked me at the bar: "Where are we going now?" the idea wasn't there. The idea made its way to me little by little. Like a stream of water under the sand. Some days later, he came wearing his track-suit like before. He said: "There's a big show at the edge of the city, with games, animals, and music."

He asked me: "Do you want to go with me to the circus?"

I told him: "I'll go with you to the circus."

Before entering my mind, his image rooted itself in my heart. Suddenly, taking me by surprise, it entered, attached itself, and wouldn't leave. At the show, we rode big rockers spinning around in the air. Strapped into metal chairs, we flew. With every turn, my heart shook, and I couldn't tell if it was from terror or delight. My heart left my chest, and I didn't know when it would come back after being jolted like this. I yelled without hearing myself, because of the wind. Aziz didn't hear me. I threw my head on his chest. He calmed me as he told me something I couldn't hear and I felt calm because I was near his chest.

We then rode small electric cars. Each of us in our own car so we ran into each other and we felt the crash in our hearts. He took me by surprise and I took him by surprise. We laughed. He hit me hard and I hit him gently. I was embarrassed because I hit him. He then got used to it and I tried to avoid him, but he's stronger than me, whether in his track-suit or his military uniform. Despite the pallor of his cheeks, he's strong. Despite the sadness in his eyes, he loves laughing. Khatima told me he looks like Abdel-Halim Hafez. I've loved Abdel-Halim Hafez since that moment because Aziz looks like him. I went to the market and bought "Why Do You Blame Me?" so I can sing it everywhere I go. At the hammam. On the street when I'm walking alone. On the street when I'm walking with Aziz. In bed when I'm sleeping or awake thinking of him. In the car sitting next to him. In the electric bumper car as I try to avoid him crashing into me. Happy, I sing "Why Do You Blame Me?" as I flee from him, and feel the blow behind me, chasing me before it comes. It threatens me, mocking my pretend fear, my heart shaking because Aziz is the one who runs behind me and hits me with his electric car. *Baf.* And I laugh as I sing to myself and wait for the crash. *Baf.*

Khatima's afraid for me since I'm young. I tell her I'm grown up, even at sixteen. Khatima tells me: "You'll grow up when you marry Aziz." Her mind won't calm down and she repeats her refrain to me. Talk to him about marriage, you rascal. I don't tell her anything this time. To myself only, I say I can't. I've got another idea. It made its way to me bit by bit. I'll tell him about it. Not now. Later. In my own way. What I'm thinking about, my idea, is for him to take my arm as he always does, lead me to the bedroom, and do with me what a man does with a woman. I think about this day and night. The idea keeps me from sleeping at night and its fever inhabits my body during the day. In the end, I told him while we were in his car on the forest road between Azrou and Fez, as the evening breeze was playing with my mind, the scent of the cedar trees and woods was all around me, and the song "Why Do You Blame Me?" was in my head. In my own way I told him, as we were going back to his house on the outskirts of Azrou, across the same evening road. "I want to tell you something," I whispered to him. My face went red from embarrassment and I lowered my eyes. Does he understand from the redness of my face what I want to say? I count the times we took the same road toward his house. It's the fourth time and I was planning to tell him. I don't know if words came out of my mouth or not. This time I believed I said it. Then, as we got near his house, I think I told him again. I hinted to him. I told him with my eyes. With my mind. With the blushing of my face. He kept staring at the road, but he understood the words I wanted him to hear. I think he understood what I was thinking and what I wanted to tell him.

I won't pay attention to what my sister says, just as I haven't paid much attention to it before. I fell in love with Aziz from the first moment at the Stork, when I saw him in the bar in his tracksuit.

His house is leaning on the woods. If you reach your arm from the window, you can touch the tree branches. That's what I was thinking about as I was clinging to him in the car. Then, as we moved toward the house, I was counting the steps to myself, thinking: Now he'll take me, to his room. A delicious tremor was running through my body. I was ready. I didn't see a reason to say anything else to him. Everything comes at the right time.

When we leave the airbase that day, we don't head straight for Azrou. We go to the port, in Mehdia. We leave the base with him happy because I saw him fly. I don't care whether he flew or not. As he talks about his plane and about the way it moved, I think he'll forget the plane but he doesn't. As in all the days God put him next to me, he's sitting with me but his mind is still on the plane. I didn't ask him to fly. But he insists. He wishes I could see him all the time flying in the sky. He says it in the café and on the road. And in the port as we buy fish. (And later in his room as he lies down next to me on the bed.) How do I explain to him I love him without the plane? I watch the boats unload their crates on the side on the river wharf as Aziz buys fish. The boat masts are erect like a forest, yearning for travel, and seagulls land on them as if they were trees in the forest. Aziz comes near me. He tells me: "At the airbase we have everything. We don't need to leave if we don't want to." He's quiet and then says: "At the base we have everything except fish." I say maybe he loves the airbase more than me. When he gets a house at the base like the other pilots, he won't have to leave anymore. Everything's there. Except fish. I might leave to buy him fish while he's flying in the sky in his plane.

Aziz goes back to the seller, laughing. The seagulls are playing at the tops of the boats as they move the crates full of fish. Cats follow the sorry fish falling from the crates as the river water swallows them before they hit dry land. I don't like fish. Except for the sardines my father used to get from the market.

In the kitchen, I make the fish Aziz will eat. I hear his footsteps in the hallway. I smell his scent before he approaches. Is he coming close? Yes, he comes near me and I feel him behind me playing with my hair. I remember I haven't told him yet. My blood rises to my face as I feel his erection on my backside. And I forget, when he touches me . . . as if heat warms my cheeks. As if a ball blocks my breath. Then I feel the breath cut up into four notes, like music. Then I feel liquid moistening me from below and I bring my thighs together in embarrassment. I say this won't happen when he does with me that thing a man does with a woman. I'll become normal, a normal woman, a woman who doesn't sweat and who doesn't get wet when he approaches me. A woman, with marriage or without. In the kitchen, I don't tell him because his standing behind me has dazed me. Everything comes in good time. I think too about the blood. Will a lot come out of me? In our village, I saw a farmer dragging a female dog to toss her into a deep pit because another dog raped her. Blood didn't come out but the farmer was swearing there was a lot of blood. Other farmers were following him, carrying rocks to stone the female dog. I won't tell Khatima anything. Khatima isn't thinking about the same thing. Khatima was only telling me to talk to him about marriage before it's too late. It's too late, sister. I'm thinking about the same thing but without engagement or marriage. Marriage, but without ceremonies. Without ceremonies or a marriage document or people getting sad. What dwells in me is like a fever. We move to his room, my hand in his, and neither of us says anything. Maybe he's thinking about my words, which I don't say. His words pass from his hand to mine. That's enough, he doesn't say them either. We're heading to the bedroom and the bed and what'll happen on it because of the fever controlling us both. He doesn't say anything. But he understands. Men know these things. Especially ones like Aziz. Even though his mind is busy with the plane. Soon we'll fly together.

3—Tuesday, 15 August 1972

My sister Khatima says Lalla Zahra's house is a good place for the wedding. So the neighborhood women can really see what's going on. And because it's a big house. At five in the morning, we were at the door of the house waiting for him, me and a girl from the house whose name is Shama. We expected him to come yesterday but he didn't. We were expecting him to appear this morning, as we'd expected last night. We waited all night. Many women were looking out from the windows and through the doors. They were trilling and singing with a drum and horn. We looked out again after five minutes. Then after another five minutes. We went on like that until the first rays of sun hit the walls of the house. Lalla Zahra said, "It's seven in the morning," and we began cleaning the house from top to bottom.

Lalla Zahra is in the courtyard of the house, sitting on her old sheepskin, smoking her first cigarette and getting drunk, saying, "Let's go girls, get going." She's ready to begin an exceptional day. Lalla Zahra still keeps control of the house and the same enthusiasm. She's puffed herself up a bit but she's still who she is. We're moving buckets around from corner to corner. The water makes us laugh. Throwing it cold on our feet and legs makes us laugh. It makes us laugh as it wets the bottoms of our skirts. We, I mean Khatima and me. I also mean Zubayda, the Shilha, Aisha from Dukkala, and Shama from Abda. Only Lalla Zahra doesn't do anything. She gets drunk, not getting her hands dirty, and giving orders. We get the impression she's everywhere. After two hours, the house has been scrubbed inside and out. The women are standing in the middle of Aqba Street, turning toward the house with its cleaned walls, windows, and door, wondering if Lalla Zahra is going on the hajj. Has she repented?

The girls say: "Oh no! Lalla Zahra hasn't recovered yet from the drunkenness of last year."

"And these banners?"

"Zina's getting married."

"You're all welcome at Lalla Zahra's house."

In the early morning, we cleaned the house with water and bleach from top to bottom. Even the fig tree in the courtyard, we cleaned it too. We climbed its trellises to get a piece of fruit that had ripened a few days earlier. A black fig sweeter than sugar. The scent of the fig leaves stayed on our clothes the entire day. Then the whitewash man came and painted the walls with white lime. We hung a loudspeaker next to the banners above the door so everyone on Aqba Street could hear Rouicha and Magni's strong mountain voices. Their voices will cut through the alley and reach the whole neighborhood. Lalla Zahra started crying early. She was happy. She'd never seen her house as a wedding venue before. She paid for the band and rented the two jurist adjuncts, who were writing the contract.

The girls were joking around: "How many weddings have happened in this house, Lalla Zahra?" It's the first. The only one in the series of dry years. That's why she doesn't want it to pass like a funeral. She bought the chicken the guests will eat. Thirty chickens and ten kilos of veal. Almonds, prunes, and fruits of the season. Then she turned to us and said: "Shama and the girl from Dukkala will take care of plucking the chicken. Zubayda the Shilha will take care of the sweets. Khatima will take care of Zina." And I, from that moment, I wasn't sixteen anymore. I grew up. Between two sentences. I heard Lalla Zahra talking about the jurists, the band, and the guests, and I grew up. Aziz doesn't know anything about the banners or the loudspeaker, the band or the sweets. Aziz appeared at eleven in the morning. As if our preparations didn't have anything to do with him. We'd been at the house since five in the morning, going in and out. Each time we said: "Here, he's about to come." But nothing suggested our preparations would speed him up.

He showed up at eleven in the morning, when we'd all but lost hope. Women looked out of the windows, but not as many I'd seen at night when I was dreaming of the wedding and banners and musicians. At the sight of the black Mercedes Khatima let out a long high trill. There were three men in it. The driver stayed behind the wheel. Aziz got out in his pilot's uniform with its medals, splendor, and brass pearls sparkling under the sun at eleven in the morning. The other man was in a uniform even more splendid. Aziz said: "This is my colonel, the head of the airbase. He came in the flesh and blood to greet you." The man was patting him on the shoulder and smiling. He didn't stay long. He greeted Lalla Zahra, drank a cup of tea with her, and left. Aziz then got up, kissed me on both cheeks, and went to the bar. "I'll come back later, in an hour or less," he said, "when you're ready, when everything's ready."

Aziz went to the Stork, to get drunk and talk with Madame Janeau.

Khatima found me naked, on the roof, pouring water on my head. My chest was flat. Smooth. My chest was like it was before I was sixteen, without breasts. They'll get bigger after you get married. Lalla Zahra has breasts the size of small milk skins. She's the one who said, to comfort me: "They'll get bigger after you get married." She said she was like me before. But like who and before what? Lalla Zahra doesn't know the shape of marriage. She doesn't even know if getting married has a shape. When we went down to Lalla Zahra's room, and the girl from Dukkala came in with the white dress she got married in seven years earlier, before her husband fled to Italy, Lalla Zahra took two thick caftans out of her old closet. Everyone got together in the courtyard of the house to let out loud trilling as they saw the white dress. The henna took a long time. We had all the time we needed, while Aziz was at the bar. We weren't following what was happening outside the room. We heard the noise of the neighbor women and the crying of their children and we imagined the courtyard was full. Zubayda, the Shilha girl, came in with dough on her hands up to her elbows. Lifting her hands up so we'd imagine the sweets she'll make for the guests.

Lalla Zahra said: "Here's the wedding dress but where's the mule?"

"Why do we need a mule, Lalla Zahra?"

"The bride leaves her father's house on a mule. That's the custom."

Then things got more complicated. We hadn't finished discussing the subject of the mule when the Shilha said that in her region, the bride doesn't leave her father's house. "She disappears first into one of the neighborhood women's houses. We go looking for her to bring her back to her house. So she remembers she has a father and a mother. So she remembers she has a house with its door open to her so she can go back if things aren't going as well as could be. Afterward, the groom comes to take her to his house on a second mule. Both have their own mules."

I imagine that, no matter what, two mules are better than one. But I don't say this to anyone. I don't say to them, for example, that Aziz has a Simca 1000. I don't say anything. I see in my mind Aziz riding his mule and I laugh. He hits his mule and screams at it to fly as I run behind him and grab him. Then my turn comes and I let my mule move ahead of his. I run and he rides behind me, and this time he doesn't catch me. I am laughing during all this because I remember the day we were in the electric cars.

Khatima, as she was brushing my hair, said, "Don't get upset. These things don't concern us because we don't have a mother or father. Or a house for us to return to if things don't go as planned."

And besides, Aziz has a Simca 1000. I said: "A Simca 1000 is better than a mule."

Lalla Zahra said: "This is your house."

The Shilha had said, "Before this, we had to take her to another house and from there we'd bring her here."

"On the mule?"

"Of course on the mule."

"And the groom?"

It's not his turn yet. His will come later. He's getting drunk now at the Stork. And parents have no place at all in this story.

Lalla Zahra turned to me: "What sort of wedding do you want?" She didn't wait for my opinion.

My opinion is that Aziz has a Simca 1000 and not a mule. My opinion is this whole circus should end so we can go together back to his house. With the mule or without. We won't leave it. Khatima asked me about his house. I said, "It's in the forest." We laughed. Yes, in the forest, far from the Stork, far from the miserable hotel, facing the Azrou woods. Far from all the miserable rooms in the miserable hotel Khatima hates. The girls helped me put on the two thick caftans. At four in the afternoon, the scent of the chickens in saffron filled every corner of the house and passed through all the rooms. And the scent of the sweets. The scent of wood, henna, incense, and rosewater. All the scents giving an impression of a joyous event knocking on Lalla Zahra's door. At four o'clock the preparations were finished. But where was Aziz? The band, the two jurists, the chicken the jurists would eat, and the sweets Zubayda the Shilha made for us with the sweat of her hands were all there. The two mules and their owner were waiting at the door. We were all waiting for Aziz. Lalla Zahra started getting drunk early. Alcohol, instead of getting her drunk like other people, makes her more awake. When the head of the band took out his violin to chase away the annoyance of waiting, she chided him with her hand on the strings: "What're you doing, one-eyed? Your fingers are eating you up? Can't the blind man wait until the groom gets here?" I told Khatima, "I'm hot." She didn't listen. She too was thinking about Aziz. About Aziz's house, which was at the edge of the forest. Finally she'll leave the hotel room. The room of lice, as she calls it. She spends the night with a candle burning at her head to scare off the lice, which nest in the holes of the room.

Aziz didn't come until midnight. The jurists had fallen asleep. The band had left. The owner of the two mules decided not to take his fee and the fee for his two mules. When Lalla Zahra handed him a green paper bill, he asked her why. I didn't do any work. He pulled his mules and went back to his mountain. Unlike the head of the band, who didn't play a single note, but nonetheless wouldn't budge until he got all his money. The two jurists fell asleep without dinner. As for Aziz, he was getting drunk and waiting for us to get ready.

At ten in the evening, he was still at the bar. When we sent Zubayda, after ten, he'd disappeared. Abdesalam told her the police van took him and Joujou down to the station. Zubayda told us what happened. She herself didn't see it but Abdesalam said Aziz got into a fight with Joujou. And he may have broken his nose. This time, they couldn't do anything since the police van was at the door of the bar. Lalla Zahra threw her djellaba on and ran to the police station. She knew the commissioner personally since he got drunk with her girls every Monday night. When she didn't find him at the police station, she went to his house.

Everyone came to the wedding. In the same police van that took them to the station a few hours earlier. Aziz, the commissioner, and Joujou, with a big bandage dividing his face in half. And the police van driver in his uniform. They came into Lalla Zahra's house, one after the other, late at night. They were laughing. The commissioner was very disappointed when he found the band and the musicians had already left. He was thinking about going after them to bring them back to finish the wedding but the scent of the chicken with saffron was overwhelming. We don't know if it was the sudden

90

turmoil or the smell of the chicken that roused the jurists. Aziz took out the two rings. He put one on my finger and I put the other on his. We become man and wife from that moment, in a way I hadn't expected. Lalla Zahra let out a drunken trill of joy. She recited the Fatiha with us drunk. So did the commissioner. And Joujou. And the police van driver.

I tell myself we became man and wife before this moment. When I walked next to him with my hand in his to his room overlooking the forest. When I slept with him and saw two drops of blood on the white sheets the next morning.

4—Wednesday, 16 August
The day of the hawk, a crazy day from start to finish.

Everyone walked with us through the alleys that night, cheering in celebration, and left us at the front door. Except for Aziz's sister Khadija, who wasn't at the wedding so she could welcome us. That's her way. Aziz said his sister can't stand crowds. She gets a nosebleed as soon as her body warms up. Aziz said as soon as a man touches her or stands in front of her, her nose bleeds.

A truly strange day. Everything in it was strange. You think this day will be exceptional before it comes. And all of a sudden, it really is but in a way you didn't expect at all. It was strange from the moment we got there, when Aziz introduced me to his sister who I hadn't heard of before. This is my sister, Khadija. She wasn't at the house before. Aziz said he brought her from the countryside to stay with us. He said she was living with his mother's uncle and that she didn't get married since she's afraid of men. It was a strange day, too, because Aziz refused to take off his uniform. At Lalla Zahra's house, he refused to put on the white djellaba and the yellow slippers we got for him. He spent the day at the Stork, wearing his uniform, forgetting about the wedding and everyone there. As if he had another wedding on his mind, one that had to do with him, not us. He spent the night not wanting to take it off.

Going into the bedroom and coming out immediately. Dragging his feet in the corners of the house, going back and forth like a clock pendulum. Maybe he was, like it, counting the seconds. *Tick tock, tick tock.* But I was happy nonetheless. Because of everything that happened. Which I hadn't expected.

Then I heard him say: "I've got to go. I've got to get back to the base."

His mind settled anxiously on this refrain. The groom forgot he was a groom. Khadija slept as soon as she opened the windows since her nose bled because of the heat. Aziz spent the night pacing through the whole house, only thinking about going back to the base. I've got to get back. He didn't lie down on the bed as people do on a night like this. He said he was afraid of falling asleep. He didn't want to sleep because he had to get back to the airbase. I forgot I was a bride. Despite the ring and the white dress and the scent of henna. I didn't sleep. Not because of the strong heat that descends on Azrou every summer, not because of the state Aziz was in. But because I set my feet in this house in the way Khatima was dreaming of. She was sleeping, relaxed, at Lalla Zahra's. She'd leave tomorrow to join me.

I saw the house for the first time from this perspective. Affected by Aziz's raving. Affected by his staggering steps, pacing around it in every direction, and repeating: "I've got to go. I've got to get back." I wondered what he wanted to do at the airbase while he was on vacation. What did he want to do at the airbase at three in the morning? My ideas didn't leave their spot. Like Aziz's idea about the airbase. Then he finally sat down and his eyes wandered far away. I thought, maybe he's forgotten. This intoxication, exhaustion, and pacing around, maybe he'll calm down and go to sleep. There was a bitterness in his face. A grimace resembling loss. No, he didn't sleep. He only stopped to begin this refrain again. He came back, saying he'd go there.

"I'm going to the base."

It didn't look like his mind and the rest of his body realized what was coming out of his mouth. He stayed frozen in his spot. Like someone dreaming.

"I'm going to the base."

Maybe he said it with his eyes only. Then he started looking around him. He pulled out his bag and started emptying it out. What was he looking for? What was going on in his head? Did he forget the base and remember other things? No. Aziz was looking for his gloves. Pilot gloves—he wanted to fly right away. At dawn we were both tired. We hadn't slept. Instead of sleeping, we kept looking for his gloves. Pilots don't fly without gloves.

"Where are my gloves?"

Aziz won't fly without his gloves, even if the plane was waiting for him at the door. I wish he wouldn't fly. With the gloves or without. I want to sit like any person who just got married and who's on vacation, who's happy on their wedding night, without going to the airbase. Not going anywhere. He asked me to look for them in his bag. His bag was empty and its contents were scattered on the ground, because of the number of times he'd searched through it. Instead of listening to what I said, he came back yelling.

"Look in the bag."

His voice came from behind my back. His gloves weren't in the bag. I turned to him. He was watching my movements with his red eyes, the eyes of someone who didn't sleep, the eyes of someone losing his self-control, possessed by demons, watching the bag and expecting honestly that the gloves would suddenly appear. We then went up to the roof, knowing we wouldn't find them on the roof. After another half hour, we went out to see if they were hanging on the clothesline at the door of the house. We knew they weren't on the clothesline.

The groom forgot he was a groom. The first signs of dawn began to spread above us. I thought maybe he won't leave Azrou because he didn't find the gloves. I was wrong. He kept looking while I went into the bedroom to cry a little. I remembered Khatima who stayed at Lalla Zahra's house. She told me: "This is your night. I'll join you tomorrow." Lalla Zahra cried because of all the whiskey she downed. The girls cried because we'd be saying goodbye to them and saying goodbye to their life, which we didn't choose. But the next day came, and it wasn't like what my sister had imagined. What'll I say to her when she comes today and finds Aziz went back to his base? What'll I say to her at the door?

With the first rays of the sun, he grabbed his bag and opened it. The woods looked over us. Our house looked over the Azrou woods. The view of the woods and the rays sneaking through the tree branches evoked a much-needed calmness in my soul. Aziz was calm too. For a few seconds, we went back to a warmth we'd forgotten. The car was parked next to the sidewalk. He took my face in his palms and said his plane was waiting for him. The colonel was counting on him and on his plane. Do you know what he said next?

"Today's our day."

Because that was what his leader, the colonel, said. "We'll fly high above," he had told him. He asked him to be at his position first thing in the morning.

"Is it reasonable to leave him waiting? He's thinking about us all," said Aziz.

Because, he added with his hand on my cheek, I was a good omen for him. He told me that that afternoon, when I was listening to the sound of a plane above my head, he'd be the one passing by. Then, when I raised my eyes, he'd wave to me, even if I didn't see him. I'd sense his hand waving even if I didn't see it. I'd recognize his voice even if I didn't hear him say: "Good morning, Zina." But I didn't understand why he wanted to go back to the base when he was on vacation. He was satisfied with just moving his head as he went to his car parked in front of him. It was ready, as if it too was in the know. Before disappearing in his Simca 1000, he said, "Lend me one kiss." I ran to him and threw myself on him and kissed him. Then he said, "I'll return it to you in the evening."

He returned my kiss when he came back, twenty-six years later.

It was indeed a new day and everything in it was strange. I don't know how long I dozed. When I left the room, Khadija had disappeared. No trace of her, not in the kitchen or in her room. I found her on the roof, bent over two turtles, feeding them. Next to the turtles were six round eggs and a small one under a small wooden covering between empty flowerpots. She turned to me and said, smiling, "They'll hatch in two weeks." I watched her in the light of the rising sun: A woman without a specific age. She might have been forty or fifty. Her skin was dark, with cracks and wrinkles dug into it. Her teeth had fallen out. She might even be sixty. But Aziz said she was thirty-two. Unmarried. Her life had always been harsh. She lived in the mountains with their aunt when their father brought another woman to their house. She's the one who kicked them out. Then they were sent to one of their relatives when their mother died after marrying another man. From time to time, Khadija looked up at the sky. As if she too was waiting for the plane to appear. A burning sun rose above us, but no trace of a plane. She motioned for me to listen. I didn't hear the sound of a plane.

"It's the hawk," she said.

I tried to listen again but I didn't hear it. I didn't see the hawk.

"Its voice is sharp and stinging, unbearable to listen to," she said.

Just as the thought of the hawk eating her two turtles was unbearable. I stared at the sky for a long time but neither the plane nor the hawk appeared.

I heard some knocks on the ground-floor door. I also noticed the commotion. Singing and banging on a tambourine. The girls came by foot from Lalla Zahra's house, led by a band of musicians and a cart with breakfast on top. Almonds, walnuts, dates, and milk. Bare sugar cones. They asked about Aziz. His absence didn't rouse their curiosity. They danced and sang. They didn't stop until late in the afternoon. Khatima said this is the custom. I didn't know any custom without Aziz. But Aziz wasn't there. He was flying. I waited for him to appear with all my heart as Khadija waited for the hawk to appear. She bent her neck up but she didn't hear anything because of all this commotion. Other women came from the mountain and sang and beat their tambourines and danced. Khadija got up quickly and went back to the stairs leading to the roof. I did the same, thinking she'd heard the sound of the plane. Khatima didn't know anything about the story of the plane or the strange story of the hawk that devours turtles. We spent the day like this, with Khadija constantly jumping up and rushing up the stairs. I joined her on the roof. When she said she heard the hawk, I listened, I opened my ears, and I listened to hear the plane and to see Aziz waving at me. Then we went back together to the ground floor. Without the stinging sound of a hawk or the drone of an airplane like the blowing of a horn, as Aziz said.

After the women left, Khatima thought she'd do some work on the house for a bit until Aziz came back. Khatima washed her hair before spending an hour rubbing it with oil and cloves. Khadija cleaned the breakfast plates and then began shaking out the rugs and the pillows, taking them to the roof to air out. I didn't want to follow her to see if the plane had appeared in the Azrou sky. I acted like a woman who had just gotten married. I revived my happiness getting to know the house. My new house where I'd settle down with Aziz, Khadija, and Khatima. The house with the trees outside. A full forest in front of the house. I looked out from the window, waiting for the plane to appear. Instead I saw the forest. It was as if I was looking out seeking solace, seeking protection from the pain of wondering what Aziz wanted to do at the airbase while he was on vacation. The plane didn't appear. Khadija kept going back and forth between the roof and the courtyard whenever she thought she heard the sound of the hawk. As for me, I didn't go out to the roof again, content with listening to the call of the horn inside my heart.

Other women knocked on the door before the evening. Without musicians. Without a cart carrying sugar cones. They too came from the mountain. They asked about Aziz. They said the pilots at the airbase attacked the king's plane in the air as it was coming back from a trip. They sat with us for half an hour. Then they wondered, was Aziz with them? Then they fell silent for another half hour and went back to where they came from. I kept looking up at the roof, waiting to hear the sound of the plane. I wondered what Aziz was doing. Why wasn't he coming back?

10

Hinda

1 a.m.

1

I NEVER UNDERSTOOD THOSE SMALL carts that follow us all over
the city, for no reason. Small overfull carts led by innocent
horses that don't understand the crime they're committing.
They take us group by group to put us to death behind the
town slaughterhouses. Once I would have suffered this calamity if I hadn't heard a dog on the street corner warn me,
yelling: "Run away, sister, run away before the Moroccans
grab you." If we'd been in Asia, I would have understood
the situation. Some of the Asians like our meat. But no, these
just kill us and burn us. God only knows why. It seems aggression runs deep in their blood. And their ignorance cannot be
surpassed. They don't differentiate between kinds of dogs.
They say dog, and that's it. I laugh to myself but I hear them
talking about us with this naïveté. What do they know about
dogs or non-dogs? They kick us about only because they say
God kicked us out of the garden.

There isn't a special continent for dogs I can go to. I'm
condemned to live among them. But instead of close contact
with human beings, like a lot of dogs, I try to limit my rela-
tions with them as much as possible. I prefer to watch them
from a distance. I don't understand, for example, why people
don't stop talking, even for a moment. I like, for example, to
walk behind this person or that, scrutinizing his movements
and gait and listening to his unending lies. I like spying on

people. I'm twelve, which is old for a dog. My hearing's still sharp, even if my gait has slowed somewhat and my eyesight's diminished.

2

I circle the room, with only the idea of fleeing from it on my mind. Confused, but with only one desire. The smell of whiskey, a disgusting smell, emanating from the commander. It's also emanating from the girl with him. I move away from the commander and get close to the door. I sit down, as if my desire was only to get away from the scent and not to leave the room. I steal a look at him. He's busy with the girl, not paying attention to what's going on in the head of a dog like me. What's going on in my head is that Aziz needs me. This time I go to the door and hear the crash of the commander, so I come back submissively with my tail between my legs as if his scream terrified me and I collapse in a heap in my corner, not far from the door. The girl with him is sitting under the air conditioner, instead of sleeping with the commander, as girls do when they come to him. She gets up, goes to the window, and pulls aside the curtain, asking about the casbah. Is it empty and who lives in it? The commander puts her back in her place and clinks his glass with hers. She laughs and they change the subject. He didn't notice me.

I always think about Aziz and about the Rifi who died before him. The previous deaths didn't trouble me as much as the Rifi's. I was in the courtyard watching a swarm of emigrating birds when all of a sudden the Rifi came out naked as the day his mother bore him, laughing loudly and running around the courtyard like he was having fun. Then the two guards appeared, chasing after him waving shovels. They followed him as he ran in front of them and avoided their shovels and their laughing. The Rifi stumbled and was about to fall down in the same happy mood. When Benghazi's shovel came down on his head, it dropped him to the ground and blood flowed from his head. They then showered him with blows and insults until he stopped moving. Since this incident, my sleep hasn't been the same. I started dreaming of him every night.

I get up again, expecting to hear behind me the crash of the loathsome commander. Instead of going to the door, I backtrack to the window, rub myself against the curtain, then get near the table and hit the bottle with my foot. The bottle smashes and the alcohol flows from it onto the rug. The commander stands looking at me in disbelief. The drunk girl under the air conditioner yells: "Oh no, oh no, oh no!" I then realize he's getting ready to kick me out of the room. I'm lucky. Before the commander's foot hits my rear, I get past the door.

I sit in front of the hole that swallowed up the Rifi a few days ago. I smell his corpse. It's still fresh. I know the dead arrange their broken remains when they go down into the grave. But that's no excuse for the way he died. I sit listening to the words of the dead and I watch the door leading to the wing. I see it's open. I see the dark corridor without seeing the room where Aziz is crouching. It's always locked. I have to think of a way to get in. I think about helping him so I don't dream of him like I dream of the Rifi. I haven't slept well since the Rifi died a few days ago. As soon as I close my eyes, I see him carrying his crushed bones and a piece of his flesh in his hands, waving them at me. All this I see when I'm awake. Eyes closed but completely awake. When I sleep, I dream of rats, lots of rats, chasing him, an army of vicious rats, hungry, their fangs bigger than them and sparkling in the dark, running behind the Rifi, carrying shovels, letting out sounds like hyenas. As he flees with pieces of his flesh and his bones falling behind him, unable to stop to pick them up.

I push the door, trying to open it. I smell every crack in it. I kick at it. Maybe it'll give. I manage in the end to get through the opening under the door. Aziz is laid out on the ground, not moving. His eyes are closed. I can't tell if he's dead or still alive. He might have fallen from the slab before dying. I go over to him. There's no life in him. His hand and toe are tied together with a string. Human beings have a lot of customs I don't understand. I put my head near his nose. Only at that moment can I tell his breath is rising and falling. The thread of life is weak but still holding him. Life is still pulsating in his body, even if in this faded shape. This is joyous. Tears well up in my eyes from so much joy.

I'd crawled inside the room in one movement. No. Before I get completely in, struggling through the narrow opening, the stench repelled me, sending me back to the corridor. It hit me in the face like a whip. A stench stronger than the stench of corpses in the trash. I tried to go in twice before I could take the stench. As for the man laid out on the wet, black, filthy ground, I could barely make him out because of how dark it was. A pile of rags tossed on patches of water. But I was happy since my hopes weren't dashed. He wasn't like the Rifi at all. First, the Rifi died and this one hasn't died yet. This one's face is long and dark while the Rifi didn't have a face at all because of how disfigured it was by the shovels. This man's cheeks are very sunken. The face of a man in a struggle with death. With a small bent body, but not bearing death like the Rifi. Aziz is shrunken, but only from the lack of light, right? I'm happy when a small shudder passes through his body. With great difficulty, I drag him back on top of the slab. He doesn't make any effort to help me. My efforts don't seem to have brought consciousness back to him. Then I start breathing on his hands and feet. And every dried-out part of him. Afterward, I spread myself out on top of him and embrace his body with my teats hanging down, then I bring my nose near his face and start blowing on him. I close my eyes and concentrate all my efforts on this sensation. Calmly, I send him some of the heat emanating from my body. I am agitated nonetheless, anxious, so I open my eyes from time to time to see the results of my efforts. To see if he's opened his eyes, to see if there's heat spreading in his limbs. Nothing's changed. The man's as still as I found him when I came in: stiff, frozen, near death, far from life, despite his breathing still going up and down unevenly. I don't despair. I wrap him up in the cover and spread myself on top of him again. After a little, I notice some change in the man. A drop of sweat glistens above his brow. This is enough to let me know life has regained its cycle. After a lot of sweat has flowed from him, he opens his eyes, then closes them and sleeps.

3

My first five years I spent at Mahjoub's, the tailor, in Khemissett. I don't remember how I got there. I was young. When the tailor, his wife, and three kids settled down on the outskirts of the city, in a house with a big barn, a dirt courtyard, and three clay rooms, they decided they needed a dog to guard the house. Because of their ignorance, they thought I'd spend the night barking. The tailor's wife was everything, inside and outside the house. She spent her time waging war against her three kids or against the neighbors. Sometimes, without justification, she turned on me, tossing at me anything she could get her hands on, a broom or a shoe, yelling she didn't want a dog that ate and didn't bark. I didn't do anything to respond to her aggression. What could I do except wait for the chance to leave the tailor's house?

They say Mahjoub is the best djellaba tailor in the area. I don't know about this kind of outerwear. I can't judge if this is true, or if it's farfetched. He worked all the time, day and night, as if to avoid the wickedness of his wife. She didn't see the tailor or hear his voice, as if he were a shadow. He spent all his time in the tailor shop. At home, he'd sit in the corner, with the day's work finished, or cutting cloth for the next day. On Wednesdays, he went to the souk and I'd spend the day watching him, as he sat under a mending tent with his djellabas around him, pretending he was selling like everyone else in the souk. But he was waiting for his second wife. A woman he saw secretly for some reason, I don't know why. At those times I barely knew him, as if another man took his place, talking and telling her jokes as they laughed together. He bought her sugar donuts and tea in the morning and meat tagine for lunch, and she wouldn't leave without him giving her a gold bracelet or earrings. After noon, instead of heading home, he'd spend time moving from alley to alley, looking behind him. He'd sit down finally in one of the houses in a narrow, dark bottom alley and wouldn't come out until late at night. When he went back home, he'd be quiet again. He'd keep to himself in his corner, cutting cloth for the next day in silence. Everyone in the house would think he'd stayed late at the mosque.

I don't know why it seemed to me I'd be in a better situation somewhere else. Instead of living with the tailor's evil wife. Her three kids were unemployed, eating from the livelihood of the tailor. The youngest of them, who was thirty, smoked hashish from morning until late at night. Something I liked about him was when hashish smoke got him dizzy and he put a leash around my neck and pulled me behind him in the street, strutting.

One day, the tailor's wife fell unconscious in the middle of the house. She shook for a while on the ground because her neighbor told her what her husband was doing on Wednesdays. I went near her with good intentions, leaned over her face, and covered her with my breath, trying to return her warmth to her. But it seemed she was so wicked that the breath of all the dogs on the earth together would be useless. When she opened her eyes and saw me nestled against her, she let out a terrifying scream as if all the evil possessing her had broken out. What do you want, sister? Benevolence isn't any use with these people. Malice dominates their nature. Instead of throwing herself on her husband who didn't move a muscle or even blink when he saw her fall, he stayed in his corner, cutting cloth, instead of digging her fingernails into his face, she turned on me and the stick in her hand would have blinded me if I hadn't jumped out of the way. I spent the night out of the house, of course, thinking about where I should go. Should I change neighborhoods or change cities? I began a new life and forgot the tailor and his evil wife.

4

The worst thing that can happen to a dog like me who has spent her whole life in a house with a roof and door is to find herself suddenly outside. Alone in the open country without being ready for it. When day broke, I'd gone far from the city and deep into the countryside. Exhaustion hit me quickly. For the first time in my life, I was full of regret because I'd never exercised. Or, at the very least, spent time wandering the alleys as dogs do instead of sitting in the tailor's house without work. While I was moving, deep in thought, I saw two dogs standing in front of one of the farms. As soon as their eyes fell on me, they began moving their tails. One of them peed on a car wheel and I didn't understand why. I got near them and they started jumping around me, their way of welcoming me. They said they were going to hunt and if I wanted to join them, I only had go up to the crate on the car parked in front of the farm before the owner of the house and his French friend left. After a bit, I was hidden between them in the pen. Two men came out from the farm at the same moment, in what looked like speckled military clothes. As if they were going to war. One of them locked the box without noticing me. The car itself looked like a military vehicle. After a bit, the car was moving quickly between the mountains. I'd never been on a hunting trip in my life. For the first time, I saw this strange thing. The two men lay in wait for birds, shooting at them. The two dogs rushed from here to there, and then one of them would bring back a dead bird bleeding in his mouth. The other followed him with sad eyes because he hadn't found a bird, alive or dead, to put in his mouth. I asked the two about their work, and they listened to me with one ear. As for the other ear, it was listening for the shot that would come from time to time. As soon as they heard the shot, they ran off with their tongues dancing in bliss. I was baffled, standing there thinking about it. It went on like that for hours. I told myself life with the tailor and his evil wife and doped-up kid was a thousand times better than this, which was like the life of lunatics. The two disappeared for a long time. After a while, I didn't hear a sound or panting anymore. From time to time, a shot came, but it was very far away. The shots then disappeared, and when the day was almost over, I was lost in the woods, not knowing east from west. Nonetheless, I came to a decision. I decided not to go back with the two of them. That's why I didn't make any effort to keep up with them as I saw them move away. I noticed I was hungry. I rarely complain about that. Since yesterday, I hadn't tasted any food. I remembered the tailor. What was he doing now? Was he still sitting alone in his corner, cutting cloth while his evil wife chewed her anger?

A night I won't ever forget. I won't talk about the wolf who spent the night howling and who would have snatched me if I hadn't thrown myself in a river that pulled me far away. The night and not the road. I haven't had an experience like this. Moving forward without knowing if you'll fall into a bluff or a hole that'll swallow you up. Late at night, I heard barking and I realized I was near the city, and then its lights appeared before me. I thought, it's not important that I go back to the same place. I was happy, as if I regretted my former life at the tailor's house. Even if I thought the best thing that could happen to me would be to find a well-mannered dog to have a good time with. No, I didn't return to the tailor's city. It was another city. I peed on a tree, then on other trees as I moved forward on the wide road.

This city was big. The buildings were tall and the streets were wide and lit. I sat relaxing and enjoyed watching the cars passing by quickly. Not far from me was one of the bars with

106

the scent of rotisserie chicken wafting from its door, stirring up my appetite and reminding me of my hunger. In Khemissett, I'd sit in front of the bars since drunks toss you bones and pieces of bread dipped in sauce and sometimes whole pieces of meat. I went near the door and looked inside. The bar was immersed in dark smoke and there was a lot of noise. And music. Among the customers, I saw a man who seemed eccentric. He was getting drunk alone. There was a lot of food and drink on his table. He was the one who drew my attention first. The man seemed uncomfortable sitting there. He had on black sunglasses despite the night and the darkness of the bar. He turned all around, taking money out of his pocket, counting it, and then putting it back, biting his lips, wiping sweat from his forehead. Some of the customers were casting sidelong glances at him and winking. As if they knew in advance what he was going to do, and found the thought entertaining. Suddenly, he jumped up from his chair and took off running to the door. His speed, much faster than most sixty-year-olds, startled me. The guard chased after him, then the waiter and other customers. They brought him back, chiding him and pushing him in front of them like a criminal. As he was moving in front of them submissively, his eyes, with the glasses off, appeared shut. He was moving his lips, mumbling incomprehensible words. I don't know if he was laughing or crying. I'm not sure. Some of them were laughing as they pulled him by the sides of his coat. The old man stood in front of the bar door, swearing he didn't have any money. But the waiter pushed him roughly inside, saying, "Aren't you ashamed of lying, grandpa?" Then I saw him standing at the bar with the same group that had been berating him a little earlier (he'd put his sunglasses back on), taking out a wad of cash from his inside pocket, spreading it in front of the bartender on the wooden counter, and saying while turning in every direction: "A round on me!" On his lips was what seemed like a smile of contentment, as he was looking at them all rejoicing and clapping wildly. He then turned to me. I didn't know what went on in his head when his eyes fell on me. He lifted his sunglasses and fixed his eyes on me. I was sure some idea was going around in his mind at that moment. He took a piece of meat and tossed it to me. Any other time, I'd hesitate and sniff it suspiciously but, in my miserable state, I devoured it without paying attention to the alarm that normally rings in my head in these kinds of situations.

After a bit, the man stood in front of the door, staring at me. As if he was wondering if I was going to follow him or not. He put his hand on my head and patted my neck. I lifted my eyes to him but without being dejected and with great caution. The expressions on his face would have made you laugh. His features were drawn. His eyes were narrow and his lipless mouth resembled a carelessly drawn line. He took a few steps away from the bar and I followed him. His body was frail and his gait was heavy. The opposite of what he was like when he was fleeing. He was walking now as if hitting the ground aimlessly. There was that strange and disgusting expression on his mouth, something you might have thought was a smile at first. I would spend the next seven years with this man, who they called the commander, and I'd often see him go into the same bar and jump out running like he did that night, with the customers bringing him back, pushing him in front of them and chiding him without me understanding why. Until now, I still wonder if I was forced to follow him.

11

Aziz
1:30 a.m.

1

IN ONE OF MY MOMENTS that falls on the thin border between clarity and oblivion. I haven't left the world I belong to, haven't yet plunged into the world of dreams. I am close. I know I'm laid out. That I am conscious. That I haven't fallen. But my body feels as though it has traveled to another realm. It's as I left it after its last palpitations, barely remembering me, because it no longer knows me. A miracle. I was sure I'd fall tonight. But it didn't happen. It'll never come like this. My certainty about an imminent departure had been shaken, but I now was sure. I dreamed I fell from on top of the basin and that Hinda came in and brought me back to my cement bed. She sat licking my hand and my face to bring life back to me. A strange dream.

A strong convulsion like an electric current flows through all of my limbs. The current became a strong shake, as happens in the moments right before the death of a ram on Eid al-Adha. The body twitches violently. The chest rises and falls in a terrifying movement, naked, the ribs appearing like sticks as they start to shake too. I feel my Adam's apple move up and down. It swells up until it becomes the size of a pomegranate. I lift my hands to feel it. My hand moves slowly but doesn't get there. Even though the stiff fingers have relaxed. After a third attempt, I raise my hand and bring it close to my face. My hand moves on its own until it reaches my mouth. It searches for the opening of my mouth hiding in the middle of my hair.

It finds it. The same reaction afflicts my mouth. It opens and then closes like the mouth of a fish in its death struggle. What's hit my body? This constriction hasn't happened to me before. I put my finger in my mouth and begin feeling around. It's as if I'm looking for an exit for life to sneak out of. In a violent motion, I throw up everything in my body. A warm yellow liquid with a disgusting smell gushes out in successive bursts and covers my eyes, nose, and chest. This is death.

And what is death in the end? Let's think about it in cold blood, if blood can be cold at moments like this. I see a light rising with the last closing of my eyes. A nighttime light. The reverberation of all the beautiful sounds I heard in my life turn toward me. I don't know where they're leading me. As I roll, rising between stars shining around me. That rising and falling has become one. Not before or after. An endless sky as I fly like a bird lighting up itself with itself forever and ever. Maybe one time I knew the other dead people that passed through the casbah, by their diseases and illnesses. They were missing the limbs they left in the casbah courtyard. Maybe we crossed through bogs and extremely wet lands. After a march of six hundred thousand years, we know we're running after the man who killed us. That we were all waiting in this great haze for the time when we take our revenge. They say the final moments in the life of man endear death to him. Let them bring it close to him in a calm and meekness that make him see himself as a child playing in the courtyard of his house. They also say that in the final moments, the taste of your mother's milk returns to your mouth. A relaxation hits you and you see your body as if it were sliding in pleasure, stretching out on land declining smoothly.

2

My cousin Driss and I were digging the hole at the water-wheel to bury the bird. From there, I could see the house and the fig tree looking over us from the courtyard. From its top, you could see the whole world if you wanted because it was big and tall. Driss was the one who dug the hole. He's the one who said: "Let's bury it here, near the waterwheel, so it doesn't get thirsty." He also said the land always stays wet near the waterwheel. After a week of life, the bird died with its wings open as if it had died flying. It came from distant lands to die here in our hands. I grabbed the bird by its wings and its beak hung down. I turned to Driss. The bird was light in my hand. Driss looked at the house. There were women at the door. Standing and sitting. I could see them when Driss didn't block them with his tall frame—he's the oldest of us by two years. His nose is long like my father's nose. I counted the feathers of the wing in my hand. Seven gray feathers shaking without wind. It might still be alive. Driss took the bird and tossed it into the hole. I was hoping it would stay in my hand longer so I could feel its wing shaking between my fingers. The bird was face down as if it wanted to hide from us because of its death. We piled dirt on it with our feet. My feet were bare. Driss was wearing shoes my uncle bought him at the souk. The bird disappeared under the dirt and the feathers of its wings stayed upright. Driss hit the ground with his shoe and stamped it until the feathers disappeared. I was jumping on the waterwheel, and my hand seemed emptier than before. Driss took out his trap. He wanted to catch another bird. I told him I wouldn't hunt another bird after today. Birds were created to fly and we catch them so they don't fly. The bird disappeared under the ground. The feel of its feathers was still in my hand. And under Driss's shoes.

When I turned toward the house, he pulled me by the hand and said: "It's better we go to the fig hedge."

There were birds of many colors there. I didn't want to go to the fig hedge and I didn't want to hunt another bird even if it was colored. Driss said: "The house is full of guests. It's better we go to the hedge."

He moved the trap in the air. What are guests doing at the door? I stepped toward the house where the guests who Driss talked about were. My sister Khadija was waving at us as if she was warning me about something. Driss ran to grab my hand. "It's better we go to the hedge. We'll find at least one bird." There was a small lump in my throat. Sad for the bird that had died for no reason. Birds always die for no reason. I told Driss I wasn't sad for the bird so he'd let go of my hand. Driss pulled me toward the hedge. Khadija joined us and said: "We're going back to our father's."

I didn't understand why we were going back to him. She yelled: "I'll run away tonight so I don't have to go back to his house."

Driss hit the air with his shoe to scare her. And Driss chased her away and she fled from him as I ran behind her and asked her: "Why are we going back to our father?" She yelled: "I'll run away tonight so I don't go back to him."

Driss hit the air with his shoe to scare her. My father won't buy me shoes since he doesn't live with us. He went to live with another woman in Chaouen. My mother told us, me and Khadija, to go to him. We went to him in Chaouen. But the new wife he lives with told us to go back to our mother. My uncle told my mother: "They're like my son, Driss." We stayed with him. I didn't understand why she wanted us to go back to live with him again. With his wife who doesn't like us. I went back to the small grave where the bird was sleeping and where Driss's shoe had been a little while ago. I put a stone on it so I could recognize it. I saw the bird was still alive under the dirt. It was singing even though the dirt filled its beak. Driss pulled me by my hand. It's better we go to the fig hedge, like Khadija said. But she didn't say anything.

Driss chided her and she yelled: "We'll run away, Aziz and me, tonight, before our mother leaves us."

Driss chided her and I said: "Who'll leave us?"

"Our mother. Tonight. She'll go to her new husband's house."

Khadija believes we'll be happy without our father and without our mother and without our uncle and without his son, Driss. Driss hit her on her head. She ran away from him toward the house and Driss said: "She's lying." He grabbed my hand again. We'll find another bird. Prettier than the one that died. With a white tail and a red chest. He put his hand in my pocket and took out the piece of bread I was feeding the bird before it died and he said: "We'll put the bread in the trap under the fig tree so the bird eats it. When we catch it, we'll have in the cage a new bird you can feed."

I looked up at the house again and at the women circling around it. I left my hand in Driss's hand. We headed to the fig hedge together.

3

We spent months at our father's in Chaouen, Khadija and me, before his wife kicked us out. Friday afternoon, we went to the barracks where he works. The barracks door was locked. We heard music inside and we said our father was training the brass band. Then we heard them outside the barracks and we realized the band was wandering the outskirts of the city, heading toward the mountain. Khadija and I were waiting for them. We looked at them from behind the trees. Then we heard them going up the mountain. We went up the mountain, running to get ahead of them. We know the road to the mountain like the band knows it, and like our father, who's leading them with the white ram. Always white and fat. The band with our father walking behind the ram. They circled where the ram circled. On invisible trails between thick trees. They stopped when the ram stopped to relax. Under the gushing waterfall. Then they went up to the mountaintop to play their music. I don't like the woman who lives with my father. Sometimes I don't like my father because he left our mother. Sometimes I like him because he wears a white uniform and leads the brass band. Khadija knows the route the band takes.

Every Friday afternoon, she'd say to me: "Why don't we go to the waterfall that the band passes?" And she'd take my hand because she's older than me. My father waved his brass rod and the fat white ram was in front with no one leading it.

When he was living with us and our mother, the light got turned on in the house. But I didn't understand the connection between the light and him being home. When our father was home, we had light. When he was late, there wasn't any. My sister said it was because of the suit he was wearing. White like the ones French officers wear. They let us leave the light on in our house but forbade us to wander around because our father led their brass band. Unlike the neighbors' house. Unlike the other houses that didn't have a father leading a brass band with a big white ram in front. Sometimes the darkness of the night would pass inside and outside the house. It covered our house and the neighbors' house. It spread its wings on everything around it. My mother said: "If your father was home, we wouldn't be in the dark." Waiting for him to come, we sit in the dark. Then she said, "Here are the French passing by again," and I heard the soldiers' shoes as they hit the ground outside. Behind the door. I heard it even if they were not passing by. To myself, I said: Will my father come if I turn on the light? I didn't turn it on. Even though the soldiers weren't walking in the dark alley now. He crossed it three times since the sun set sun. Light wouldn't come on in the neighbors' house. Nor in our house. My father would come to turn it on. I took advantage of the opportunity to ask what would happen if I turned it on. My mother said the soldiers were coming and they'd break the door onto our heads. If our father was here? Then no one would break in his door since he wears a uniform like theirs. Sometimes we didn't turn on the light even though our father was home because it was daytime. If it was night, we'd turn it on despite the passing of the soldiers, my mother said. No one would break our door with the butt of his rifle. He came during the day, sat for an hour, and then went back to his ram. We didn't turn on the light to see him as he left. As we didn't turn it on to see him coming. He sat for an hour without us turning on the light for a single minute to see if the soldiers would break down the doors or not. If they smashed the door onto our heads or not. There was no way to know because it was daytime. He lit it this time because mother was sleeping in her room. I then got close to the door and listened for the sound outside. Did I hear the noise of the soldiers' shoes or the noise of my father coming back? Khadija was sleeping, not seeing the light from the depths of her thick sleep. I listened and heard a lot of rustling. That was my sister tossing and turning under the sheets. I heard the rustling and I expected her to say something. She didn't say anything. The sheets returned to their silence. They were sleeping too. The feet then got close and I didn't know if they were the soldiers' or my father's. Thick, monotonous, regulated, they kept getting closer in the night. Maybe all of them together. I imagined the ends of their rifles were raised, while my father was standing in front of the door to stop them from breaking it down.

4

I leave Driss setting up the trap behind the hedge and I sneak to the house, fleeing, and I climb the fig tree so I don't have to go to my father's in Chaouen. In the courtyard of the house, they come in and ask where I've gone and leave again. "Where'd Aziz go?" From the fig-tree branches, I can see them in the courtyard of the house, on the ground floor, coming in and leaving, wondering: "Where'd that devil go?" When they've had enough of looking, Khadija looks up to the tree to see me hanging at the top. I pick an unripe fig. She doesn't say she saw me and starts gesturing but I don't understand her. Or I understand this: We'll flee to the woods to live with the monkeys. Maybe we'll find birds that love to live with us without needing to fly and to flee as we get close to them.

My mother leaves the room and sits by the tree. Her shirt's new. The scent of the man whose house she's going to emanates from her. All our neighbors circle around her. Women I don't know. Two men wearing thick djellabas, not sweating in them despite the summer. There's a lot of henna on our mother's hands and feet. I can smell its fragrance from here. She thinks I don't see or smell her henna. My uncle comes outside and I hear him say to my mother: "He doesn't have to know." But I know. My uncle says: "He doesn't have to know because he's still young." But I've grown up more than my uncle thinks. I'm about six. In two years, I'll be Khadija's age and maybe bigger than her. I know my mother will leave us to go live with another man. The smell of the other man wafts from her and his flavor reaches my perch on top of the fig tree. She'll leave us just as my father did. This time, she wants me to hear her say she wants to settle down on something firm. Under the fig tree, my uncle shakes himself. What's this firm thing? She ironed his shirts and socks while he trimmed his mustache and jumped from one woman to the next. What's this firm thing? "She can't," says my uncle. "This creature can't keep her man because she spends her day sleeping. She doesn't do anything that makes her man stay home." I hear my mother say she's been getting up before dawn to iron his shirts and socks. My father now lives with the other woman. Now she irons his shirts and socks too, while he trims his mustache in front of the mirror and his mind's with the ram waiting for him at the barracks.

I get ready to spend the afternoon in the tree branches because I don't want to go to the woods with Khadija to live with the monkeys. I don't want to go back to our father's. I'll spend the next day and more in the branches. There isn't fruit in them to eat if I get hungry. They're still the size of the peanuts we picked from my uncle's hood when he came back from work covered with dust from the road that enslaves him and the other workers. When he comes back in the evening, he says: "We worked hard today. We opened up half a kilometer in the mountain." Instead of listening to him, we throw ourselves on his djellaba hood.

Our neighbor tells her: "Take him to his father. Him and his sister. He has to take care of them." Another neighbor says the same thing. My uncle says they're like my son Driss. I imagine my uncle loves us more than my father. My mother says she doesn't want to bother anyone. I imagine my mother doesn't love us either. The neighbor women say: "The two kids have grown up. They've got to have a father." I imagine he's now in the barracks training the brass band. Or washing the ram with soap. I imagine him on the forest road, his brass rod in his hand, directing the band. My uncle comes back to the courtyard, wondering: "Where'd that devil go?" I remember I love my uncle. Because he always comes to the house with a handful of peanuts. Driss and I dig our hands into his pocket to take some and run away to the corner of the room like cats to eat them one by one. Sometimes we don't find them in his pockets. We exchange glances and wonder: Where are the peanuts? And we find them in the hood of his djellaba. When my uncle finishes work on the road, he buys peanuts in the souk and hides them in his hood for us to find. The smell of the road always wafts from my uncle. His scent's there in the house, even when he's gone. When his work is near the village, Driss and I go to see the bulldozers and diggers with their long iron arms. One like a giant locust. Another like a scarab. My uncle and the other workers are extending the road that'll go to the capital.

We ask my uncle every night: "Has the road made it to the capital?"

And my uncle says happily: "Soon, soon."

We see the road creep toward the capital little by little. The workers sit to drink tea in black mugs, talking about the road that's passed and the other that'll pass under their thin forearms. There are rags on their heads so the sun doesn't burn

117

them. Then one day, the road passes in front of the house and the workers stay with us for a few weeks. They sleep under the big machines that look like locusts. During the day, they work with empty bags for cement or the rags we'd seen before on their heads. Under the wall of the house, they bend iron and make from it high walls that become long when they extend them on the columns, then they become a road we'll take to the other side of the river. My uncle says this is a bridge. We start to say we'll pass on the bridge. When we go to it, we find the workers eating lunch under it. We say the bridge was fixed also for workers to have lunch under it. The butcher Si Moussa comes and, in its shadow, he slaughters the goat he'll sell in the market. We say the bridge was repaired so that Si Moussa could slaughter his goat under it. He hangs it under the bridge so its blood flows. Sometimes two goats, because the workers also buy the meat from Si Moussa. My uncle sees the road extending and says it'll reach the capital soon, and he's happy because he said that. We're happy too because there's a city, and it's the capital, with the road going there.

When he comes back in the evening, he says: "We worked hard today. Tomorrow we'll work more."

We ask him if the road has reached the capital and he says: "Little by little."

I love my uncle a lot but I don't love my father and I don't love my mother.

From the branches of the fig tree, I look at the waterwheel. The waterwheel stays in its place. Like the fig hedge. And the olive trees. I look for the stone we put on top of the bird. I can't make out the stone because it's far away. Maybe the bird got up from its nap, moved the stone off, and flew away without me seeing it. I hear a bird tweeting among the fig leaves. It might be our bird, which we buried near the waterwheel. Far from the waterwheel, on the horizon, a specter crosses. I enjoy watching its quick progress. After a bit, the specter becomes a man moving on his mule. My mother cries under the tree.

The neighbor women console her and my uncle chides her. My mother cries and says she longs for her son and I'm surprised by her words. She says she prefers to stay with her children and my uncle says he always has enough to provide for us. The man who was advancing on his mule is moving now next to the waterwheel. He finally stops at the hills of the olive trees, dismounts, and sits on a stone, wiping off his sweat. As if his journey ended right here. In front of our house. My uncle doesn't look for me anymore because he's busy with my mother's crying. Does Khadija know why the man has come? To sit among the olive trees looking at the house? Did he come to take our mother with him? Until now, she has only been using gestures. My mother is crying even before she joins him, begging him to take her far away on his mule. His scent wafts from her. The neighbor women say: "It's better we go back to our father so he takes care of us until we've grown up."

The man stares at the house like someone waiting for a woman to come out to take her away with him. Not like someone waiting for kids. Because we'll run away to the woods and live with monkeys, not our father and his wife who doesn't like us. Maybe the ram liked us as we liked it. Is the ram still in the barracks? Does the ram still occupy our mother's thoughts even after her husband left with this woman? The ram doesn't know if my mother is thinking about it or not. It doesn't know and it doesn't care. It doesn't know if we go from house to house. For my part, I don't understand why a ram had to be at the front of the brass band, or how it knows what route to take. White, fat, and washed, it knows the way.

A woman comes and put a container of broth and a lot of bread in front of the man and goes back inside. She doesn't say hello to him and he doesn't say hello to her. He washes his hands in the water coming off the waterwheel. Instead of a djellaba, he wears a blue smock. He rubs his hands and his beard on it and begins to pray. His mule is rubbing its body on the bark of the tree and looking at him as he prays. When he leans over the container, his face disappears. My uncle comes and sits next to him. My mother pulls Khadija by her arm and kisses her as she cries. The two men get up and go toward the house. They stand in the courtyard under the tree. The man lifts his eyes to the tree and gestures that I should come down. I come down. My uncle says: "You're going to live with your other uncle, your father's brother."

12

Baba Ali

2:30 a.m.

THE OWL SCREECHED AS IT does whenever one of the prisoners dies. I asked Benghazi: "Why don't we bury him like Muslims are buried?"

He went back to playing checkers. With two colors. As if he was leaving some time between us so he could understand what I said.

"At least we should bury them like Muslims."

"How do you bury Muslims?"

"With a shroud."

"Why does he need a shroud?"

"At least he'll die at peace and won't come back to us at night."

Was Benghazi making fun of me, asking if the dead come out at night? We went back to playing but I couldn't summon the same enthusiasm. This time, we heard the sound clearly. Distinctly. At night. From the middle of the courtyard. My heart shook and the hair stood up on my head.

"You hear it?"

"Yes."

Benghazi heard the owl this time and he couldn't pretend he didn't. But it didn't stir anything in him. Not a single hair of his shook, even though it was the last death. We kept wondering, whenever the owl screeched, when there were a lot of them. Whose turn is it this time? There was no more contempt in my heart since I started seeing them at night. My mind kept

121

seeing Aziz dead. After burying him, would I be able to relax? Even if not a single push from the prisoners came, would I be able to relax? We'd been burying them for twenty years. One group after another, and I always said: "They're the last group." Always lying to myself. My mind kept following the screeching of the owl too. Its echo following in the heart of the night. It was like a string of lights that lit up and went out at night. It lit up and went out in the heart of empty desert nights, causing a strange stinging inside me. For the first time.

Benghazi got rid of the checkers in his hand, cursing, using words I didn't understand. I didn't understand what Benghazi was saying, even when he wasn't cursing. He got up as if he remembered something. He took the lamp and went out. Benghazi said he wasn't afraid of the dead. He wasn't afraid of anyone. Not of humans and not of the jinn. He was only afraid of his uncle, the commander. He's not his uncle but he calls him uncle to flatter him. I don't like him, whether he's his uncle or not. I don't like Benghazi. I got up and went after him. His big body was tottering in front of me like a bear in the night. From behind him, I said: "Let's bury them like Muslims. Let's at least bury them like Muslims."

He didn't respond. We stopped in front of the cell. In front of its small door. He said: "Go in."

I said: "I'm not going in."

He kept looking at the door and rubbing his chin. His head is big, like the head of an elephant. As he was thinking he grabbed his head as if he was afraid of falling from the weight of his thoughts. He held the lamp out to me and snuck inside the cell. I directed the lamp at Benghazi and saw him bend over the dead man and look through his pockets. He came out, took the lamp from me, and went back inside. My eyes kept seeing him searching the dead man. What was Benghazi's hand doing in the dead man's rags? I saw the other hand put out the lamp. As if the colluding hands fell on something they didn't want me to see.

I insisted on asking: "What's your hand doing in the dead man's pocket, Benghazi?"

The lamp came back on again. This time, Benghazi was holding Aziz's thigh and lifting it up high. The dead man didn't move. Benghazi was turning toward me as if to convince me he wasn't interested in the pocket but in the dead man. I kept asking him what he had taken from one of his pockets.

The sergeant said: "It's over, he's dead." He turned the lamp on the dead man's face.

At that moment, I forgot what was in Aziz's pocket. Aziz looked like he had been extinguished. His usual hopeful expression had disappeared. No flash of teeth, no tormented look. Nothing. His face was smooth. Expressionless. A thick liquid clung to the thick hair on his face and his torn clothes. As if he had fought death for a long time. We wrapped the blanket around him, forgetting his pocket or what was in it, or if he even had a pocket to begin with. His wrap was worn, torn, and black. We pulled him toward the courtyard. Toward the hole. Benghazi said, laughing: "You like this torn shroud?" I don't joke about things like that. I don't make fun of the dead. The shroud should be clean and white, always.

He was trying to explain to me that we've always buried them without a shroud or a wrap. But my mind was telling me: Aren't we used to tossing them without a wrap, and naked too?

Without trying to understand him, I repeated: "We have to bury him like a Muslim. With a white shroud at least, as a Muslim . . . with the shroud and verses from the Quran."

"The shroud, white . . . if you have one."

"I don't."

Then I didn't hear him anymore. I said: "Let's wait until morning. We'll buy him a shroud. We'll bury him like a Muslim. In a new white shroud with the scent of cloth, not the scent of shit."

That's what I said. If we bury him in a shroud, it will be like we were burying the others in a shroud too. Because God will see our final act and forgive us for our previous sins. He'll see we were forced and we did what we were told to do. We'll have done a good deed on our own because the dead man's dead and it doesn't matter to him if he's buried in a shroud or not. Do you understand, Benghazi? The dead don't know. We do this for us, not for someone who doesn't care anymore about sleeping naked or covered. Do you understand that at least? As if we forgot the dead are buried in shrouds and we finally remembered. Do you know? God will see all the effort we make. If it came late, it'll show our best intentions and He'll forgive us for what happened before. He'll think about the matter from every angle and He'll see in the end there's no escape from forgiveness. Especially with some verses from the Quran. . . .

The pits are there. Always ready. With a barrel of lime next to them. When we were about to toss Aziz, the dog appeared. She came out from behind the palm tree. The sergeant put the lamp on the ground and a spot of light glowed. Night spread around us—me, Hinda, and Aziz on his back in his disgusting wrap. He won't be buried like a Muslim. In a white shroud and with verses from the Quran. The darkness was doubled outside the spot of light covering us. Benghazi disappeared behind the palm tree to get the shovel. Benghazi doesn't need light. He moves in the night like the owl that was screeching or like bats. Or like any vermin. I turned toward the lamp and saw the dead man's face. His eyes were open. As if he was looking at me. His lips moved. As if he wanted to say something. Even Hinda came up to him and began sniffing him. I thought I heard a call. Aziz was calling me. The dog jumped back, letting out a strange sound, and terror took hold of me like a current of electricity hitting me. The dog sounded as if he were wailing. I went back to staring at the dead man. His lips were moving. Aziz was still alive. No doubt about it. When the sergeant came back with the shovel, I told him: "Aziz is still alive."

"He's dead, I'm telling you."

I took the lamp and shined it on his face: "Look." His eyes were closed this time. His mouth was frozen. No movement at all. As if he'd died a second time.

"What am I going to see? There's nothing for me to see."

I lit up his face again. It was frozen. My mind is imagining things tonight. The night of the dead. My mind isn't there anymore. It's been shaken. I told Benghazi: "We'll hurry to bury him before disaster strikes us." As if he was only waiting for direction. I tossed the wrap over Aziz's face and we pushed him into the hole and threw a big pile of lime on top of him. We piled the dirt on him.

For a while, I kept looking at the shovel on the pile of dirt, unable to move. As if my limbs were paralyzed. What am I doing here? Benghazi said: "We don't need to talk to ourselves because we came together to the casbah to double our salary and other things."

Did I forget? With a bad beginning, you quickly forget how you started, not knowing how you'll end. You begin as a cook or a guide like Benghazi and all of a sudden you become a gravedigger, and then you bury the dead and you end up burying even the living. Benghazi put out the lamp. We went back to the room.

"Play."

But I don't play because I don't see the board anymore. I see Aziz fighting to get out of the hole. His mouth is full of soil and lime as he fights. I think: The least that can happen is for Aziz to come in to us covered in dirt and lime. Naked except for a white wrap instead of a shroud, and a covering of the lime we tossed on him. My head was on fire, hot like an oven. My limbs became weak after the previous convulsions. Sweat was pouring from my forehead and I felt it moving freely, flowing down my chest like a secret stream. Sweat didn't flow from Benghazi's forehead. As if burying the living was his job. Benghazi said if I think about it, he was going to die anyway. If not now, then in an hour. If not in an hour, then tomorrow as that's how the world works. What's the use of this dead man adding another hour or two to his life?

"Play, Baba Ali. The man's dead and that's it."

He lit the hash pipe and handed it to me. "Want to smoke?"

I took the hash pipe, and after two puffs, my anxiety went up instead of going down.

"What's wrong with you, Baba Ali? Forget the dead man, Baba Ali. Forget him like I forgot him."

But when I tried to forget him, I thought about him more. Maybe because of the hash, I saw him coming through the door and shaking the lime off his shoulders. I played so I didn't see the door. I forgot Aziz. I forgot the white dust tossed on us. He was the last prisoner. My mind will relax after him. My mind won't relax after him. This idea alone was enough. I searched inside me for calm but didn't find it. I told Benghazi: "We won't bury anyone after today." I believe I smiled but I'm not sure. The sergeant laughed, repeating: "We won't bury anyone after today."

"Play, Baba Ali."

I tossed the checker. I looked at my hand. It was shaking.

Hinda started barking outside.

I didn't know if my eyes were open or closed. My body told me they were closed. My mind said the opposite. I saw Benghazi like a line of smoke, letting out sounds like the owl that was screeching a little while ago. Then there were other sounds outside. Some steps outside, rattling, creaking, rustling, making my body leave me. It was Aziz breathing. Do you hear him breathing behind the door? His eyes were enveloping the room so I couldn't leave. They were looking out from the window and the door. Is there time to get out, and where should I leave from? There's a roof, walls, light on, light off, lime, dust, specters, running, and screaming. . . .

13

Hinda

2:30 a.m.

1

I STILL WONDER AFTER ALL these years if I was forced to follow him to this wasteland. I'm now in a faraway place. Far from any city. A casbah erected in the middle of dry land. No farming, and no water at all except for some palm trees growing in the courtyard. Its clay walls are high. The soldiers who bring us water put the full metal cistern at the door, take the empty one, and leave. Important officers come from the capital but they don't leave the commander's office. Except for me and the two guards, Baba Ali and Benghazi, no one comes in or goes. The commander stays in his office. On Saturday, he goes to Meknès to visit his family, and he comes back Monday at dawn. I haven't gone with him for a while. Not to his house and not to the bar where we met for the first time. Sometimes he doesn't go anywhere. He gets drunk in his office with one of the girls from the nearby villages. Baba Ali and Benghazi are in the casbah all the time. They go home twice every three days. They live in a nearby village, not far from the casbah. They spend all their time in their room playing checkers. I don't like Benghazi. I especially don't like it when he puts his hand on my back. Baba Ali isn't like Benghazi. About once a month he comes in to see us in the commander's office. He asks him: "What do you want, Baba Ali?" Baba Ali hands him a piece of paper, saying he only wants the government to send him on the hajj so he can cleanse his sins before it's too late.

I don't regret it. I don't expect a lot from people. I only wonder what the commander was thinking and what he needed with me as he was opening his car door for me. Maybe he thought I was a hunting dog. It wouldn't be his first mistake, in any case. Here's an important man, everyone respects him here in the casbah and outside it, doing what he wants like a king in his kingdom, but he didn't catch a single bird during the seven years I was with him. How many times did I laugh to myself, watching him doing his stupid sport? As soon as he's ready and he lifts the rifle, the birds fly off. I laugh more when I hear the other birds in the nearby trees chuckling. For the first time, I see human stupidity. About a year ago, the commander hung up his rifle on the wall.

The courtyard is full of the dead. Lots of people come here to die. In the courtyard, I watch the dead moving under the ground. There were more than 370 when I came here seven years ago. When death comes for one of them, they drag him by his foot to the edge of the hole, toss him in, and pour lime on top of him for him to burn. This is a way to bury the dead I hadn't seen before. Twice I saw them bring out a dead person from one of the rooms, pushing him in a wheelbarrow. (Just as they used to do with us when they were taking us behind the town slaughterhouses to put us to death. A small, gray, overfull cart just for our execution.) The wrap came off and dragged on the ground while the dead man kept swaying back and forth on top of the wheelbarrow, naked. A pile of bones, covered by hair. Alive or dead, a dog stays a dog. But this dead man was turned into something else I didn't recognize at all. Not human and not animal. A lump of festering hair, emitting a disgusting smell, more putrid than the stench of the corpse. What was left of his rags was hard like wood. The stench of piss and human feces and pus and decay all piled up, the stench of something disgusting. I hadn't seen anything like this before. I retreated. As for Baba Ali and Benghazi, they moved to the hole like they were carrying a sack of potatoes.

One night, they were so busy playing they put off burying a body. When they came back the next day, they found the rats had eaten his entire stomach.

2

When they're not burying people, they're playing checkers. They're in their room now, absorbed in playing. I see the dull light of the room on the other side of the courtyard. My mind is troubled tonight. I feel something unusual is happening. Alone, I'm thinking about the darkness. Actually, I'm thinking about the man buried alive. I'm thinking about the still-fresh dirt on top of him. The rats begin looking out from their lairs when they smell the banquet and think in their little brains they'll dine on fresh meat as they did before on the stomach of his friend. The rats are called to an exceptional feast tonight. Anger never overwhelmed me like it did at that moment. I lived with humans. I spent my entire life with them. I know them, or I thought I did. Humans don't bury people alive. Tears of horror well up in my eyes. There isn't a living thing that buries another living thing alive. Not bugs or animals or inanimate beings. I am boiling inside. Dogs aren't humans but they have feelings, even if they're simple. They know what pain and misery are. And joy and happiness. I start barking to scare the rats. And they actually disappear for a while. Or they retreat so as to attack again. When I start digging, I hear them digging on the other side of the grave. As if we have the same goal.

Darkness envelops everything in the courtyard so my attacks on them are useless. But I am determined to drive them off. At the same time, I think about him and try to dig around his head to open a small hole to let him breathe before his soul departs. I smell the scent of life under the soil. I dig. But there are more and more rats around me. I attack them from one side and they flee to the other. They stop for a little until I think they've fled, and then I hear them scratching in the darkness. The growing sound of their paws. The smell of fresh meat stirs them. How many are there? All the casbah rats have come out tonight. The name of the feast awaiting them is Aziz. I hit the ground and the air around me and I bark with all my might and I dig. I dig again, despite the lime burning my eyes and the rats, whose sharp sounds I hear around me like the meowing of blind cats. I dig. And they dig. I smell life diminishing under the soil. I dig. I dig. I see my strength double before their increasing attacks against me this time and I feel their fangs gnawing at my feet. Sharp stings. I bend backward and find the shovel. I lean against a nearby palm tree and catch my breath. Everything's dark. I don't see what the rats are doing, though I can feel them jumping around me feverishly and can hear persistent movement. My miserable mind pictures it like a continuously fading roar underneath me, and I imagine the rat fangs are doing their job and there won't be anything left of the man by the break of dawn. I can't do anything. My misery's growing and injustice is getting the better of me as I see the night extend and stretch as if it's helping them carry out their disgusting mission.

Then, suddenly, it starts to rain. Thick rain, like stones. It might be hail, coming down at just the right time. A shudder of joy flows through my entire body as I hear the sound of the rain and I wonder if the repulsive animals have retreated under the downpour. I don't hear them anymore. What happened to the man buried alive? I approach and they retreat at the same time. Do they think water, even if in this storm, is enough to bother them? No, even the flood wouldn't stop them from their extraordinary feast. I don't care if the sky pours its anger on us, as long as it stops the rats from attacking. Suddenly, the light from the room illuminates part of the courtyard and the two guards appear, making loud sounds that precede them in the night. Baba Ali, with Benghazi following him. They are fighting. One of the blessings of the rain has been to make the two men appear at this critical moment. This time the rats flee. They disappear completely.

Benghazi only comes back after a long while and the light of the room stays on. I think, yes, the rain didn't force the rats to retreat but it forced the guards to come out. It's the same thing. When Benghazi comes back alone, he is laughing or cursing or something, I don't know what. I don't care because I've made a lot of progress. I work with increasing abandonment, I need to finish before the light disappears and the rats attack again. When I grab his hand and start pulling, the day has begun to break. Aziz is light. He doesn't weigh as much as two chickens. I see his eyes sparkle in the light of the rising dawn. I'm delighted. My enthusiasm increased. This time I don't care about the rats, which are pulling on his other side. I attack them and pounce on one of them with all the strength in my fangs, until its stomach explodes. Aziz is smiling and his eyes are sparkling at the first sign of day. And I, with my eyes, encourage him to keep up his optimism. Then he closes his eyes as if to relax.

14

Zina
Dawn the Next Day

1

I DON'T REMEMBER CROSSING A river or a bridge. I wake to the hum of the engine, which has become noisy and constricted as if it's turning in empty space. My mind screams and burns and the earlier anxiety is starting to vanish, as if I'm seeing it through a long tunnel. I look at my watch. Outside, night begins to withdraw and day spreads sparse light around the bus as if it's sneaking in through unseen cracks. The birth of a new day always causes joy. That's what I think when I open my eyes. The woman next to me is fast asleep. Her head isn't rising or falling or nodding to the right or left like other passengers when they give in to the strength of sleep. Her head is leaning on top of the chair and it seems like she's awake, but with eyes shut and resting. The road we're moving on is narrow and rising because we're traveling through high mountains, a thick, dark mass, surrounding us from every direction. Veils of thin fog at their peaks increase the magic of their mysteriousness. The harsh coldness of dawn enters the window and pierces my bones. I try to close the window. I see the bus moving on the edge of a bottomless abyss. My heart is rising up in my throat. I move back. I look in front of me and the bus seems like it's suspended or rising in the air. I don't look at the chasm below but it doesn't disappear from my sight. At each turn, my chest contracts as I imagine the bus turning, flipping over and rolling down, and then a boulder or a tree stops it and we remain suspended in the air. I then imagine it falling into the bottom of the river, with passengers strewn about from the windows. I plunge into the river, not knowing if it's really there at the bottom, and I come out safe, waiting for the woman to emerge from the water too. I look in every direction, but don't see her.

I imagine myself dead, calm and peaceful.

The driver's face is expressionless. His eyes are focused on the road. As if he's herding a tame animal and they've known each other for a long time. One hand's on the steering wheel while the other's on the shift stick, moving it forward and backward. The engine changes the sharpness of its noise with each motion as if it's following the orders of its master. We turn and the bus starts moving more quickly, even though the curves of the road don't disappear at first. After that, we move onto a flat road in the middle of a forest with trees like umbrellas, with tall trunks and dense leaves. The driver takes out a box of snuff and tips some powder onto the back of the hand holding the steering wheel. He puts the box away and takes a deep sniff, wipes his nose, and goes back to concentrating on the road. At the end of this forest, an iron barrier coming out of the ground like bent nails stops us. There is a patrol of police and soldiers with dogs. There are trucks and jeeps transporting them to the edges of the forest at the side of the road.

The driver leans to the right and stops the engine. The woman wakes up and turns toward me, smiling. When she's in a bus or in a car, she tells me, she always wakes up when the engine stops. Birds in nearby trees chirp with a high-pitched song. In the morning, their singing is denser. The zeal of some of them becomes more intense before they set off to look for food. I think about the progress I've made and what's left. Another day with me far from Azrou, near an undefined place. A casbah in a village or in a forest or a desert? All I know is I'll recognize it as soon as I see it. I have this hunch I saw it many times in my dreams and my eyes won't mislead me. I don't know how much time I'll spend looking for it. For the first time, I ask myself how I'll get back to Azrou. Can I get back the same day? And if not? I see myself knocking on a door, at times big and at times small. Sometimes someone looks out and sometimes it stays shut. And then? I'll see when it happens.

The driver looks out the window and talks to two people from the patrol. One of them takes the box of snuff, laughing. The cop pours a line from it and then gives it back to the driver. They exchange a few words and then he gets up and leaves the bus. After a bit, a cop, a soldier, and another person wearing civilian clothes get on the bus. They stand at the front and look at us for a long time, one after the other. The man in civilian clothes passes between the rows of seats and asks this passenger or that about where he's going and asks for his ID. He backtracks, focusing on every face with the same harshness, then joins the others and leaves. The bus remains parked in its spot under the tree. The driver's still gone. When he finally gets back on, he says three prisoners have escaped from the prison and that the army, with the help of locals, has been chasing them for two days in the mountains. He lights a cigarette and sits in his seat.

The bus isn't moving but there's a lot of commotion on the road. Soldiers cross and disappear between the trees. Others shout back and forth. Dogs bark after all the yelling. The ones standing near the trucks are exchanging words in a loud voice. What can I do besides imagine the prisoners escaping, with Aziz among them? At each bark, I imagine the fangs of the vicious dogs tearing into his flesh and the flesh of those escaping with him. Not surprisingly, I remember the dream I had. After some passengers have descended and mixed with the soldiers and the police, we leave the bus too, the woman and me. The first rays of the morning sun break through the branches, angled streaks throw interlacing speckles of light on the damp grass. We go to a small clearing. Through the branches, we can see intermittent movement on the road. A bird flaps its wings above us, making a sudden movement in the middle of the silent forest. The woman asks me if I am thinking about Aziz and I move my head, not knowing what I'm indicating. We speak awhile without me knowing if I preferred him to have fled or be crouching in a cell waiting. What will the prisoner wait for except to escape or not? She then says: "Does he deserve all this effort?" Silence. Does he deserve it? I'm not really thinking about her question. I blame myself because I forgot him the past four years. If not for the man who appeared last night at the bar. Then I excuse myself, because I kept running, looking for him for fourteen years. I say to myself: *I take refuge in God from Evil Satan.*

I hear the driver's voice, so we go back toward the bus. He says maybe we'll be delayed and maybe we won't be able to keep going. I don't know why the woman knits her brows and seems miserable when she hears this. Some of the passengers protest and others suggest helping the soldiers catch the prisoners. Most of them jump on the soldier's truck, shouting "There is no God but God" and "Allahu Akbar," but the officer tells them to get down and they return to the ground without hiding their enthusiasm. A strange silence reigns. Like an anxiety hiding behind the trees. We go back to the clearing. The women spread out around us collecting herbs. One near us yells that she found some mushrooms. Others join her and they talk for a long time about poisonous and nonpoisonous mushrooms and decide the best thing is to collect wild wormwood, because it's a medicine for the stomach and the intestines and eases digestion and urination. I have forgotten the woman's question. Now I imagine the passengers bringing him back, bound, with bloodied hands and feet. I see Aziz as in my dream, fleeing from vicious dogs chasing after him. Sometimes their fangs almost sink into his thigh and sometimes he disappears into the top of a tree or plunges into a river so the dogs lose his scent.

To my surprise, the woman says she isn't happy with her life: "I'm not happy about anything in it." She got married twice and brought into the world eleven kids without wanting to. She was tormented by her first husband and her second husband was tormented by her. He put up with her submissively and bore her flare-ups willingly. Is there a third way? Do you know what my desire is now? To remain as I was at twenty. Without a man. Then, as she looks at the far-off mountains, she asks: "How would life be out there? The same as our life or different?" I think it's different. A hut with a tree shading it and near it a spring of water flowing forever. I would prefer to live there and to give birth to a single girl with the first person who passed by my hut and then to forget him. A moment of silence passes. But there is no opportunity for this, no second chance. Does the sea get another chance, to change its scope or its islands? Or does the forest get to change its place? A little while ago, when the driver announced the trip might be cancelled, she said she felt a great resignation and strange bliss. As if someone was pushing her forward and, at the same time, warning her and restricting her. However the course of our life may be, we'll always remain slaves. Another long period of silence.

She asks me afterward if I know where she's going. I shake my head.

"Back to him," she says.

"Who?"

"My first husband."

"Who . . . ?"

"Yes."

She straightens her back against a tree behind her and lowers her eyes as she starts playing with the grass with her feet. Her eyes are bathed in tears. Beautiful, even with her tears. Her beauty still follows her, even after forty. I imagine she'll stay beautiful, I imagine her beauty will follow her to the grave. I go over to her and put my head on her chest. She calms down and I calm down with her. We stay in this position for a while. Calmly, I look at a butterfly that has settled near her foot. Her foot has stopped playing with the grass. As if it recognizes the life nearby and has stopped playing in order not to crush it. The butterfly flies up and lands on the back of my hand, which is resting on her chest. A small butterfly with fine rings of yellow, red, and blue. The butterfly doesn't know it's carrying elegant and brilliant decorations. It's not concerned with the woman or me. All this engraving and beauty is threatened by obliteration as soon as its heedless feet move.

I hear the horn of the bus. Its engine is turned on. The driver yelling that we're continuing the trip. I see the passengers hurrying back to the bus as if they're afraid it'll leave without them. We go back to our places too. The bus sets off after the driver says goodbye from his window to some of the men on the patrol and wishes them a good day.

2

At seventeen, I passed near the barracks. A few hours ago, I was in Azrou and now I've made it all the way here. Far from Azrou now. No one with me. Khatima didn't come with me. I have only a foggy idea of where I'll find Aziz. After his disappearance, I cried. Even though I'd thought there were no more tears in my eyes. Khatima kept telling me to forget it. The neighbors were saying the same thing. Two days after his disappearance, Khatima and I went around to all the administrations, establishments, and ministries. From the central prison to the Ministry of Justice. No one we asked knew anything about the person we were looking for. Aziz? There's no one with that name. Khatima started saying she didn't trust men who talked this way. They repeated the same words the prison guard said the first time. There's no one with that name. There were many ministries and even more offices but we didn't find anyone in this office or that to tell us something different. We only said we were looking for a pilot named

Aziz. The Ministry of the Interior first said: "What does the Ministry of the Interior have to do with the disappearance of a pilot who works in the army? Why don't you turn your feet toward the Ministry of Justice?"

We spent more days like this. From ministry to ministry. Rabat is a small city but it seems big, like a rumor that keeps spreading. You don't even know where to begin. At the Ministry of Justice: "You knocked on the wrong door. You want the Military Ministry of Justice."

"Where's that?"

No one knew. Like that, from office to office. From administration to administration. Until we wore out the soil we walked on. We went back to Azrou. And Khatima told me to forget about it.

But I didn't forget. I went out to the airbase. And here I am in Kénitra. A mysterious city. Like a village for summer vacation without vacationers. I didn't imagine I'd get here so quickly. The bus was moving slowly. Sometimes it almost stopped. I was thinking: I won't ever reach this Kénitra that I don't know. But I made it. Quicker than I'd imagined, and without my sister.

My inquiries to find Aziz started with his unit. From that road leading to the airbase. Passersby were looking at me, not knowing I just came from another city. I didn't have any trace indicating that. They look at my swollen stomach but they didn't know. Maybe the swelling wasn't obvious enough and I didn't say anything. But Aziz was growing inside me calmly. I sat on a stone to relax from the exhaustion of walking. I'd walked from the station to here, and I still hadn't arrived. At the station, they didn't know anything about Aziz but they stared for a long time at my belly. The airbase had been surrounded by soldiers since the coup, as people would tell me, whether I asked or not. They knew everything about the airbase and about the coup but they didn't know anything about Aziz. What did I have to do with the coup? I was looking for

Aziz who works at the airbase. Someone told me: "Follow this road but you'll find the base surrounded."

I came from the station all the way here on foot. Always along the same road until the river. Then you follow the river to the airbase. Its zigzags, which Aziz and I saw not far from the airbase. Once. My hand in his. Happy because we were near the river. Far from the base.

How much time had passed? Three or four months? Khatima didn't want me to travel without her. She didn't want me to move around without her because I was weighed down with the life in my belly. She told me to forget it. She didn't want me to move. But Aziz hadn't appeared. I waited for him. After our attempts to look for him at the offices and administrations. Then after our miserable waiting at the house. Two months we spent waiting. I'd just turned seventeen. Day after day. Week after week. All of it. Day by day. Hour by hour. Time passed faster than I'd imagined. And there I was sitting on a stone, alone, between the station and the base that would look over me after a little. A woman selling snails handed me a plastic bottle of water while I was sitting on the stone. I thanked her. She insisted I drink because she guessed my stomach was full. So I drank. I was happy with her water, scented with wild thyme and orange. The woman was happy as she saw me drink and water the life in my belly. She smiled at the child I was carrying with her many wrinkles, moving her old head. I told her: "His name is Aziz." We smiled together.

I didn't go near, since getting close to the airbase was forbidden. I stood far away from it. At a distance from the gate, and that's why I didn't know if Aziz was inside. People don't disappear for no reason. Going near any government building is forbidden. When we went looking for him, Khatima and I, we spent the day far from the central prison because approaching its gate is forbidden. Is Aziz there with you or not? They didn't say anything. Neither the guards nor the families of the prisoners who passed by carrying baskets of fruit for their relatives. We asked them if they'd seen Aziz, but they didn't say anything. It was the same with the guards, who looked at my swollen belly.

At the bus stop, a man we didn't know approached us. I didn't know people disappeared for no reason until I heard it from this man's mouth. They leave their houses and they don't return. They're in prison, and tomorrow they don't come back. Where do they go? They're disappeared. What do I do in that case? Aziz disappeared when he was in his plane. As if a star swallowed him. His mistake was that he loved flying. He was piloting his plane while I was on the roof waiting for him to appear. But he didn't. Not in my sky or in any other sky.

I remember his car as I see it approaching. His Simca 1000. Coming out of the airbase gate toward me. Slowly. In a non-threatening way, spreading calm in my soul. As if it's not coming from an airbase that's forbidden to enter, but from a tranquil dream. Like a small miracle. I stood up, beaming, sweat pouring from my pores. I imagined my anxiety would end here. It would be over. The car stopped at the curb. The same car we rode in together, the same color, but it wasn't Aziz, who I was expecting. The same blue uniform, yes. But the man who got out of it didn't look like Aziz. My anxiety was only beginning.

I was anxious, but not hopeless because I'm mature now, as my sister says. After marrying Aziz, she doesn't say I'm young anymore. She didn't like the work she was doing anymore. She kept saying she'd work in a rug factory until Aziz came back. But she worked at Madame Janeau's, at Stork Bar. Aziz was her go-between but he didn't come back. Khatima and I went to a fortuneteller. After she put her plate in front of her and moved on it her herbs, colored pearls, and strange seeds I wasn't familiar with, she said only God would assist us. But no one would help us. I didn't despair though, because I was mature. Pregnant and mature because of Aziz.

The man I thought was Aziz was standing in front of me, in his uniform and his many medals. He put his hand on my shoulder. His hand was cold. The material of my clothes felt wet when the coldness of his hand pierced it. His white teeth weren't his own. That's why he seemed like he didn't know if he was smiling or not. I didn't smile because I was still thinking about the car without Aziz. The man says, as if reading my mind: "Aziz is a friend of us all. What happened to you happened to everyone."

I felt anxious as I stood listening to him. "You have to be patient. Wait. When things calm down. You'll soon find your problem solved. There isn't a problem without a solution."

This was the opposite of what the fortune-teller told me: "Only God will assist you. No one'll help you." People's opinions differ like night and day. He seemed good, trustworthy, the man with the white teeth. He asked: "Where are you living?"

"Me? I don't live anywhere."

"Go to the Golden Sands Hotel and wait. I'll bring you news this evening about where he is."

I found the Golden Sands Hotel after some effort. I saw the river. Then the port, and an incredible boat emptying its load of wheat on the curb. I saw the wide streets and a lot of storks and two bridges before I found the hotel between two clouds, between two bars with thick smoke coming out of their doors. The hotel owner was nice. She gave me a chair to relax on. She could see that I'd been walking for a long time.

"Yes, from the airbase on foot. . . . It's a long way, right? . . . My feet have been busy. . . . Yes. A pilot at the airbase."

After the chair, she gave me an orange. She was a nice woman. She said it was best to find me a room on the ground floor. For the child in my belly. So I didn't have to go up to the first or second floor.

I lay down in the bare space that looked like a room in a hotel should. Little light. The bedcover was cold. Like the man's hand on my shoulder that afternoon. As I remembered him I heard a knock on the door. I opened the door but it wasn't him, the guy with the white teeth, the man who was driving the Simca 1000 and who I thought was Aziz. What I felt wasn't fear but anxiety, because my anxiety hadn't settled inside me. There was a glass of tea in his hand. As if he was a hotel guest who had just stepped out of the next room. He calmed me down and gave me a glass of tea. He then asked me for my marriage certificate to be sure we were really married, me and Aziz. I handed him the certificate. I blushed as I waited for him to read it. Then calmly he tore it up into little pieces and put the small bits in his pocket, saying, with the same calmness: "The son of the bitch who's in your belly doesn't have a father anymore."

From then on, if I was caught wandering around the airbase or one of the ministries. . . . I didn't hear the final part because sweat started pouring out of me again. For the second time today, sweat was pouring off me. A sharp whistle pierced my ears and a thick wrap began falling over my eyes. And Aziz? He was far away. Then I understood the words of the fortuneteller. Aziz had moved even farther away. Instead of moving closer.

3

Yes, I spent a while bedridden, semi-absent. Khatima said I hadn't left the bed since the miscarriage. Aziz's sister said it was the high fever that caused it. But I wasn't paying them any attention. For a long time, I kept feeling my child and his weight as he grew. His kicks as he moved. Khatima and Khadija didn't feel this. Their bellies hadn't swollen even once. So they could say what they wanted. I stayed hidden in various states of consciousness. When I woke up, I got up and started moving slowly so I didn't bother him. My sister insisted the fetus miscarried and I'm not trying to disagree with her. I heard him kick inside me and I told him to be calm.

"Relax, Aziz," I told him. "They're only your aunts, Khatima and Khadija, joking with you."

When I felt I could get up, I got up. Khatima went to work at the bar in the morning and didn't come back until late at night. Khadija and I would stay behind. She too says I spent ten months raving. I didn't leave the bed for ten months. It's her way of talking. We then went to the roof and, to convince me I spent ten months in bed, she'd show me her second turtle and say she bought this female for her male tortoise and she watched her every day. Yes, ten whole months passed and they hadn't laid their eggs yet. "This is the female, small, but she eats a lot. She especially loves lettuce and tomato peels. This is the male, big like a pig, but he doesn't eat a lot since he doesn't need to eat. He won't lay an egg. He just eats and shits only." We laugh. Then Khadija lays the piece of wood over the plant pots like a cover that'll keep the hawk from seeing the promised eggs. She raised her head up to the sky but she didn't see the hawk. She then asked me how many months a turtle needs to lay eggs. I don't know about turtles. Or about crickets. We went up in the afternoon to see if they'd eaten all their vegetable peels, which we'd scattered around them. And for Khadija to see if the hawk had appeared in the sky.

I went after Aziz again, after I heard about a barracks in the middle of the woods. I didn't know how to get there, which direction I should head in. Should I go east or west? And I didn't know how many forests I'd cross. Or how long my trip would last. It wasn't important. I only knew I needed Aziz and that I had to find him, and that he was abandoned in a place that I had seen in my nightmares. I had to find him on my own, without anyone's help. Like the fortuneteller said. Only God would assist us, she said.

I was walking in the shaded forest. Tall cedar trees. The road was dusty and wet and the scent of dead leaves rose up from it. There were trees on each side. Their roots were thick. The trees were bigger than anything I'd seen before.

Human arms couldn't reach around some of them, not even four arms. Behind them, behind the thick trees, girls were laughing and showing their small faces and thin hands reaching out from behind the trees, begging for dirhams from passersby. They laughed yet seemed afraid at the same time. And the morning was spring-like and invigorating, arousing pleasant memories in my soul. This idea brought a small happiness to my heart.

I was walking to a place I had seen in recurring nightmares. But I didn't see trees in my nightmares. Nor did I recognize the many faces that flickered in my memory and that didn't resemble the faces I saw in front of me on the side of the dirt road that zigzagged between the cedar trees. The skinny girls asked for dirhams with what look like veils of dried mud on their faces. The biggest one pointed back to where huts of wood, thick rags, and colored plastic were spread out. As if she wanted to show me the misery they were living in. And then I saw the camp. The mothers sitting in silence, picking lice off their many kids. There were no men. Then a small laughing child began pulling me by my sleeve. Her eyes were blue. Their blueness and the blue of the other eyes seem clearer because of the veils of dried black mud covering their faces. The girl holding onto my hand was five at the most, but her laughter was older than her years. She said she was big and strong and wasn't afraid of the woods, as her father said. I asked her where he was. This time, she pulled me in the opposite direction. We left the camp behind us.

"We don't see him anymore," the girl said. She laughed, as if her laugh was what led us. After the road, we saw the barracks. My disappointment stopped me as I realized the girl was leading me to the wrong place. But the girl kept pulling me by the hand toward it.

Two tall hangars with bent tin roofs and a stone wall with a tower in each corner surrounding them. In the middle was a round space with no trees. As if they had been ripped out from it. At the same time, we heard dogs barking. The big wooden door was wide open. There was a lot of commotion inside. I grabbed a handful of soil and rubbed it on my face to look like the child leading me toward the barracks. No one noticed us coming in. They were busy. We just looked like two local kids, after I'd put mud on my face. Men of different ages wearing khaki clothes, uniforms of the auxiliary forces. They were holding thick sticks and hurrying in every direction, yelling happily as if playing a childhood game. They then stood in front of one of the two buildings in two long rows. Showing off their clubs. What were they doing? There were lots of dogs under the wall. More than twenty dogs spread out on the dirt and watching the work of the auxiliary forces with empty, lazy eyes. Then a whistle rang out, and at that moment the members of the auxiliary forces began moving their clubs as if beating someone, yelling: "Run! Run, you son of a bitch!" They laughed. Until they reached the second building. They then repeated it three more times.

The heedless dogs, stretched themselves out under the shaded wall. Or licked their bodies with their long tongues or pulled fleas out of their hair, watching as if it were a sporting event.

"What are they doing?"

The girl didn't pay attention to my question. She was drawn to the movements of the auxiliary forces. Should I ask her about Aziz? Or wait for her father, who was also playing with his club? Or ask her if their game will last a long time?

Then the dogs moved without a sign from anyone. They got up, raised their ears, made a lot of noise, and bared their fangs. This time, a sheikh wearing a blackened Sahrawi gandoura whose sides hung down came out of the building. He might have been a hundred years old. He was thin, with a dark face and a few white hairs covering the bottom of his chin and reaching down to his chest. Thin like a reed.

The girl said: "A weak breeze will push him to the ground."

They move the clubs over his back and on his face and nape as the auxiliary forces chase him and yell: "Run, run you son of a bitch!"

They hit him on the head. On the head. The dogs were riled up and dragged away what was left of his rags and bit his thighs. But the sheikh didn't run. He didn't do what they wanted. Or what the clubs wanted. Or what the dogs wanted. The malice of the auxiliary forces and the zeal of their dogs increased. The sheikh moved with dignity and pride. The clubs hit and the mouths let out their vile words. What were they doing? This was no game. The hitting was real and the yelling was real. The blood flowing from the Sahrawi sheikh's head, bare arms, and thighs was real. A bitch ran off with a piece of flesh from the man's thigh and other dogs followed her as she growled, excited by the scent of raw human flesh.

The girl looked at me and said: "They spend their days playing like this. They don't get tired."

Do they play with Aziz like this? I didn't ask her. This wasn't the place to look for him. There wasn't a place like this in my dream. The woman who saw in her colored pearls what my days were hiding said he's in a far-off place and there's no way to get there.

As we come back, the five-year-old girl tells me her father comes home in the evening. When he sleeps, she hears him cry.

15

Aziz

Morning the Next Day

1

A BLACK BIRD SNEAKS IN under the tin roof and starts building its nest on one of the wooden columns holding up the clay roof. This bird fills the place with questions that don't exist. With a new air. It fills the place with an entire life that doesn't exist, at a time when someone needs to clutch at straws. It doesn't stop flapping its wings in that tight space between the two roofs. I see under my eyes everything it brings to make its nest. Pieces of straw, twine, wires, matchsticks. I don't know what the surrounding land is like. I haven't left this kitchen since I got here. I got here at night. I imagine the place surrounding us is a big trash dump because the bird also comes with very strange things, like cork or pieces of plastic. Sometimes dead scorpions. It does this coming and going, not forgetting to cast a glance down at me. I discover by chance it has one eye. That its pupil has a strange glimmer. Is it the light of another day making it sparkle in that exciting way? The glint in its eye gives the raven a look of evil intent. To excite its curiosity, I tell it I don't like ravens, especially the annoying ones like the creature moving above me. I waited for its response for a long time but it doesn't reply. I tell myself this luckless, black, one-eyed raven doesn't like me. When I think this, I hear it say: "What makes you think I'm black?"

I don't know how to respond to its unexpected and dumbfounding question. Hesitantly, I say: "Maybe it's the lack of light."

Or maybe I've forgotten the colors. It seems my answer doesn't convince him and his crying out increases.

I think about what happens outside, outside the kitchen, in the other kitchens. How many of us are left? I know our number's have gone down by a lot. Are there black or green birds above us debating with the other prisoners? But I don't know how many we were so I can't know how many we've become exactly. And how many birds are in each kitchen? Maybe five, maybe less. Is there a raven above all their roofs, building its nest, making the same chaos this damned one is making? Do they have the same problems I have with this bird?

Silence inundates the corridor. There are other guests I don't see. Maybe they were here and they didn't come back. I had been hearing the whisper of their movement but I don't hear it anymore. I was listening in on the nightmares of their sleep. I don't hear anything anymore. There's a light movement in the corridor but you'd never know if it's a snake moving away or scorpions falling from the nearby ceiling or rats running or a human being in the final agony of death. Or a cook walking on his tiptoes.

The bird keeps collecting its strange things that attract my attention and increase my curiosity. I decide to forget him, to forget his lit-up eye. I decided to concern myself with myself and what's been happening to me after I came back from my coma and found dirt and lime covering me from top to bottom without knowing where it came from. No doubt the cook sprayed me with lime to kill the lice that ate half my testicle. I took my clothes off and tossed them into the bottom of the basin and sat naked.

I raise my eyes and see something flashing through the holes of the clay roof. I do everything I can to focus on it. This time, the bird doesn't turn toward me. It keeps at its work, moving the piece of curved tin it brought in with its beak and feet. In this direction and then in that. It seems it isn't straight enough to make it happy. It leaves it hanging there and goes away. It continues collecting straw and twigs. It finally stops moving. It's enough to watch the raven's work. And what I discover is that the piece of curved tin is reflecting sunlight. Then that bird's color wasn't black. The day acquires a color and a presence. The light reflects off the bottom of the piece of shining metal and a sun appears at its base. A captivating, transparent light, between violet and blue, fills the place. I sit in the middle of the kitchen, naked, thinking about the bird that fetched the day to me. I discover its charming light on my entire body. Bit by bit. I look over my testicles as if seeing them for the first time. These are my feet and these are my legs and this is my penis and this is what's left of my right testicle. This is a piece of skin from my left testicle. I put it back and grab it so it clings to its brother. The sickly yellow color of the skin disappears and the scars disappear and the wounds disappear. I look with surprise at the change that's happening to the worn-out skin. I have no way to take some of these rays and keep them for a day when the sun finally disappears. Perplexed, I discover the wounds are healing. The skin's coming back. And the boils are recovering and the pus is drying up. I stretch my feet out in front of me as I look at this miracle. I look at my hands this time, extended in front of me. The right, then the left. I turn them over in every direction, enchanted by their appearance and by their color, changing from light yellow to brown like someone who spent the summer under the sun. I move on to my fingers. I move them one by one. I see all their old movements have come back to them. They point in the same old directions. They speak the same language. I discover a gold ring on one of my fingers. I don't know where it came from. Isn't that strange? I had it on all this time without noticing it. A big part of my memory is split apart around this. I don't remember where I bought it. I don't remember if I bought it or if someone gave it to me. I don't even remember if it's stayed on my finger all this time. Maybe it belongs to someone who was here before me. Should I hide it so the cook doesn't see it? Should I throw the ring in the corridor or give it to another guest who knows how to hide it better than me? I call out to my neighbor. No one responds. Except for the hum I heard in the corridor and that I don't understand, I don't respond. *Haaa.* Another guest discovers for the first time the sunlight and the miracle it makes before his eyes after a bird like mine alights on his roof. *Haaa.* Maybe it's connected to the echo of my voice. I spend a long time trying to get the ring off but it's as if it is attached to my flesh. Every attempt produces more anxiety than pain. When I am able finally to get it off, I put it to the side. I have the whole day to think about a good way to hide it.

The bird flaps its wings. Maybe he's noticed the extreme heat that starts rising with the new day. When it seems he's getting ready to leave, I ask him his name. Faraj, he says—"relief"—and beats his wings twice, or laughs twice, and flies off.

2

I stand under a tree without a name watching my uncle's house, the house of my father's brother, dozens of meters away. I stand under a short, thick tree with no breeze blowing under it. Leaning on its trunk, I look over the farm in every direction. I take breaths. My uncle hasn't come yet. He might come after a while, because he's heard the news. Now he knows. I don't have much time before he comes. He knows. The time has come for him to know. Nonetheless, there's still time for me to go in and say hello to my uncle's wife. Maybe I'll kiss her head and move away before my eyes catch his. If I get close enough and look into the stable, I'll see his donkey isn't there. I'll calm down because he's not in the house or outside it or around it. I'll feel even calmer if he hasn't arrived yet. He won't come back without me seeing his mule crossing the descent with his head low, submissively. It's better to wait until I'm sure.

A stream of water passes two steps from my foot. From the foot of the tree. I get near it and then backtrack toward the tree. I'll drink later. For now I'll watch the building. The sun has faded the color of its bricks. Light red and dilapidated in a number of places. Next to it is the tall eucalyptus tree. I haven't been able to climb it as I climbed the fig tree. Tall, but without much shade. As for water, I'll drink later. From this stream or from another, when I'm moving freely as I have to.

I say hello to my uncle's wife, kiss her head, and leave before her husband comes. So I can say later I didn't leave without having seen her. At least. She's a good woman. She was my sanctuary and aid during the six years I spent at my uncle's farm. She always pressed a piece of fruit or candy into my hand when my uncle had his back turned, counting the chickens that laid eggs and the ones that didn't. At her house, I'd always find her hand over my hair as I slept. I'd always find a piece of bread with butter or a glass of yogurt milk handed to me when her husband was gone. When he came back, I'd sneak away because of my horrible fear of him, fleeing from his violence. And from outside the house, I'd hear him. You're feeding the snake while I'm gone? You're fattening him up at my expense? Sleeping in the stable, I kept hearing him. You're taking my daily bread to feed the pig? He's stealing from me. I don't need proof to know he's stealing from me.

The scent of my uncle's wife is always in my nose and between the folds of my clothes. The scent of my uncle's wife is the scent of bread and milk. The scent of a woman crying. Crying as she kneads bread. Crying as she cooks. Crying as she pretties herself to join him in bed. She kept crying in silence the whole ten days I stayed in bed after my uncle dragged me by my leg on top of the stones and thorns until the bones of my back cracked. She cries with no tears so my uncle doesn't hit her. That day, my uncle found me milking one of his seven goats. I don't know if he saw me drinking the milk. I didn't feel the blow as it came down on my neck. When I fell to the ground, he grabbed my foot and dragged me, threatening and frightening me with the hell I'd live in with him and the straight path he'd put me back on. My uncle's wife came out to the river and gathered medicinal herbs that looked like mint and put them on the wound on my back. She doesn't have kids. She never complained about that. Or anything else. She gets up before dawn to knead bread for my uncle, to milk the cows, to bring the breakfast milk, and to spend the rest of the day sweeping, cleaning, and mending his clothes. When my uncle built a new room opposite his old room and moved into it, he forbade her from crossing its threshold. When he was there, he'd spend his time praying in his new room and watching his wife so she didn't go in and desecrate his prayers. Before leaving, he'd put two locks on her door. I was in the woods tending his herd. From dawn to dusk. My uncle has nine goats and three cows and he needs someone to take them to protect the milk that I drink secretly. Because it's me that tends the herd, he says I was the one stealing too.

It's better I don't wait much more. When I've said hello to her, I can go. I've been thinking about leaving the farm for months but I don't know where I'll go. During the day I think about it and at night I think about the pavement where I'll wind up. At night I dream I'm flying. I spread my wings above the farm and fly above my uncle's head as he threatens me and orders me to come down. The more his threats increase, the higher I go in the sky. After a while, he appears as just a tiny dot moving like a bubble in the sea. After a while I don't see him anymore.

Through the trees, I can see the bends in the road. It's better I wait until I'm sure he hasn't made it here before me. I think about the stable. Should I look there? If his donkey isn't in the stable, I can be sure he hasn't arrived. I don't look in the stable.

The teacher told me: "Your uncle knows." He said my uncle was stretched out on the bench next to the mill, clutching his heart so it doesn't stop. He almost passed out when he heard the news. He didn't open his mouth until the miller gave him a glass of water with pine tar. When he drank it and opened his mouth, no sound came out. The owner of the bakery was there. The owner of the mill and his assistants were there. All of them were there and they heard him say, after he drank the glass of water with tar: "School? He's going to school? He's been going to school for five years and no one told me?"

He then stretched out on the bench next to the mill, shaking, with his hand on his heart. Maybe he hasn't recovered from the shock yet. Maybe I still have enough time.

3

As if we didn't have anything to say to each other anymore, me and the teacher standing in front of me. As if there were no more words for us to say. The time has come for us to grow up. The time has come for my uncle to know. He passes out and drinks water with pine tar to get his voice back. The teacher's standing in front of his house as if he's just finished work he had to do. I heard the story as if I was expecting to hear it. Ready to hear it at any time. That child who his uncle brought five years ago to tend to the three cows and nine goats, day after day, from dawn to dusk, was also going to school. Under the cover of night while everything was dark, I snuck out of the stable on my tiptoes, night after night, covering fifteen kilometers on foot to the teacher's house, and returning fifteen kilometers on foot to get home before my uncle's wife woke up. Every night, long and short, for five years. Every night, I went to the teacher's house by night and came back by night.

Five years ago, I left my uncle at the market shopping and went to the Algerian teacher's house. I stood in front of him without saying a word. He looked at me, surprised, and asked me what I wanted. I didn't say anything.

"You speak Arabic?"

"No."

"French?"

155

"No."

"Are you Shilh?"

Yes. I didn't say it but the teacher read something like that in my eyes.

He then spoke with me in Shilha:

"What's your name?"

"My name's Aziz."

"What're you doing in the market?"

"I came with my uncle."

"What do you want?"

"I want to learn to read and write. But I can't go to school during the day because I work."

Five years went by quickly, after I met the Algerian teacher. And after I started going to his house in Azrou, I didn't care about my uncle or his power anymore. Because at the Algerian teacher's house I was learning to read and write. Learning a lot of enchanting things. I wrote on paper vague things, but as soon as they were read aloud, their meaning became clear. All of a sudden the table and the kitchen and the sky and the rainy season and the cow and the garden were with us, without them being physically there. The world widened to captivating limits. All of a sudden, birds flew on paper. And butterflies. All of a sudden things came to have meaning and then meanings and they took on dimensions and sizes. Five years passed like that. Fifteen kilometers going and fifteen kilometers coming without tiring me at all. My uncle's wife was sleeping and the women workers on the neighboring farms were also sleeping. The world was sleeping and I, what was I doing during this time? Learning the names of things. I would be sleeping in a cow's shadow, or under a tree, lulled by the music of an apple being written in my mind.

Then my uncle caught me sleeping and said: "Follow me."

I followed him to the house. It happened his wife was standing watching his stick as it was coming down on my head, powerless, pleading with me to cry for him to stop. But I didn't cry. She pleaded with her face and then with her tears but I didn't cry. My uncle's stick came down on this side or that, and blood followed it. For five years, exhaustion, pain, and blood simmered in my body. But my mind was alert. And now I've forgotten my uncle completely. Where is he now? Is he the one panting behind me? I don't think so. I don't have an uncle. Or mother. Or father. My sister Khadija is in the countryside. She might have gotten married at ten or twelve. She might have died. Yes, she probably died so I have no family tree, or branches. The entire story ended. Maybe I needed my uncle so I'd learn all this. Maybe I needed my uncle's wife so I'd see something nice could spread in the hearts of human beings. Or maybe all I needed was the time when I crossed the door and said hello to my uncle's wife and kissed her forehead.

My uncle's wife had her back to me, bending over the stove, baking the evening bread and wiping her worn, emaciated hands on a dirty rag. There were two chickens next to her, pecking at fallen seeds. Her clothes were worn and her sandals had holes in them. I didn't see her face or her forehead. I imagined her face was calm. I didn't expect words to come out of her mouth. There weren't words for her to say. Even if there were, they wouldn't reach anyone. I imagined a phantom of an old smile on her lips, sometimes visible, sometimes not. The memory of a smile that doesn't want to be obliterated. I don't know if my uncle had seen her smile before. As for me, I knew it even if I hadn't seen it.

I didn't go in more than two steps since I had seen my uncle approaching at the bottom of the dusty road on his donkey. I went out, running toward the stable. From the crack in the door, I saw him crossing the courtyard. His back was crooked and his head was bent forward from the shock and the mule was walking heavily as if my uncle's suspicions had possessed him too. The sun was setting behind them, casting the shadows of two creatures getting old fast. I heard him striding back and forth in front of the door, brandishing his stick.

"School? Who in his parents' family went to school? For five years, I've been giving him food and drink so he can go to school? For five years, the son of a bitch has been robbing me."

Without even seeing him, I imagined his pale face and yellow froth hanging from the corners of his mouth.

"Where is he? Where's the son of a bitch? For five years, he's been robbing me. From the day I brought him, he's been robbing me and giving my money to the Algerian. Where's that son of a bitch?"

I imagined his wife bending over the stove to hide her tears. Then I saw him leaning on his stick and going to the stable. His shadow preceded him. His chest wasn't wide like it used to be. Or his shoulders. A lot of white had appeared in his beard. As if we'd crossed a long distance of time together, not a mere five years. He stood now at the door of the stable and listened. From the threshold of the stable, I saw him. We both knew the time had come to settle our score. I'd grown up and had a strange feeling that our time had come to an end. Maybe my uncle was imagining the same thing. I also knew he wouldn't risk coming into the stable. He was cautious as a snake. He grabbed his chest and sat on the stone supporting the stable door. He looked more senile and wretched than I'd imagined. I thought how his shadow was greatly shrunken, how he didn't have a shadow anymore. His back was bent. His thighs were small, spread out in front of him. My thighs were bigger than his. I thought he didn't dare come into the stable because of my thighs, which had become bigger than his. Time passed with neither of us moving, each clinging to his spot. He knew but maybe he'd ask me to sneak outside the stable and he'd pretend not to see me and I'd pretend not to see him. As if we'd reached this point without an agreement. Or carrying out an earlier agreement we'd kept putting off all these years. Then his hand fell next to him. Did I see this too? Or did I imagine it? Did I imagine his death in this random way? Sitting on a stone supporting the stable as if he were basking in the sun, without there being a sun? I was looking at him, at his gaping mouth, his hollow chest. At what was left of my uncle.

4

Father Joachim opened the door of the charity seven years ago, and I think how lucky I am. From my uncle's farm to the charity. I didn't spend a single day homeless. He told me: "Here you can eat, sleep, and study." Father Joachim is seventy, thin as a cane, with a thin white beard, a bald head, and eyes that don't settle. His face is scarred by the fragments of bullets he took in the war. You don't know if they increase his reverence, his dignity, or his reserve.

I stayed close to him from my first days at the charity. At nineteen, I still need someone who cares about me, asks me about my interests, and gives me advice. Maybe he got close to me when he saw me staying away from the others. I don't get involved with them. I don't show my feelings to anyone. My concerns stay inside me and I keep them with me. I was always afraid of getting too near to my peers in the charity. I was looking for the fastest way to get through studying, to pass the exam, and join the military school, because I've decided to become a pilot. From then, I saw myself flying far away, turning my back on everything around me.

We gather the winter wood together, Father Joachim and I, and we go to the market together, wash our clothes, and spread them out on the side of the river. I go with him on his appalling outings when he gets drunk in Immouzer or El Hajib. He asks me to keep an eye on him so he doesn't go too far. He takes it too far without me noticing. And I spend the night looking for him, only to find him naked in the middle of the woods yelling, pleading, protesting, and mainly angry. On other days, when he's clearheaded and calm, he usually spends time praying. And sometimes, when he's not praying, he sits next to me in the evening as I'm studying. Then suddenly, he pulls the book out of my hands and asks me to show what I've memorized even if it's connected to my Arabic lessons. Father Joachim's memorizing the Quran, but in French, and he learned a lot of words from Shilha, but he doesn't know Arabic. Even though he doesn't know Arabic, his eyes follow the lines of Arabic letters, and he'll turn and tell me, "Here, you've made a mistake," when I make a mistake.

I have two months until the final exam. I stand in front of the crooked mirror in the hallway and see my face in it and I say out loud: "I've really grown up since I left the apple farm." My beard has sprouted and reddish fuzz has appeared above my lip. I now have a wide forehead.

I left the students in the canteen watching television and talking about politics instead of reviewing lessons for the exams that are almost upon us. Of thirty teachers, half of them belong to the N.T.U., as they call it. They say N.T.U. so we who don't belong to it don't understand what they're discussing. I know they mean the National Teachers' Union. But I don't say so as I listen to their fiery conversation. Inside, I'm jealous of them because they belong to a group, even if no one knows what this N.T.U. is or what it does. I only know they're against the regime. I feel miserable in front of their confident stares. When I get near them, they grow quiet. Or hide the papers they're passing between them. Their gaze strikes me like stones. I wonder if I should go back to the canteen. I stay in the corridor, pacing back and forth, then enter the canteen. A lot of people leave and the only supporters of the organization remain. I notice their annoyance as they watch the royal activities on television. Inaugurations, receiving ambassadors, and then other events and government and nongovernmental meetings. I hear one of them say the public money is being wasted on this nonsense. Then he turns to me. I feel anger, and heat rises to my face as if I was one of the people on the screen. I hope the police raid the charity and put handcuffs on their wrists. We'll get rid of them before their aggression spreads throughout the charity. I leave the restaurant to wander around in the garden. Without meaning to linger, but aimless, like an outcast, and with some regret for something I don't know or want to know. All I want is to cut a path without noise, without drums, and find a place for myself under the sun. I didn't have to listen to them, as if I was joining them in their extremism. I don't have an opinion to share with anyone, extremist or not. I don't belong to the left or the right. If I gave my opinion to one of them, he'd kick me out. Or if he was nice and understanding, he'd tell me: "You belong to the left without knowing it. Because you're poor and you want to change your situation and the situation of your family, like us all." What'll my response be at that point? Do I tell him I don't have a family?

Father Joachim was the one who told me about flying for the first time. He predicted I'd become a pilot. As if he'd directed my rudder onto a particular path. He planted the seed of flying in my blood. He'd been a pilot during the Second World War. A young man, twenty-two, not imaging at the time he'd wear the priest's cassock. He was only dreaming of flying. He said when he flew for the first time, he heard voices coming from far away. He said, at that moment, human eyes widen in an inhuman way. It's not because of fear or pressure but because you see another side of human history. Then he said he saw waves in the sky like the sea. Roads and forests and rivers where groups of lobsters are raised. He said: "You can move around in them like a shepherd or an aimless traveler. You move around between the strata as if you were moving around among cities. One thing that's not there is the wind."

Father Joachim looked up at the sky for a moment and asked me: "Did you know people grow up in the clouds? Look at these swallows standing above our heads."

I lifted my head up to the sky. I saw how they played as if they were swimming in a water basin. They were rising up now and moving away, getting smaller. Were they the ones getting smaller or were we?

He spent a period of the war in southern Algeria and there he tossed off the military uniform and put on the priest's. As if he exchanged the priesthood of the sky for the priesthood of the desert.

The night's thick around the charity building. The night's always thicker at its start. Nonetheless, the moon is near the ground this time of year. The little light comes either from the restaurant where I left the unionist students talking. Or from the top floor where the three priests overseeing the charity live. The garden is wet but the day's storm passed safely and didn't leave much of a mark on the trees and flowers that started blooming some days ago.

Someone knocks on the outer door. Father Jerome gets there before me and opens it. I don't see who knocked. I don't hear the news he brought. No one hears it except for Father Jerome, who hurries across the garden as if he's been expecting a catastrophe all day long. He's been spending day and night praying. Without turning to me, he says: "Father Joachim's returned. But he can't go up there."

Then Father Raphael joins him. The two fathers stand in the garden, as if they've always been expecting news like this and waiting for it, looking up at the sky and getting ready to go out, prepared for rain or a storm on the road. They'll take the donkey with them since they have to bring him back on it. They ask me to pull the donkey because I know the road better than them. And also since the donkey will be useful no matter what. Dawn's still far off. It might rain again because we're high up. I see them coming and going in the garden, talking about Father Joachim as if he'd lost his mind. And then as if he'd been tossed aside outside and was dying. Stained with his own blood after getting stabbed in the forest. I'm worried about Father Joachim too, even without thinking he might have been stabbed or drowned, without the other catastrophes in the eyes of the clergymen wrapped in their black abayas.

162

We're in the highlands. I'm at the front, followed by the mule and the two monks. Wrapped in their thick black clothes. We're not in winter but we haven't entered the period of heat yet. The two monks wear black in all seasons. And it rains a lot in this region. We pass above an old airport. There aren't the usual markers of an airport on the ground. Father Joachim's the one who told me this is the airport. Only the rich French land here in their private airplanes for treatment at the Bansmim sanatorium. When one of Father Joachim's fits comes on, he heads up to the airport and passes the day there. Sitting, looking at the sky. Once, when I was sitting next to him on the airport grass where the scent of wild thyme and wild mint spread inch by inch. I heard him say: "My faith has been shaken."

Father Joachim was telling me, alone, far from the charity and the fathers: "I no longer believe in God. No one wants to understand me."

What do you want men who dedicate their lives to prayer and getting close to God to understand? "What do you want them to understand, Father Joachim?"

He seemed miserable, not like someone who'd lost his faith but like someone who'd lost his trust in humanity. Father Joachim has been like that since the day I met him. Nothing will soothe him. He devotes himself to prayer and reading for long months, night and day. Then, like someone who's lost his good sense, he raves for days, before disappearing for a number of months. He comes back afterward with a radiant face. Calm. Not even mentioning what happened.

"Where were you, Father?"

"I was looking for where I found faith for the first time, in the desert, in the remote south of the desert. The sky is close there. And God comes out. God only comes out in the desert. There are people who can hear what you say as you hear what they say, without needing to speak."

"How can this be, Father?"

I remember the day monks detained him in his cell when he announced he wanted to change the monastery into a shrine where everyone can take refuge, Muslims and Christians, people exploring, believers and nonbelievers.

I don't remember how many times he disappeared during my seven years there. What was Father Joachim looking for? Not for God. He says he's looking for people. Father Joachim kept telling me, as if to dig his words into my mind, that people, in their nature, seek good and aspire for perfection. Because the important thing is that you believe in some kind of perfection. In a being of infinite perfection, and that you aspire for this perfection, call it what you will. I don't understand him and I don't understand his way. I see him sometimes as a Muslim, sometimes as a Christian, and sometimes as a heretic. In his prayers, I hear him mix the Quran with the New Testament. Sometimes in a language I don't understand. Especially when he's drunk. When I ask him about the language he prays in, he says all languages can take you close to the Creator.

When he isn't in the charity, he might cross the mountain and go deep into the desert, looking for the nomads. He might not find them. Sometimes nomads aren't in the areas where he roams. He spends months living on barley bread, water, and fruit from trees, if he finds them. He comes back like a drunkard. He says what he found on his last trip is invaluable even though I don't understand what it is he found. He can't explain it. He only yells: "It's everywhere. It's everywhere."

I try to understand him but I don't. Sometimes I say the man has lost his mind.

Before his latest disappearance four months ago, I asked him: "Haven't you found what you're looking for yet?"

This time, traces of grief didn't appear on his face. He didn't tell me he'd lost his faith. Or that his belief had been shaken. He was happy. He said he'd decided to leave for good. He'd head to the south, and there he'd build his shrine. A shrine of clay and figs, he'd build it with his hands near a spring, and next to it he'd plant barley and harvest it with his hands. And he'd welcome transients of all nationalities, colors, and creeds.

We found him stretched out near an olive press, passed out, with wounds on his face and his clothes muddied. There was a lamp at his head and some villagers up late around him. They said a gang of robbers had attacked his tent and took the little money he had. A traveler was passing near his tent and brought him here on his camel.

The rain started falling. We were on our way back at dawn. I was pulling the donkey. We were crossing the same road we came on. The ground was wetting my shoes. I see him rocking back and forth on the donkey, Father Joachim, his face bloodied, clothes ripped, covered in mud, and his head bent forward a little, looking at me with the hint of a simple-minded smile on the sides of his lips. As if he was saying he finally found what he was looking for.

16

Hinda
The Next Morning

1

DARKNESS KEPT ME FROM LEAVING the casbah. I said I was waiting for sunrise and, maybe, I thought a lot about where I'd go. The morning I was waiting for has risen and I don't know yet which direction I'll set my head. I remember the life of the dogs waiting for me and I wonder what's better, the unconfined life outdoors or the life of the casbah. A few days ago, I saw a bitch wandering around nearby, and the free life she was living overwhelmed me. She could go where she wanted and sleep where she wanted. She told me she'd come here to see the casbah because yesterday she'd heard an incredible story about it. She said: "I heard its architect was well known throughout the south. But I only see ruins in front of me. Who lives in this casbah?"

I told her: "Some government types."

I didn't want to disturb her morning with stories of burying people alive. And she wouldn't trust me if I tell her what I witnessed. She'll say I hate human beings or something like that. We wandered around for a while among the palm trees and then she asked me to come with her to where she lives with a Sahrawi family. We crossed a piece of desert with golden sands, and during the trip I asked her for her name. She told me it was Rustam. The name seemed strange to me and I told her so. She said she really found it strange at first too, but with time. . . . We stopped above a sand dune and rolled down to its bottom laughing and then kept going. She said a man named Glaoui had built the casbah without spending a single penny from his pocket on it. Rustam stopped, turned to me, and asked me what the shabby covers and rusty tin plates filling the courtyard were for. I didn't know how to respond. I said: "They're covers from the days of the pasha and no one wanted to take them because they didn't want to bring misfortune on their house."

"And the smell of death?"

"What smell of death, dear Rustam? I don't know what you're talking about."

She grew quiet and looked at me as if she doubted what I was saying. She then said there was an unmistakable odor. We kept going. We reached an oasis with lots of palms around it, surrounded by black Bedouin tents tied to the ground with ropes and pens for herds of goats. Others for sheep. Smoke from ovens and women sitting at the tent entrances making a thick soup from flour and clarified butter with their children on their backs. Their daughters were playing in front of them and other kids of different ages were running in every direction, yelling. Rustam turned to me and said proudly: "They're all my family."

I was thinking about Rustam now and about the happy life she was living among the kids and the Sahrawi clan. What a simple life, simple and complete. Rustam was a nice dog and she entered my heart from the first moment I saw her. I was thinking about all this as I hid in the corridor so the commander didn't see me after I intentionally broke the bottle of whiskey he and the woman with him were drinking yesterday. The door to Aziz's room was shut. I looked over it from the lower opening and saw him on his slab, sitting naked as the day he was born. He was swimming in a circle of sunlight coming down strongly on him from the ceiling. There was no trace of the festering wounds I saw on his skin at night. He was sitting like a man sunbathing and after a little while, he'd put on his clothes and leave the slab. Yes, I didn't have anything else to do here. No one needed me. A few months ago, the commander was going to give me to one of his friends. He told him: "Save me from this bitch, she's not good for hunting or guarding." But the friend apologized and told him I was an old dog and it was better for me to die here. He's right. The exhaustion of the years is weighing on my shoulders. I'm not strong anymore like I was when I was young and lived with the tailor Mahjoub and his evil wife. But I don't want to die here and be buried with the others in an infested hole and be sprayed with lime like the hundreds of corpses I've seen. Despite my old age, I still hope for a happier life.

I moved forward on the edges of my toes and looked over the courtyard. I didn't hear the sound of the guards. No movement in the courtyard at all and the hole was as I left it yesterday, overturned. The guard's room was empty. So was the commander's office. In the whole casbah, there was no one. That was strange, but I didn't have time to think about it. I'll think about it after I leave this hell. Wherever I go, it'll be better than this. I learned while living in these wastelands that I can get by on hunting bugs and vermin. I managed to shrink my stomach so a small mouse would be enough for an entire day. Desert rats are among the most delicious meals I've had in my life, in addition to being healthy. I don't really need anything else. I haven't relied at all on the guards' generosity because they're stingy. The commander eats lunch and dinner with whiskey. Since I came here, I've relied on myself.

That's what I said as I approached the big gate of the casbah. The courtyard before the gate was clean and sprayed with water and the trash strewn in front of the casbah had disappeared. Flags fluttered as if we were welcoming an important guest. Only a few minutes passed before I saw him cross the courtyard wearing white slippers and a light-yellow djellaba. A man wearing white from head to toe was accompanying him, carrying a small metal briefcase and a small chair.

They went deep into the corridor and reached Aziz's door. The man put the chair to the side of the door and withdrew.

2

His Majesty has arrived, greeting you and asking you if you have thought about us.

"Maybe it is the last time I will visit you and ask you to say the single sentence I am waiting for from you: You are the king and I am one of your devoted subjects. Is that too much? I do not understand why you do not love me. I have thought about it for a long time but I have not found a convincing response. There is no one in my kingdom who does not love me. Why are you disturbing my life and making me spend time thinking about you instead of the affairs of the people? Why do you hate me? Everyone loves me. My ministers, my poets, my palace jesters, and my slaves. Why do you not love me like all the people love me? You should love me, just like that, simply and without question.

"What do you want? I ask you only what do you want? That I be like the king of Sweden? No one sees him because he spends his day driving around on his motorcycle. Are you Swedish? Or your father or grandfather? Or do you want me to give power to the leftist parties who will sell us out to the Soviet Union? If they are even able to run the country. They will sit on chairs spreading revolution and watch the country head into the abyss. While the money I take, I spend on the protestors among you and the sick. Do you not remember how many singers, composers, and painters I sent for treatment abroad at my expense? Unfortunately they all died, but that did not stop the doctors in Paris from taking all their fees. Do you think the deaths of singers and painters will make their hearts merciful like mine? Oh, by Almighty God, they have not forgiven me. I paid the bills to the last penny. In addition to the bills, I paid for the airlines that transported their dear bodies and that is without talking about the funerals and mourning ceremonies. All this I paid for from the money I collected and saved for the day you would need it. Do you remember the coffin that held the body of our friend, the film director Reggab? How beautiful it was! Who was dreaming of a coffin like this? With ebony and a glass peephole Mohamed could look through at us, we who were loving him and treating him like our son. Would the socialists or communists think about a coffin like this? Never. Do you know why? Because I think of everything. You are my children and part of my heart, and what I ask from you, friend, is not much for a citizen who loves his king. But you do not love me, you wretch. A soldier who does not love his king. There is not anyone like that from China to Norway. That only happens in this country, which does not remember the blessing God has bestowed on it.

"What do you want? Do you want my reign to end so you can begin yours? I see you from here, imagining the day I will flee. Coming out of a narrow back door. With cheers following me: 'Grab the dictator. Grab him before he gets away. Stone him and stone his children.' That is if the riffraff do not grab hold of me and lead me to the gallows, shouting at each other and spraying saliva: 'Kill him and his family!' Is that what you want? Why? Am I not the father of you all? Your father who loves you and stays up late for your comfort? Who treats you as a father treats his children? If I hit you or jailed you, it was for your own good. Do you not hit your children from time to time if they act out? Do you not lock them in a room or the kitchen or the well? Speaking of that, do you know the Americans have started asking about you and the others? Is that reasonable? Are you happy? The Americans intervening in our affairs now? They sent a commission and reports and lots of bad things because of you, you piece of bad luck. Are you not ashamed? Is that what you want?"

He calmed down for a moment and his voice seemed sub-dued as he told us he hadn't slept the night before. During the day, he only drank a glass of milk with honey. For long nights, he hasn't slept. The guest rested his back against the wall. I looked at him from my hiding place. I saw he'd passed out. The man who was with him was leaning over him, giving him an injection in his arm. After about fifteen minutes, he woke up and asked the man to help him change position. The man didn't know what position he was talking about. The man who might be his personal doctor asked him to take a bit of rest. The guest put black sunglasses over his eyes and I said maybe he's doing that so the doctor doesn't see his tears. The guest then turned to the nurse getting ready and asked: "How are things on the streets?"

The man said: The situation on the streets is calm."

He then said: "The repulsion was completed with a hundred tanks at the entrances of the cities." The guest smiled.

I felt my eyes closing and my body went limp. I was still tired from the effort I'd made that night. I've become senile. I'll be lucky if I can fit in with that simple Sahrawi family.

17

Benghazi

10 a.m.

1

THEN THERE'S THIS WOMAN WHO comes looking for her husband.
I don't see her at first when she gets out. I am lying down in
the room and I think: Today's the day I go to the city to try my
luck. The only thing on my mind is the horses that'll run in the
afternoon. I drink a cup of tea and leave my room. I find a bus
full of tourists. My uncle told them we don't need tourists, most
of them are spies. He's in his office, my uncle. Either they're
French or Italian or Indian. What do we do with them? They've
come to marvel at the impenetrable walls and what's left of
the pasha's tiles and his decorations in the catalogs they carry.
They're sweating a lot. It's May. The tourists don't understand
what I say but the guide responds to their questions.

I say: "They're spies and we don't have any prisoners here,
thank God."

The guide doesn't know how to explain so I say: "All this
was left by tyrannical colonialism. As for now, thank God, the
country enjoys freedom and happiness."

And the guide: "The casbah's closed because today's
Friday."

And the tourists protest: "Today's Sunday."

And I yell: "Regardless, today's a Friday in this region.

And the tourists scream: "We protest strongly."

And me: "May God bless your parents, go. The journey's
over."

My uncle's in the office. They're trying to charge the door as I tell the guide to stop them from coming in if he wants to end his day safely. Tomorrow I'll open the door for them because it'll be their Friday. No races, no horses, no numbers. There's no one left, nothing that the French and Americans will be able to accuse us of. God willing. For now, entering is forbidden and that's it. My uncle knows half of them are spies who've brought their evil intentions and preconceptions and my uncle says they'll sow evil words in newspapers, whether we open the door for them or not.

I say goodbye to the guide and his tourists at the door, and when the bus moves, it leaves the woman behind. Standing on the other side of the bus where it was stopped. The numbers are going round in my head. Dogs running and horses following them and sometimes running together in the same race. And the woman is standing under the sun. Dogs, horses, donkeys, and chickens. She looks up at the casbah walls in the morning light. She doesn't look like the tourists who come to see us from time to time so we can show them our historical achievements. Her skirt's long with white buttons, covering her from top to bottom. Her modest bag and her smile full of hope. Her bag is of black leather. Her tight held hair in a decorated bandana. Maybe she's Shilha from Immouzer or Timhdit. And when she says she's looking for her husband, Aziz, I know she isn't Shilha. I know immediately. She says her husband's name. I pretend I don't know him. Why would I be responsible for knowing him? I don't know anyone, ask my uncle. Or whoever's above him. Or above us all. I pretend I like what she was saying because the casbah's a place tourists from all over the world come to. Even from Japan. I ask her if Aziz is a Japanese tourist or a guide like me in the ministry of tourism. Because I've been a guide in this casbah for twenty years without seeing a colleague with that name. Aziz, you say? She's looking at me, breathless, and wondering and hoping and disbelieving. Then sympathy fills my heart.

We buried him only yesterday. If she'd come the day before or two days ago. But that's another story, as they say. She says she spent the night on the bus because she was coming from Azrou. She's not hungry or tired. She only wants to see her husband. A mature woman, her chest mature and full. I remember him in his hole in the middle of the courtyard where I left him last night under the ground, rotting in peace. I ask her about his work and why he disappeared and why she has kept looking for him all this time. Because a man doesn't disappear unless he has a plan. I tell her about men I know who have disappeared because they had a plan. They wanted to change their lives completely.

She said her name was Zina. I didn't feel like carrying on saying the same thing, while she looked at me with her teary eyes. And I, in my mind, saw her, instead of my wife, sitting at my house, waiting for the happy birth. I see her through new eyes. As she presses with her fingers on her black leather bag and says: "The woman who showed me the place."

I don't hear what she says. So no one can say I heard. I tell her that standing here, near the casbah, or far from it, is forbidden. Do you know getting close isn't permitted, even for tourists? Nonetheless, as my uncle says, they're put on a list from the Ministry of the Interior so spies and enemies don't sneak in.

Welcome to you in any case, if you want to visit. But I tell you now you won't find who you're looking for. Not even half of him. All the wings of the casbah are empty, thank God. I tell her this when it becomes clear to me that moving away is better than standing here very close to him. And to the hole we threw him in. He might get up at any moment, as Baba Ali says. My uncle might be spying on us from his window and abduct her because he'll think she came to drink whiskey with him. It's not necessary for us to keep standing here. I don't have a solution for her. As I told her, we don't have any people for her to look for, except for the dead. And may God have mercy on the dead. Is it possible to say more than that? I told her: "This is a tourist place." And tourists come here for the beautiful palms in the neighboring oases. From the casbah roof, they seem beautiful at dusk. Do you want to see dusk from the casbah roof and other things, as they call them? The tourists sit on the roof to drink Moroccan tea we make for them as they watch the red spread from the sun setting on our beautiful oases. Maybe there's another place. With the same name and the same descriptions and with this man who . . . What's his name? Aziz. I tell you men don't disappear like that for nothing. You say twenty years? Really? That's a lot. No one looks for someone for twenty years. He might have gotten married and had kids, and he's now playing in the stadium of the Royal Federation of Soccer or studying medicine in Belgium or selling hashish in Rotterdam.

We move away then and I let the current lead me. God alone is able to find a good solution. In the taxi, my elbow touches hers. The horses are running in my head, and time runs. I've got enough time to get to the bookie in the city. Two hours going and two hours coming back. And other things. Nothing's turned up in its place. And my arm's leaning on hers. Like two friends busy with the concerns of the world. And I speak with her about everything happening around us. My wife's pregnant. That's right, seven girls. The boy, I'll call him Ismail. Imagine, triplets in a single night. If there is a boy. And I'll buy a ram from the market this morning for us to slaughter in case there is. And she says she came this whole distance to see her husband. All night and by bus. Without eating or sleeping. And I say: "God will make it right. If God wants you to know where he is, you'll know and if He wants you to see him, you'll see him because God doesn't waste these things and other things like them. God willing."

My wife is in her ninth month. In her last day or the one right before the last. She leans against me when the taxi turns to the right and I lean against her when it leans to the

176

left. I feel for her and I'm sympathetic to her. Her smile at this moment is closer to submission to the command of God and His decree. Her breasts are like pomegranates shaking under her dress. If he was alive, I'd tell her. Or I'd drop a hint so she'd know and calm down a bit. She stops twisting her fingers. But he's dead, and by God on high, I saw him with my own eyes and we buried him with my own hands and there's no use going back to the past. Baba Ali alone saw him alive again, but he's always talking nonsense. If the matter was in my hands, I'd have tossed the two of them into the same hole. And I'd have tossed in my sinning uncle, the commander, and the old dog and been finished with the whole thing.

As the taxi moved us away, I say: "A time will come when you'll forget this illness whose name's Aziz. There's no illness human beings won't heal from."

If only she'd let me propose to her another life without Aziz and without a wife who gives birth to girls. Life's beautiful without boys or girls. If she'd only let me sleep on her chest and hear the beating of life. We'll start over. A new start. From the beginning. Without pits or bodies or my godless noisy uncle. And I see everything's possible this time. With her, I'll go back to the beginning.

2

We found Baba Ali lame. She stands, and so do I. His wide red eyes fill with tears and a yellow fluid comes out of them. What's wrong with you, Baba Ali? He's like someone who's been stunned by something. He says he was always expecting the administration would send him on the hajj. What administration? We don't have anything we call the administration. No papers and no register with our names so they can identify us. If Baba Ali's a cook, he has to write to a ministry concerned with cooking, and if I'm a real guide, I have to go to the Ministry of Tourism. Baba Ali says they have to send us together on the hajj. "Why? Did you commit sins, Baba Ali?"

Since I first saw her behind the bus, she hasn't sat down. I ask her to sit. Does she think I'll tell him something about her? That she came looking for her husband, who we buried yesterday? I tell him her name's Zina. Her name comes off my tongue easily.

This catastrophe is happening to Baba Ali because he doesn't remember God. How will he remember God if he's not praying? He lives alone like a mouse after he left his children in Taza. My house is better than his. His house is a room five meters long, it's two rooms in one. In addition to a kitchen and bathroom he shares with the neighbors. It's as if God the Almighty told me: Here's your chance if you want to change your life with a good woman. With her shyness and her way of lowering her eyes. And he's here, extended before us, losing control over his right side. Before three o'clock, if I hurry, I can reach El Hajib and Midelt before three. I've got in my pocket the winning numbers. Twenty years she's been waiting to come to the casbah gate to say she's looking for her husband. And I say she's not looking for her husband. A lost woman, she's looking for someone to save her. And I, as if I were striving to save her. God put me on her path so I can grant her the life she's looking for. Without asking her where she came from or how she spent the past twenty years. Ready to accept her as she is. With her sins and reckless deeds. Should I leave her with Baba Ali like someone waiting for her husband to come back from work? Should I go to El Hajib or Midelt to get rid of the numbers playing in my mind and go to the hammam and then to the barber? The woman is looking for stability. Food and a house to take refuge in. And then it was fated for her to settle down with me in Midelt or El Hajib. Or a distant city so we don't see the casbah. Or the men buried in it. God will find us a solution at the right time. Not before or after. And Baba Ali's looking at us with his unparalyzed half. If he'd said *In the Name of God the Compassionate the Merciful* yesterday when he thought he saw the dead man moving, the matter would have ended and that would have been it. But God didn't run this sentence on his tongue because He doesn't love him. Baba Ali was as good as finished when he saw the dead man alive. Baba Ali has lost his direction. We buried the man she was looking for. And then Baba Ali ran out of the room in the middle of the night. Have you, Zina, forgotten to bury a dead man and found him the next day without a stomach and with his head covered in mud, without any eyes? Yes, this wonder happened to us. But it's the past. And with the help of God, I'll become someone else. Instead of the mouth, there was a hole full of dirt. What was left of the body was mangled from head to toe. I swear to God the Most Great. I'm very lucky because, at that moment, I said: *I take refuge in God against Evil Satan*. If not for that, I'd have been struck like Baba Ali. Bones sticking out like branches with the remains of pieces of flesh hanging down from them and spots of blood darkened by soil sticking to them, God protect me from that. Baba Ali won't ever say a word. Because when someone is right with himself and his family, these things don't happen to him. I won't leave her with him in case he says something. I'm not sure God finally tore out his tongue. Because if the left sides of human beings' brains are paralyzed, you don't know what's going on in their right brains. As happened to Baba Ali, whose mouth fled toward his ear and whose eye was red and hung down and widened, looking in another direction. His hand became lean and slept next to him, frozen, unmoving. And we, as if we've come to comfort him for half an hour, in a friendly visit. As long as he thinks we're good friends and we haven't abandoned him in these disasters. Afterward, we'll go back to our house in Midelt or El Hajib. And I took a checkerboard from under his bed and told him: "Play, Baba Ali." What would he play with since his fingers were stiff? I told him: "Your left hand, Baba Ali, is still good and you can move checkers with it, and thank God it hasn't become stiff like the right one."

179

I put the board between us. Baba Ali glanced at the shut door. I asked him: "Should I lock the door, Baba Ali?"

I got up and locked it. It let out a strange sound. Like moaning. I opened the door again and sat on the couch next to Zina and she arranged the pieces on top of the squares. He kept looking at the wide-open door as if he was expecting the dead man to appear in front of him to ask him for the shroud. He kept indicating toward the door. No one was at the door. The sun was ablaze and I heard the chirping of the bugs and nothing else. I didn't know exactly what Baba Ali wanted. Maybe he had no desire to play. "You don't want to play, Baba Ali? Should I ask my uncle to pay for the pilgrimage to Mecca for you?"

This time, he yelled in his voice hitting the ground. I heard him say: "Do you think God will forgive us?"

If he doesn't go on the hajj, everything he did will follow him to the hereafter. "They're the reason. They're the reason for everything that happens to us, Benghazi. The man who—"

I yelled in his face not to say his name. "What's He forgiving us for, Baba Ali? Did we do something forbidden that our Lord will punish us for? Did we do something not mentioned in the Holy Book, Baba Ali?"

He returned to his senses and we went out and the woman didn't ask what Baba Ali wanted to say. She got up and followed me. No one likes Baba Ali.

Are we the ones who brought them to the casbah?

I left her standing at the door and went back to Baba Ali. So I know I felt pity for him. That I was changed because of this new feeling. The new heart beating in my chest.

"I didn't bring anyone here and we didn't kill anyone, Baba Ali. With the help of God, you'll get up and resume your life and it's no use going back to the casbah because no one lives there anymore."

I swear, he'll talk to the others. Everyone will get what's coming to them, northing more and nothing less. Are you comfortable now, Baba Ali, because I've explained it to you?

His voice was only a whistle. I didn't know Baba Ali had a voice that whistled. What's wrong with you, Baba Ali? Maybe he's lost his mind. Should I put the board and the checkers back under the bed or should I leave them in front of him? Maybe they'll help him regain his mind.

3

The house was as I left it fifteen days ago or more. There was nothing to indicate that she'd given birth to what was in her belly. No trilling and no congratulations. No scent of sauce with chicken and saffron. And Zina was standing at the door. The house was hers. Until now, there has been no other house. Later, when we settle down in our new house, in El Hajib or Midelt or any house she chooses. . . . And for the first time, I told her: "Zina, go in." If my mind had been helping me, I'd have seen she was surprised as that name came off my tongue again. She was looking at me with her pleading eyes and look-ing at my pregnant wife on the mat, her forehead moistened with scraps of cloth. The television in the living room was telling its stories to my daughters Ruqiya and Fatiha. Other than them, there was no one. I said: "The house is empty this morning except for the noise of the girls."

My two girls kissed my hand and said their sisters were at their grandmother's. Then they said their mother was waiting for a boy. And my wife was in labor in the middle of the long room and sending her calm looks toward me. But I don't trust the looks of women. She told me with her eyes that it would be a boy. But I don't trust the looks of women. At that exact moment, I didn't care. Because I heard the name in my ears a third and fourth time. Zina. Zina. I told my wife: "This is Zina. She's looking for her husband."

I said it because the name stayed in my mouth. Zina was still standing there, laughing with the girls near the door. And the actors on television were laughing. They were happy with the new arrival on the way, preparing for her a special place among them. When I went back to the living room, Zina came back with me and sat down. We carried on watching my wife from the window. As if we were looking at another woman far away. In some hospital. In some wing. With no connection to us. She and everything that's in the room. As if she'd forgotten the reason she came.

I gave her a glass of tea and some sweets. She had no desire or appetite. She only came to look for him. She was not the first woman to find herself in this position, far away. Maybe the time had come for her to go back to Azrou, as they call it.

"God will make good things happen. But now it would be better for you to relax and change your mind about going back. This will be your place, as soon as I come back."

She ate a piece and waited for my return, when God would enable us to be together. Instead of moving, Zina's eyes kept watching the TV show. This was good too. I went out and closed the door behind me. Men and women passed before me, celebrating in their colorful clothes and their kohl-lined eyes and all the other things that happen in a marriage festival. Why didn't we get married in the middle of the music, dancing, and beating drums? This was a unique occasion. She was on her way to forgetting. And the girls were crossing the alley, laughing. And groups of male and female singers headed to the square with red and white flowers around their necks and ululations rising up from every direction. I don't want either a boy or a girl anymore. God has put the marriage festival on our path as a sign.

I was sure she'd calmed down when I left. Maybe she wasn't thinking about him anymore, but of all the goodness before us. Her presence in the house was a good idea. When I got back, she was standing and getting ready to go somewhere. It seemed to me there wasn't anything between me and her anymore. I came down to her from the sky to solve the problem that a man left her without a protector for twenty years. Who would provide for her? Who would protect her from the cold nights and the summer heat? It was as if God had put me here at the right time and place.

4

This was something that hadn't happened before. I couldn't find the girl who spent the night with my uncle to bring her back to her family. This was another job I had to do. Instead of her, I found big cars in front of the casbah gate. Tanks. Ambulances too. My uncle said a high-level American commission had come to get one of its citizens. And the commission said he was with the group of prisoners. His grandfather had traveled to America on a research trip and become intimate with an American woman and so he remained in their protection. Neither I nor my uncle understand the Americans. And you'd think the American commission would be made up of Americans, but they weren't. The ones I saw in front of me were Moroccan. A group of officers and important officials, tall, with blond hair. In military uniforms and other things. As for the commission, as they call him, he was a short man, thin like a branch, whose face was covered with freckles like a sieve and whose thick glasses were like two jam jars. He wore khaki shorts and a khaki shirt as if he was going to hunt butterflies. It was a high-level American commission because the important Moroccan officers were surrounding the short man and raising their heads at every word and laughing at every sign. Was this the commission that was asking for the American?

My uncle said: "Do you know where the short man came from? From Congress or Conogress. It's the equivalent of our parliament." So it's not equivalent to anything. We don't have an American or even half an American prisoner. We don't jail Americans. And the man, the commission, was sitting behind my uncle's desk and joking with the American officers in American, and my uncle, who doesn't understand American, was near the window moving his head as if he understood and was laughing and the American saw he didn't understand so

183

he spoke with him in Moroccan and this time my uncle moved his head as if he'd remembered he could understand. The officers suggested they make a visit to the casbah so the American Congress could see our magnificent heritage. I thought my role as guide had come. But the Congress apologized. It didn't have any time to waste. My uncle came up to me and we went out to the roof.

We were alone now, and he asked me: "Where's the notebook?

"What notebook, Uncle?"

"The commission's been looking for it since they came."

"What notebook, Uncle?"

"The notebook we've been registering the names of our prisoners in."

"If my memory serves me, Uncle, we tore it up, so no trace remains of them."

"Baba Ali was recording the names of the dead in a special notebook."

"But Uncle, you tore it up. I'm a soldier. I don't know how to write, I told you, Uncle. I agree with you. Since that day, we've been burying them, not writing them down. I never thought about them, dead or alive. Because since the first day, you told us, Uncle, these cursed ones have come here to die. Without a notebook or anything else. I only understand that."

I also understand my uncle doesn't buy food for them with the money from the state. Sometimes I don't understand him because he builds houses with this money. He builds complete neighborhoods in Meknès and doesn't give us anything from the state's money, even though we're in the same boat. Of course it's not the same boat when it's about money. I don't like to think a lot about these things. I only enjoy the memories that will come. This woman who came at the exactly the right time to change my life. I hope what I'm thinking about is good. She'll need a house to shelter her. The money I'll earn will be enough to find an appropriate house in Midelt or El Hajib.

And I'll leave my uncle with the Americans and I hope they eat him alive. God willing, the Merciful and the Compassionate.

My uncle said: "Go bring them their American." His face didn't turn red or green, as I thought it would.

This wasn't my uncle anymore, my uncle who didn't open his casbah to the Minister of the Interior in its length and width because he only takes orders from the king and here he was opening it before a man who wasn't more than a hand-span high? Because he was an American and he came from Congress and he was wearing shorts? I didn't tell him: There's no trace of them, Uncle. I didn't tell him they're all dead. In the notebook or not. I went down to the courtyard to dig up the dirt. And that was how, for the first time since yesterday, I remembered the ring. I knew God had put in my path everything I needed. I also remembered I couldn't get it off the dead man's finger because of the night and the dog and Baba Ali who ran off and all the other things. I could sell it. I saw that God was looking at me with the eye of compassion. And Zina was waiting. I also saw I wouldn't disappoint her. She'd see she'd done a good thing by coming. *There is no power and no strength save in God.*

The hole and the lime and the clay were dug up. There was no trace of him in the courtyard. God doesn't close a door without opening others. The man was dead yesterday but here he was no longer dead or alive. And the hole with its soil overturned, that was how I found it in the courtyard with no trace of the dog. *In the name of God, the Merciful and the Compassionate.* Did the earth swallow him? Or did he move to another hole?

In the corridor, I lit the lamp so I could see him returned from his hole. With his lime and soil. The door was open. And he was sitting, alive. With his wife waiting for him at my house. Only yesterday he was dead, as he should be. But the morning dawned and here he was alive because his wife came asking about him. May God be praised. He wasn't spread out on the slab. He was sitting, turning toward me with his disgusting eyes. I didn't like his eyes. I put out the lamp and his eyes still shone like someone who didn't realize he'd died a few hours ago. And his eye wasn't worth more than four thousand dirhams in the market. The right or the left. Four thousand dirhams for a single eye. That was the price in the market. She was watching the TV show and waiting for him. My anger increased. This wasn't the time to think about eyes. I didn't have a ring or money or an eye and they weren't grieving. The man seemed in perfect health after twenty years of torture. As if he'd repaired all his parts in half a night and sat resting. My heart started pounding.

All the hatred of the previous night froze in my heart with its heat and sweat and curses. *There is no power and no strength save in God.* How would I get the ring I left on him? I felt my nerves tense up as morning wouldn't dawn until we'd rid ourselves of him. If I'd sold his eyes, he wouldn't have the chance to see me. Four thousand dirhams for a single eye. A thousand dirhams for Baba Ali so that his other half would be paralyzed. A thousand dirhams for my uncle so he'd know he didn't think badly about me, like I thought about him. And two thousand dirhams for the woman who came from Azrou on the night bus. In addition to the price of the ring. The delicious things that would come with it. All this causes happiness.

Would Baba Ali give me a thousand dirhams if he was the one who sold the eye? I'm the one who always gives him thousands upon thousands without him thanking me even once. And there he was in his house, paralyzed. His mouth was drooping toward his ear. God struck him with paralysis in his mouth because he's an infidel. I won't visit Baba Ali after today. He'll die alone like a dog. Is he better than all the ones we, me and him, tossed into the pits in the courtyard?

Yesterday, I left him in his hole. And here he is with those eyes of his, full of impudence. I know this kind of person. My uncle told me not to trust them. I told him as I looked over the door: "The Americans are waiting for you."

I opened the door completely. "Get up, Mr. Aziz."

This time I addressed him politely so he'd understand there wasn't any animosity between us. That we were brothers in religion and creed and lineage.

"Or do you want to die here in peace?" It would be better for him to die. It would be better for him to go to America or Brazil or to face some other calamity.

Then I remembered the ring. I saw it flash on his finger. The ring I left in his pocket as I was digging the hole. I heard him say: "Take it. The ring's not mine. I found it in the wall. May God be praised."

Here was the man who yesterday gave me the ring, but I didn't take it. And here he was back in his cell, waiting for me to come take the ring, and this was a miracle. So I prostrated myself twice to thank God for this, as they say. We were like the rest of His servants. We live to wait for death. And I was expecting anything from this cursed one. Even that he'd get up again and go back to his hole. These devils are capable of anything. I didn't go in to take the ring, even though it flashed on one of his fingers. So I didn't fall into his trap. Or the Americans'. Or someone else's trap. This was also a blessing. My life was upright from this perspective. I couldn't be blamed for anything. I perform my five prayers at the right times. And I fast during Ramadan. And a part of the month of Shaaban. I observe the traditions. And soon I'll pray every Thursday and Friday. When we're in El Hajib, me and Zina. In our new house. If God wants to say something, let it be and it is so.

The Americans came all the way here to look for him so why doesn't he go with them? No doubt he left his hole to go with them. Who'd take him except the Americans? That's what I told my uncle. When I took the ring, I went out running so he didn't go back on his word. I saw the short, small commission with the thick glasses shake its head and say in American: "Good. Very good." I told the American we've found him and he's as well as can be. He was only waiting for the order to leave, which my uncle will sign off on when the time comes. And other things like that.

5

This time I forgot too. Did I lock the door or leave it open? I always have a problem with the door. I always leave and come back to see if I've locked it or left it open. It's a problem, I swear. I'm in the taxi heading to Midelt. With the numbers in my pocket. And all the horses in my head with their names and weights. After four hours, everything's changed. I won't go back to the casbah. Let my uncle do with his casbah and his prisoners whatever he wants. Because we won't ever finish with this story. They kept coming for twenty years and they'll keep coming for a hundred more. I won't bear their sins after today. The day when man opens his eyes and sees has arrived. This is a great day. My heart is beating to a special rhythm for the first time. There's no need to go to Mecca for God to pardon you. You say it with your heart and that's it. In the upcoming long winter nights, Zina will be sitting with me and listening to my incredible, unbelievable stories. It's not important anymore for my wife to give birth to a girl or boy. We've forgotten all this. I'll tell her before I divorce her. Good men are for good women and wicked men for wicked women. For her to understand the meaning of producing something she doesn't want from her womb. And afterward, I'll go to the countryside because Zina loves the countryside. She likes the long winter nights in the countryside. *There is no power and no strength save in God.* In the taxi I remembered the door again. I can't go back in any case because the Americans have come. And they'll take their prisoner with them. And that's it. And the lime we were tossing on them doesn't have a role anymore. Because the last fear was carried out with the coming of the small American commission.

When I got out of the taxi. When I went into the barber's and sat on the chair. Like that, without introductions, everything ended. In one fell swoop. *Taf!* The lights went out.

18

Aziz

12 p.m.

1

I SEE HER COMING DOWN with the waterfall of light, sneaking through the peephole, between the roots of the palms bracing the clay roof. As if she's coming down with water. She waited long enough that night dissolved and darkness turned to light. Then, on what remains of the ceiling drowning in calm darkness, I see her moving. Or taking a stroll, as if in an airy courtyard. Her hair spread out, her hands isolated, flying. Her hair as it was, wheat colored. Surrounded by a halo of light she attracts from outside. Her thin body sways with the sway of the thin white cloth. I close my eyes. Her breasts under the cloth laugh. I reach out my hand to her but she doesn't come down from her heavens as I expected. She sits down cross-legged above me, in the air. She's looking over me. Or maybe she's relaxing after the exhaustion of a long and tiring trip. I sit on the cement basin watching her. I watch her next steps. Zina didn't like planes or flying in the high air. But she loved the big wheel at the fair that was once set up in the square. I took her to it and we took our seats in the incredible wheel. I didn't pay attention to it as it was spinning around. When Zina was there, everything disappeared. Neither the wheel, nor the men flying with us, nor anyone else was able to turn my attention from her for a minute. I was looking at her hair flapping in the air. At her smile, her delight in the dizziness the wheel made as it spun around. She let out a cry between happiness and fear as the wheel dropped to the ground. I loved Zina. I loved everything about Zina. Her happiness was the happiness of a fifteen-year-old girl. I find myself smiling without realizing it as I tell myself I'm lucky because I met Zina at a time when I needed her. As if I'd lived in Stork Bar for months, only to find her there one morning. Having her next to me is enough. Zina was the first girl I knew. Another girl would never fill my eyes after her. I found what I was looking for. What I was looking for was something like the dizziness of the wheel. After the wheel made another turn, I saw I wasn't the one who was smiling. It was her smile reflected onto my face and my lips whenever she beamed next to me. I carry in my heart a small paradise whose name is Zina. This is something that makes me sad too. I told her I'd buy her a gift when we left the fair. She didn't hear me. Two nylon socks or a handbag from the bazaar. But she didn't hear me that time either. Why don't we go to the cinema to watch Abdel-Halim Hafez sing "Tell Me Something, Anything." I yelled in my loudest voice: "I'll buy you a bottle of Rêve d'Or perfume." Finally, I told myself that what with the wind and the dizziness and the spinning wheel she couldn't hear what I was telling her. I kept following her happiness.

Why doesn't she come down from her heavens?

I go back to the roof. All of a sudden she disappears, only to reappear, this time near the door. With her two braids hanging down on her chest. Her two braids on her chest rise and fall calmly with the rhythm of her eager waiting. I don't ask her to come in. She's looking at the washbasin gravely. As if she's thinking. I don't see the expressions on her face because she's in the darkness. I don't move. I close my eyes. I pretend to sleep so she calms down and comes closer. This place and its stenches don't have to disturb her. It's better she stays at the door for a moment until she gets used to it. In this delicious slumber where I see for the first time beautiful things, I hear the voice say: "Get up. Get up. You're free, you . . . The Americans have freed you, you son of a bitch. . . ."

2

They were all laughing in the snack bar because I don't like landing. I hear their laughter in my ears spinning around.

"How do you do it, Aziz? You're good at taking off but not at landing?"

I say nothing. I envy Captain Hammouda because he has an opinion about everything. How was he able to learn all these things? Where does he get all this information? Did I grow up in a well? Sometimes when I find something important in one of the newspapers, I memorize it to recite it to my colleagues. But when I'm among them, I discover that my attempts to memorize it were futile and it's been wiped away like dust scattered by the wind. Even when I have an opinion I don't express it for fear I'll stir up the scorn and hatred of those around me. Because Captain Hammouda will object. He'll ask me: "Where'd you get that nonsense?"

Captain Hammouda's my friend and he says what he likes. He speaks his mind without worry. He can turn white into black and black into white.

All this disappeared one day when the colonel put his hand on me gently. A number of times, the pilots saw me with him in the snack bar drinking coffee and chatting. The colonel asked me, as they were listening, about my family and if I was married. I told him I wasn't. Then I told him I'd met a girl named Zina a few days ago. The colonel said he was happy to hear this news (as the other pilots listened) and asked me to introduce her to him. We then ate lunch, Zina and I, at his house. Yes, at the colonel's house, the head of the airbase.

Once as we were drinking coffee, he told me he understood my misery and the wretchedness of young people like me because we live in a world where we have nothing. We're miserable so others can be happy. Is that why God created humanity and exalted us? I didn't understand much of what he was saying or what he was aiming at. But I was happy with him. In my bed, I cried from happiness and I hoped I was at the level of deserving his trust. He invited me to his house a number of times and I ate dinner with him among the members of his family.

I told the pilots in the snack bar: "The colonel's the only person who opened his house and his heart to me and confided things to me."

With mouths agape, they swallowed every word. Yes, he confided to me unsaid things, such as, for example, when he was a young man, he wanted to join the communist party. And that he went all the way to Vietnam after World War Two and met Ho Chi Minh personally. There are other things maybe I can't say because they're secrets between me and him.

I noticed as we were in the street walking side by side that the colonel and I were the same height, we were both tall, and felt the same sense of pride. The colonel and I come from the same region, almost. He's Fassi, stout, and never laughs. He told me he the jokes he makes are the talk of the airbase for the whole year. I didn't know if he was always like this, or only when I was with him. I think he did it to make our connection stronger.

Once, a woman came asking about her husband, a colleague of ours at the base. The colonel called him and before he left him with his wife, he told him: "Whenever you want your grand, I've got it." He left the woman asking about the grand, asking her husband how he let himself hide money with his boss while they're drowning in debts up to their ears? Whenever he tried to explain it to her, she pulled her hair out and slapped her cheeks. There was no way to explain or interpret the colonel's intervention. Another time, he told a woman who came asking for her husband, a pilot, but she hadn't found him at the base. "Your husband?" he asked. "Who? Pilot so-and-so? He's married to someone else," he said seriously with the same Fassi accent. We turned, and all of a sudden her husband was coming toward us and she threw herself on him, dug her fingernails into his face as the colonel and I stood there watching. Then he winked at me and we took off, leaving the two of them. But the strange thing in this story was that the pilot apologized to his wife because he really was married in secret. The colonel swore he hadn't known about it and that he'd said it only in jest.

Between morning and night, the position of the pilots changed. Their stares were no longer haughty. Or malicious or mocking. As for me, they didn't act the same way anymore. The moment I came into the snack bar, they rushed over to ask me about the colonel: What does he eat and drink at his house? Is his house like any other? How many servants does he have? What do you do when you're together? Sometimes I didn't respond if I didn't feel like it. I saw they'd come to respect me and show their enjoyment at every word I uttered. That was how I started hating them. I hated them as I hated my father and my uncle before. Suddenly, I came out of my shell. Some things that I didn't know about, the colonel made me aware of in our private sittings. Often he put his hand on my shoulder and I felt its strength flowing inside me. His hand was strong, manly, and compassionate, like the hand of a father I didn't have. I'd have kissed it if he let me. With love. With passion. When I was with him, I was no longer as I was, shy, silent, loving privacy. I drank his words to the end, word by word:

"Our exalted officers call me severe. They're right. Justice is severe. Moral excellence is severe. All the basic things in people's lives must be clothed with severity so we can change something in this country. Is it just that a handful of officers and businessmen exploit the riches of the country and live on incredible returns from fishing without seeing the sea or from quarries without seeing a stone and building palaces on shores they visit ten days a year? Most of them have foreign citizenship and, with illicit money, they buy luxurious houses overlooking Hyde Park or the Champs-Élysées or on Fifth Avenue in New York. I'm among the few who say we have to cleanse the country from these parasites. I went once to a poor family to hear what they had to say. I spoke with the head of the family for a long time. Do you know what he told me at the end, that simple man? He said if only he could kill them with his bare hands and toss their bodies to the dogs. But he has no opportunity, no weapons, and no power. I'm not like you, an officer in the army, he said. I have all the weapons I need, machine guns, tanks, and airplanes. Yes, the simple farmer said this with sweat on his neck, which bulged until it almost exploded."

At moments like these, I heard his words and an intoxication like a storm before it blows overwhelmed me. I became strong, terrifying. I could move mountains if he asked me to. I saw him sometimes in his office frustrated, broken, and I asked him what was wrong. He remained bent over for a moment, staring off at empty space more than he looked at the papers in front of him. He asked why it wasn't permitted for soldiers like him to become parliamentarians so their voice could reach the people who didn't know what was happening around them.

3

"This is your day, Aziz. And tomorrow is our day, all of us," said the colonel as we were heading to Azrou.

A week ago, suddenly and unexpectedly, after all the friendship and affection he spread before me, he called me into his office. My forehead was sweating when I saw his darkened face. He said he was angry at my behavior. The world went dark before me. The slanderers and enviers got between me and him, that's what I thought at that moment. Then he said: "You're an upright young man. I appreciate uprightness in a soldier above anyone else. But I'm angry because you didn't invite me to your wedding."

I became embarrassed and I blushed and told him: "You're the first person I'd invite, my colonel."

I didn't understand this sudden change in his behavior. As I didn't understand his change seven or eight months ago when he told me: "Forget the plane. Forget the sky, Aziz. The ground is better for you." I spent a dark week after that before he called me again and asked me how I felt after being forbidden from flying for a whole week.

The water of friendship flowed between us again.

Should I understand his vicissitudes as a series of tests? Maybe he did that with other officers as well. Then he said, as we were heading to Azrou: "Today is your day and tomorrow is our day, all of us. Tomorrow will be a great day you'll remember for your entire life."

The driver was gripping the steering wheel as we were in the back seat talking. In the black Mercedes, like two close friends. Yes, he took me next to him in the state car so Zina and Khatima saw us. So everyone saw us. We got out together, me in the captain's uniform. With brass pearls sparkling under the morning sun. The colonel was in a uniform splendid with medals and majesty. The colonel in the flesh and blood had come all the way to Azrou to greet everyone. All that and with his hand on my shoulder, as if he was my father. And he really is my father and more. He honored the house of Lalla Zahra, despite how she is. He drank a glass of tea with us. Before leaving, he told me: "Don't forget tomorrow. Tomorrow is our day, all of us."

That was enough to make sleep flee from my eyes. Inside me was a current eating me up with fear and worry about tomorrow. I didn't have a problem with myself anymore. We were all in the same boat. A single concern unified us, the colonel told me. This doubled my anxiety and my apprehension. I couldn't take any steps forward because I was always hesitating. Is this the right step to take? To save the country, as the colonel said. The country's counting on us. He and me. As if veils had been covering things and were lifted all of a sudden. I am the colonel and the colonel is me. I spent the night in my

195

uniform. I had every hope of spending an unforgettable night with Zina, but couldn't do even that. As soon as I put my head on the pillow, I saw the plane. I didn't take off my uniform, afraid sleep would take me if I didn't feel it on my skin. I told Zina I had to go back to the base. Without telling her about what we were going to do. Nonetheless, I lay down for some time, and with the first signs of dawn, I jumped out of bed. Zina and I looked for a long time for my gloves, to no avail. I took Zina's face between my palms and told her she only had to lift her eyes to the sky in the afternoon to see me flying.

I reached the base at around two and the colonel hurried over to me with his face pale from anger. He screamed: "What are you doing here? Get over to your plane."

This change in him terrified me. I ran without feeling I was running toward the plane that lay near the storehouse waiting for me. It had been waiting for two days, nervous, angry at me. The other pilots were flying above us. I joined them. I flew. I went far away. I went high. The plane's engine played in my blood like music. When I heard the shots and the colonel on the radio ordering us to attack, a pleasure like an intoxication of the heavens took hold of me. "Crush them," said the voice on the radio, "Aim at the plane under you." The colonel was my father, my leader, and my guide and his voice was in my ears: "I'm one of the few who says we have to cleanse the country of these parasites."

If I died, I'd die a martyr because I did what I was supposed to. And the voice of the simple peasant: "If I could, I'd kill them with my bare hands and toss their bodies to the dogs." When I started firing, I felt as if the souls of the humiliated and the victorious took control of me. There's nothing better than the vastness of space to hear the reverberations of the bullets as they echo, making multiple cracks. The spirit of the sky seized me. Or the blue disease, as Father Joachim would call it when he was a pilot in the war. When the blue disease takes control of you, you can only submit to it and obey. I squeezed the trigger of the machine gun without any concern except what the disease that had taken control of me dictated. I was liberated from my fear. I was liberated from my doubts. The colonel chose my liberation in this form. I welcomed the bullets echoing under me and to either side. To the creative anger leading my hand. The lure had disappeared and there was no longer any land or sky. It's the moment one chooses to say he doesn't need to eat, drink, or sleep anymore. He doesn't need anything anymore. He's ready for death so someone or a handful of his officers and businessmen don't exploit our resources and use them to build palaces they don't live in. I'll die a martyr because I did what I had to, and what the colonel would have done if he hadn't been our leader and the torch that would light our path toward majesty. A viciousness I hadn't known was in me woke up in all its vigor, intoxicated me, and filled my veins with a holy fire, filling me with an indescribable happiness. I fired on the grounds of the airport with its buildings and heard its glass flying everywhere in my head and I turned on the walls of the royal palace and attacked it with all the violence I had. I wrote my name on it bullet by bullet and I bombed its wings and bricks and plants and pool and branches and water and air. I heard on the radio a voice ordering me to land but I didn't land. I was in my world. In my sky. I don't know how a pilot lands after he's flown.

19

Zina

A Few Minutes after 4 p.m.

1

I'VE ARRIVED. HAVE I REALLY made it? And where am I? My body tells me I'm where I've got to be. And I, until now, don't know why I followed the guide Benghazi to his house. Did I have another choice? His looks before leaving the house also told me I've reached my final stop. I wonder if I've really made it. An abandoned casbah that still stirs up the curiosity of some tourists. The man who came yesterday to the bar spoke about a season of flowers and a casbah. Is it the casbah he meant? He handed me a piece of paper without any date, the wrapper for a pack of cigarettes with "We're in danger, save us" written on it and without any signature. Is that enough?

We got off the bus and the woman going back to her first husband and I stood in what looked like a square with a lot of people in it. Men and women and a number of taxis. A cart carrying oranges. And a butcher. And a cheap café with a number of tagines set up in front of it. Behind us were some low houses and in front of us were some bald mountains with God Nation King written lengthwise in stones stained with lime. Most of the men rode horses and wore white djellabas and yellow slippers with daggers sparkling under the sun in their belts. And the women had kohl-rimmed eyes. With tattoos on their chins and the happiness of the festival they were heading to in their faces. They didn't know yet the man who would be theirs. That was why they stole glances at the cavalry and laughed as they put their palms on their hearts. Trilling, songs, and banners. A man who was with us on the bus said, "After a little the dancing and the Berber marriage, dances will begin," and he shook his shoulders laughing so we would know what he meant. We walked to the intersection outside the village and the woman pointed at the casbah erected in a spot bare except for a few palms and she went back to the village.

And here I am, in Benghazi's house, as if I'm standing in another world. Oh, I've come all the way here and in such a short time. My body tells me there isn't another village or another casbah after this one. There isn't another desert after this one. My body doesn't feel any exhaustion. New things tell it what to do. In a house like a hut, I stand between a living room and a bedroom. I don't hear the noise of the twins as they jump around the television. There's a lit lamp and a brazier and incense and the smell of spices in the room. There's also the guide's wife, spread out on the mat with her wet hair hanging down in a mess on her face. As if she's sleeping. I say to myself: I have to leave this house. What am I doing here? But I don't leave. Are they the spirits keeping my body from moving and making it turn against me without me realizing it? Instead of leaving the house, I go into the room. I reach my hand to the woman's face and wipe away her sweat. When she opens her eyes, I smile at her to encourage her and to wish her birth goes well, whatever the sex of the baby. After I find myself like that, a stranger in a strange room, in front of her questioning glances, I say: "I've come looking for my husband. He disappeared twenty years ago. But he isn't in the casbah, as your husband told me."

It seems as if she doesn't hear. Then I say: "I don't know anyone in this village and your husband told me . . . ." But she isn't listening. "I could spend the night in your house if that's okay with you . . . ." But she isn't listening.

The sight of her lean breasts attracts me. This makes me uncomfortable in myself and in my body. The first sign of change I feel, without knowing its shape, is hunger. A deep hunger like a big hole in my stomach. I've felt a hunger like this before. But I haven't thought about Aziz, as if I've lost hope of finding him. That's an idea I don't like. As if the germ of resignation has snuck inside me. Embodied by two dry breasts.

Then I find myself asking for food without feeling ashamed or shy. As if I'm at home with Khatima. Something is happening to me I don't understand. The woman reaches under the bed and gives me bread and olive oil. On the bottle is written in green letters: Oil of Blessing. Isn't this another sign strange things are happening around me? Everything that happens after this takes me from one surprise to another. I ask her about the midwife and she tells me that she normally goes to the hospital on her neighbor's mule. She doesn't know if it's time or not. She says she doesn't feel it is.

I say, as I see the muscles of her face tighten from pain: "It's better we go now." I am sharing something very important with her. I'm not a stranger in her house anymore. I smile at her and say things, but I don't know why I say them. The woman lifts the bed cover as if to resume something she'd begun before we came in. She pulls out a big, full package and a reed basket whose sides were made of cloth. We go out behind the house where the mule is waiting for us. I help her get on the animal. We put the bundles and the baskets on its sides.

This hasn't happened to me before. I discover that, for the first time, I am moving without intent and I'm not looking for Aziz. I don't know why I'm following a mule carrying a woman who will give birth far from her house. The twins are moving behind us. I hear them wondering if their mother will give birth to a girl or a boy. The first says: "If it's a boy, our father will come back home."

The second asks: "And if it's a girl?"

"He won't come back."

The first says she doesn't like boys. The other says she doesn't like girls either.

I am surprised by how the mule can find its way along the edge of the cliff without looking where it is putting its feet. We stop a little for the woman to relax. A strange calmness fills me. I can smell the peppermint and mint mixed with other scents. The scent of stone pine trees always reminds me of the morning at the summit of a mountain, spreading like a light drizzle. I look at the plants sprouting up around my feet and I stand on each of them to recognize them and the simple life they are nourishing. Migrating birds cross the sky, forming a symmetrical triangle. Some kind of disturbance spreads in my body. Is it the altitude? Or the nice scents? We keep moving. It's as if the entire world is shrinking down to just me, the woman, and the fetus she is carrying in her belly. Even the noise of the twins behind me diminishes little by little, and then disappears. I only hear the movement of my going forward to the rhythm of the mule's hoofs and the shaking of the woman on top of it. And the fetus, what's it saying now? Does it like this shaking?

2

Khadija discovered that the turtle she thought was female was in fact male. When she had completely given up hope about it, she took it to the souk and got another one they said was female. And, after four months, it did lay six small round eggs. The next day, Khadija remembered the hawk, so we waited for it but it didn't appear. Six eggs were lined up, one behind the other, and after two days there wasn't anything left but shells tossed on the roof. Khadija cried, saying she didn't think about hiding them from the hawk's eyes under wooden roofs or between flowerpots or changing their position because she thought their alignment this way would adhere to the customs of turtles. Lined up, one after the other, in a unique system, like a knot. And it wasn't enough for the hawk to devour eggs. It pierced the head of the turtle as it was defending its offspring that hadn't seen the light of day. When I went up to the roof,

I found the turtle turned over on its back like a stranded ship, empty, with worms coming and going out of its holes and what was left of the eggs it had laid a few days ago next to it.

I didn't feel the same hopelessness overwhelming Khadija. At twenty-four, I still clung to the hope of finding Aziz with both my hands because, whenever I put my head on the pillow, I heard him say he needed me. There was no one other than me who could save him from his darkness. And what surprised me was no one knew where he was. Ministers, heads of cabinets, lawyers, heads of political parties both close to and distant from the palace. No one. Then I contacted two members of parliament from the opposition who were getting drunk in a cabaret on Mohamed V Street in Rabat. They shook their heads and said: "Have a drink first, beautiful." No, I didn't despair. After more years of questioning, I stood in front of the village of a general whose integrity I'd heard a lot about. I didn't notice I'd grown up during these years when I was looking for the general and collecting information about his life and asking for news about his family and relatives and groping my way to him. I didn't notice I grew up as I waited with great desire for the moment I'd get close to his circle and put my complaint into his hands, dreaming my sufferings would come to an end at his hands . . . until I heard he built a farm on the outskirts of Meknès.

There, far from Azrou, on the outskirts of Meknès, a farm was being built. It wasn't far if I compared it to the six years I'd spent looking for this officer, the only man they said could find a solution for my problem because he was from the king's family and was charged with everything related to the royal palaces. I'd reach him in any case, if reaching him would lead me to some kind of result. Except for occasional moments of weakness that overwhelmed me, the fire of looking for Aziz and the certainty of finding him didn't leave me for a single day. The fire simmered down and flared up according to the seasons. According to the great deceptions and weak hopes each season brought. And the sweat? I stopped counting the days my bed was covered in sweat. Especially in the spring when a fundamental change happened to my body. I felt this in the disorder of my cells as I lay in bed. When Khatima saw the changes happening to me, she said: "It's true you need a man." The fortuneteller said the man refuses to return to his house on his own for one reason or another. In this case, all the woman can do is look for another man. True, your husband will not stay there in the depths of darkness until there's no ending. But in any case, what if he doesn't appear? I'm not saying Aziz will stay in his darkness all these years. One day, he'll leave for the light. Your husband is no exception. He's a human being and he loves the light like all human beings in the world. But if he refuses to appear? I agree with my sister and the fortuneteller. Light attracts all living beings that don't like the darkness.

I reached the farm early so I didn't miss my chance to meet the general. People worked here and there and I walked among them. For half an hour or more. A lot of workers. A whole army of farmers were planting trees and flowers. I stood on the side of their path. I didn't know if they were workers, farmers, or soldiers. Maybe a mixture. Why did they seem mostly the same? Maybe because of the blackness of their necks and arms as they stayed outside, bent over under the sun. I sat to take a break. I was thinking about the general and his wife after this distance I'd covered. After the recent information I'd collected. I felt my energy waning. The workers around me, close to me, were bent over, fixated on their plants, turning them over with their hands a number of times before they moved them to the ground very gently. An entire garden flowed in their imaginations as they bent over the ground. I stood up again. I asked them the way so I didn't go in the wrong direction and I headed where they told me. They didn't mention the general by name. When I asked one of them if the general had arrived, he responded arrogantly that he had been working in the farm of his "master" since dawn and had no time to waste to know if his "master" has arrived. Then his neighbor butted in, talking about the farm and the number of its rooms, which were more than a hundred. And about the dining hall that would be built above the pool of rare fish. The other added that when guests came, they'd savor their banquet as they watched fish from all the continents swim under their feet. He hadn't seen these strange things yet but they were working night and day before they moved to another piece of land to build another farm for another general. They spoke enthusiastically in order to appear like the ones in charge of this whole creation.

I haven't been doing any work for a long time. My sister's the one who works. Madame Janeau can't do without her now. While my sister's standing behind the bar, I sit at home planning the coming trip. And then I find myself sitting near the workshop, carrying optimistic ideas. As if our nightmare would end soon. Aziz's and mine. At any moment, I expected the general to appear before his house. The one I saw was his wife. She didn't look old because of the softness of her skin or maybe because of an air of sadness spreading from her eyes. Syllables came to her lips but they were broken because she was a foreigner. She listened to my complaints in the entryway that was wide like a stadium, with much commotion and noise because of the ironsmiths, carpenters, and men putting ornate plaster on the ceilings. She went back inside after my words ended without me knowing if she'd gotten anything from my complaint.

She wasn't gone long. Because the general appeared behind her yelling excitedly. The workers stopped their work so he didn't waste a single syllable he was saying, the general I'd spent long years searching for. I heard him now, yelling in his wife's face: why had she received me at her house? Looking at the woman's bent back, I saw she was crying. Did she want to destroy his house? Were we accustomed to receiving these kinds of people? What happened to his wife that she forgot herself and subjected herself, their life, and the lives of their children to danger? Did his wife not know my husband was going to kill the king if God hadn't been kind to him and to us? She cried. I froze in my spot. I became a piece of ice. As he threatened me and said he knew how to deal with the likes of me . . . He then turned to the workers. Why did they stop working? The noise returned as it was, screaming, violent, piercing the surface of my ears.

I went back, dragging my feet among the workers and farmers who weren't paying attention to my disasters. For a number of days, I'd wondered what would happen when I finally faced the general. I wasn't sleeping at night and I was spending the days turning the matter over and over. I imagined all the possible endings except for this, as it always happens. I then said to myself: I just have to forget this episode. I know I'll get past the state of temporary frustration because I'm thinking about Aziz. I'm sure I'll wind up finding him, as the fortuneteller said. I had to cling to all the paths I'd taken until now and forget about the one that led to this man's farm.

As I moved away from the farm, I heard kids at the bottom of the river yelling out: "Aziz . . . Aziz." It filled me with surprise and then it made me happy. The name rang in my ears at a time when I needed him. The child whose name was Aziz disappeared behind the tree trunks. He asked me to be quiet, putting his index finger to his lips. That made me laugh. He might have been twelve or thirteen. The other kids kept yelling at the bottom of the river: "Aziz . . . Aziz." They found him easily and pushed him in front of them. Where were they going? These devils didn't say where they disappeared to, so the torrent might have swept them away or a tree branch dealt one of them a heavy blow. Maybe they had a meeting with some girls in the woods. Who knows with these little devils? Maybe they were going to the river to bathe. Was there a river in this area? I'd find it if it existed. But I was severely exhausted. My head was heavy as if it wanted to abandon me so it could get rid of its burden.

Khatima handed me a small piece of cheese, saying: "The one who needs to be gotten rid of is Aziz."

3

Then Khatima said, as she looked through the window, "Look."

But I didn't see. Then she said: "There, under the grapevine. On the other side of the street."

Then I saw him. He was standing where she said. On the other side of the street, not far from the soldiers' houses. Yellow walls with brick roofs rising over them above which storks built their nests. Old dilapidated houses from the days of the French. Families spent their lives between these walls in hidden peacefulness. You almost didn't know they were there except for the washing spread out under their windows or in front of their doors. It's the fourth day, she said. She saw him under the grapevine when we left for work. Why didn't I see him too? My sister also saw him when we came back. Late, since we now worked together at Stork Bar. She said: "He's following us all the way to the bar."

He didn't leave his spot until we left the bar. Except for this, he didn't go anywhere. She didn't know when he ate or drank. She didn't know if he had things to do, like everyone else.

I too started seeing him every morning. It continued for days. I noticed afterward the times he was there weren't fixed, as Khatima said. He left at different times, and it was impossible to discern a fixed schedule or a set plan. He might sit until noon and then disappear for the rest of the day. He might come at a later time, at sunset for example. He might not come for an entire day, or two. He might spend the day standing, watching the bar door. I told my sister he might have news about Aziz. My sister said: "The man's sending information about your movements in reports he gives to his bosses."

What was he writing about? There's nothing in my life someone could write about except me looking for Aziz. What good would these reports be? The goal's to sow fear in your soul. There isn't any other goal. It's possible I felt fear in the initial days or the first year following Aziz's disappearance, but mainly I felt anger. So I went down from the house and crossed the street, heading to the tree where he was standing. When he saw me cross the road, he took a step back, confused, then when he realized I was heading toward him, he moved away, shaking, as if I was going to arrest him. He stopped when I stopped. When I got under the tree, he disappeared behind the residence block of soldiers' families. Maybe he went into one of their houses. I said he might be a relative of one of the soldiers' families. A number of times, I saw him talking to one of them. He might be an uncle of this girl or that. A number of times I saw him playing with their children. There was the young girl who brought him food. She too didn't have a set time when she came. A girl who wasn't yet eight, with a neglected appearance and shabby. I didn't see her go in or out of any their houses or come out but she wasn't very different from the girls of the block. It wasn't very different in the following weeks. When I was going to work, I'd take short strolls around the block of soldiers' residences or in the nearby neighborhoods. I'd turn to see him behind me, washing off the walls. Then when I was coming back home afterward. And when I stole a glance, I usually saw him coming back under the vine. I wouldn't have noticed this vine if it wasn't for him there under it. I hadn't noticed it before. As if it had sprouted up with him. Its leaves appeared and turned green with him still hanging around, its branches that were bare white before they took on a dark green color and wrapped the man in their shade. It might disappear with him. I then became interested in the storks. I noticed them moving around. They were above the entrances of the military houses, raising their young. It wasn't yet time for them to migrate. Where do they go when they leave the brick roofs? Only God knows. I noticed he always wore the same clothes, not changing them with the change of the seasons, the same gray pants and jacket.

These short strolls of mine, under the fig trees spread out along the main road of the city, lasted for years. A few steps separating us. The situation would seem strange at first before you got used to it. I stopped and so he stopped. I moved on so he followed behind me. He no longer made any effort to hide the fact he was following me. There were ten meters between us, sometimes less, as if he wanted to confide some secret to me. Then he'd backtrack, in a moment of hesitation, as if he'd changed his mind. The most overwhelming thing in all this was the state of knowing someone was behind you. As if you were walking in the street naked and everyone was watching you. Or something like that. In the morning, I'd open my eyes and remember the man waiting for me outside under the grapevines. As if I'd exchanged one waiting for another. Like two lovers. Two lovers of a unique kind. They cross the streets and roads, going under the mulberry trees, moving from this neighborhood to that, stopping in this place or that, thinking about the oppressive presence of each of them. A delicate thread only the two of them see binds them.

I was outside a lot. I took many aimless strolls. Only with a goal to feel him walking behind me. With a goal to feel something had come to bind me with Aziz. I felt his presence whenever the man was walking behind me. As if I got close to my goal. Khatima asked me whether I'd set my mind on a new husband. She wanted it to be like that. So she could stop worrying about me and say I'd become an ordinary woman. I told her yes, with a nod, pointing at the same time to the man standing under the grapevines.

4

The appearance of our father troubled me, surprised me, and disturbed my mind, so much that we forgot about the man standing under the vines. Father said he had worked very hard to find us. We didn't recognize him at first. When we realized who he was, Khatima asked him why he was looking for us. He said hunger and repeated years of drought drove him out. Our mother died and his second wife and her children went back to their family after he couldn't provide for them. So this was what had become of our father. He'd become shorter, his head small and bald, and his eyebrows white and thick. His misery didn't touch us at all. We left him at the house like we would any transient. We didn't respond to him when he asked where we were going every morning. The day he found out where we worked, he came asking Madame Janeau to give him our pay because he was our father and he had the right to oversee us and oversee our work. When Madame Janeau and Abdesalam kicked him out of the bar, he told us it was his duty to forbid his daughters from working at bars, even if by force or the intervention of the authorities.

Since we told Khadija this, she and our father became inseparable. They ate together and went up to the roof together and talked about turtles together. He bought her another turtle and built them a wooden cover so the hawk wouldn't see them. Together they came to wait for the eggs they'd lay. He bought a television, which they'd watch in the evening when the roof got dark and they couldn't keep watch for the hawk anymore. Khatima and I came home one evening and found the two having dinner and watching television. Khadija wore new white clothes. Our father said he bought her a dress from the souk for their wedding.

From that day, they started planning to kick us out of the house.

I was in the covered market checking out a piece of cloth when all of a sudden I saw them together. Father was with him, the man from under the vines who'd been writing reports about me, and the two were checking out pieces of cloth in the neighboring stall. They didn't seem to care about me. As if chance had brought us together. I then found them together in the evening, sitting and drinking tea at home. This time, I saw the man up close. So close that I could see every detail of his face. He was nearly forty, his clothes neglected, gray pants and jacket, tall, thin, and looking like the many drunks I saw every day at Stork Bar. His face was blue, his pupils black as if he was swimming in murky water. His hands trembling. Old age had settled on him though he can't have been older than forty. They became three, then, forming a circle around the table, eating sweets Khadija had made, drinking tea Khadija had prepared, and planning to file a complaint against us because the house was her brother's and we had no right to it.

Luckily that was when Madame Janeau chose to die, so we moved to her house.

5

We heard the king pass by our house. Helicopters were flying above our heads and the army and rapid-intervention troops were coming and going along the main road, sweeping it and painting the trees while we, Khatima and I, were looking over the road from the mountain above, wondering what the army was doing on an arid road with animals constantly being herded on its sides and only a few trucks passing on it from time to time. The villagers were wondering what was happening on the main road. This happened a long time ago. I was ten. The next day, we heard the king had come through, on the main road, under our house. We also heard that our neighbor, who was twenty, threw himself on his car and handed him a letter. We then heard that when the king looked at his letter, our neighbor, Mohamed, went to Rabat and got a position in one of the ministries. For a while, Khatima and I kept imagining him wandering every morning around the streets of a city lit up with different lights before going to work. Everyone in the city worked in the ministries. They walked the streets before going to work in their clean clothes. They went back to drink evening coffee on their balconies. I've never seen the king in my life. I thought about him when I remembered Mohamed's story. And here I am, waiting for him, as Mohamed waited for him twenty years ago, but without streets with lots of lights or people drinking coffee on balconies.

In another city and behind another tree, in an empty street, I wait for the king to come by. Without a letter. My letter is in my head. I memorized it well. I read it and I practiced reciting it so it became like water flowing easily in my mind. I'm hidden between the street and the barrier of plants. My heart beating, pounding. My entire body shaking. As if it is independent from me and from my mind. Just imagining myself standing in front of the king makes my blood freeze. In order to encourage it to regain its balance, I remind it what happened to Mohamed. From herding goats to an employee in the government. He might have become a director or general secretary. When you go to Rabat, it's to become an important man. Everyone's important in that city. I say this to calm my mind as I wait for the royal motorcade to appear. Then I tell myself that I'm not looking for a position. I'm looking for Aziz. You don't have anything to lose anymore after all these years. I tell myself: You're still hoping. It's not for me but for Aziz. Do you remember him? He was a pilot and he was with you. He disappeared fifteen years ago. The day after the night we got married. Yes, for fifteen whole years I haven't seen him. I might have been late in coming, but no matter. These are the words I think about from time to time, and they make me feel disturbed and troubled. My husband disappeared fifteen years ago somewhere and I only want to know where he is. That's what I'll say. I practiced my role for a long time. I didn't ask Khatima's opinion when I was first contemplating how to reach him. I brushed my hair and put it in braids that hang down on my chest, and I wore a short dress so I'd look like an innocent girl who'd stir up the compassion of anyone who saw me. What'll the guards do when they see a girl who looks fifteen cross the road to kiss the king's hand? I practiced some movements too.

At eleven thirty, I see him coming toward the golf course. I think at that moment of backtracking. I can't. I've been counting on this meeting. Isn't he the king? Can't he solve any problem? Am I not one of his dear people? We're your flock who you tell your guests you're proud of. There's a group of soldiers and policemen in civilian clothes and special guards around him. Foreign dignitaries. The place is different from how it was a little while ago. The men surrounding him are hurrying in every direction. One of them notices me and asks me to move away. I say: "I never saw the king up close in my life." This scene and this sentence, I memorized them and practiced them. He asks me not to move from my spot. I am shaking from top to bottom as I see him approach. A terrible weakness overwhelms me. Then the king appears, surrounded by his entourage. Very close to me. I run to him like an arrow. None of his guards notices until I drop to his feet and kiss his shoes. In the middle of the surprised procession. The officer next to him pulls out his gun and points it at me and then puts it back in his holster when he sees anger on the king's face. As if he was telling him you should have done that sooner. I tell him what I've memorized. From the first day we got married, then the next day when Aziz disappeared and all my attempts to look for him over more than fifteen years . . . and I cry. I haven't even thought about this. I didn't imagine I'd cry. I cry as I see the king affected by my state. He is repeating: *There is no power and no strength save in God.* He asks me for his name.

"Aziz. He was on the plane."

"He was on the plane?"

"Yes. On the plane."

"He didn't even know he was going to fly that day. He was on vacation. He asked for time off for us to get married. We got married without him knowing he was going to fly. That's why he went without his gloves."

"*There's no power and no strength save in God*. Where is he now?"

"Where is he? I don't know . . . in prison somewhere. . . . In the Sahara, in the sea, in the sky. Underground . . . I don't know."

"*There is no power and no strength save in God*."

One of the officers grabs me by my shoulders gently and takes me to his Mercedes, consoling me and saying that my problem will be solved today.

He says too: "*There is no power and no strength save in God*."

He then says the king will receive me in the palace as soon as he finishes with his guests. I imagine myself in the palace, sitting with the king and the queen and the princesses around a glass of tea, exchanging stories like old acquaintances. The officer starts asking me questions and taking down my replies in a big notebook. Family name and given name? Date and place of birth? Father's name? Mother's name? Her profession? Number of children? Schooling? I didn't go to school. Address?

Instead of the palace and a tea party, I find myself in a small room like a cell. There's a table with two chairs in it. Instead of the king, someone else comes in. He's wearing the same uniform the officer was wearing. Four hours later. He begins his series of questions. The same questions. He takes down my answers in a notebook he pulls out of his pocket. The same notebook. Family and given name. Date and place of birth. Father's name and profession. Mother's name and profession, if she has a profession . . . He asks me if I have a marriage contract proving I was married to this person I claim disappeared. I don't have the marriage contract with me because it's lost. A man attacked me at a hotel and he tore it up. It sounds very strange even to me as I say it. Then the man leaves. A third person appears late at night. I keep clinging to this hope. I made it all the way to the king. After fifteen years. I won't leave empty-handed from this adventure. This person asks me the same questions and takes them down in a notebook he pulls out of his pocket.

"Who told you the king was passing by?"

I'm not ready to answer this question and I say, "I was waiting for him to pass by for many months." It seems my reply convinces him.

He takes me in another car and goes in a direction I don't know. Darkness surrounds me, as do trees and a dark road. I go over the events of the day from the beginning. I start to wonder why the king's face changed when I told him about Aziz. Was he expecting something else? As the car cuts through the darkness, the sequence of events seems strange and alarming to me. As if I've fallen into some trap. For the first time, I feel fear. A fear maybe I kept hidden during the years I waited for Aziz. The car stops and the soldier gets out and asks me to get out too. The engine keeps running as I leave the car. I am waiting for him to pull out his gun. I imagine the echo of the bullet in the calm nighttime forest. I keep standing, waiting for the moment when my body will collapse and I'll feel the grass under my feet. Long seconds passed before I notice the car moving. That it's lighting up the sides of the road in the middle of the woods. That it's disappearing into the night.

6

When the newborn girl came out, I was ready without knowing it. Maybe my body was aware. We'd crossed a bend on the top of the mountain with a woman collecting wood nearby when the first signs of labor pain started. Together, we got the woman down from the donkey. We laid her down under a tree. The woman collecting wood lit a fire while I was getting the baskets down. I then sent the two girls deep into the woods to play. The woman reached her hand into one of her baskets, took out incense, and tossed it on the fire. When she brought her face close, the scented smoke rising up thickly around her sweating face invigorated her.

The woman was in labor now on top of the cover I spread out under her. Grabbing with both hands a rope hanging from the tree. The wood collector, who had hung the rope from a branch, was behind her. She straightened her back, telling her to push. The other part of the rope was in the woman's mouth so she wouldn't scream. The twins were among the trees, collecting flowers. I was in front of the woman, mopping her sweat with a wet rag. The shadows of the branches were moving above her face. I grabbed her thighs and repeated what the wood collector was saying. Push. Push. And the woman was looking at me with the same terror in her eyes as when we were in the house. As if the fetus had guessed what was going on in its mother's head and decided not to leave its mother's womb. I wonder why it was late coming out. The woman said her husband wouldn't come back home if it was a girl. The wood gatherer said it was better for her to be quiet and push. After an hour of torture, the girl still hadn't appeared. As if she knew what Benghazi had devised for her so she swore she wouldn't leave her mother's belly.

I became tenser. My body noticed a sudden fever spread to every part of my body and I began dripping with sweat too. As if I were swimming in a very hot bath. A strange pain squeezed my body as if I were melting from the inside. I stood up, terrified. I felt milk come out of a source inside me and rise up. I felt my breasts swell, and an aching pain came over them whenever their swelling increased. After a little while, they became like two full water skins. As if my pain extended to the pain of the woman who was biting the rope. After another hour of pain and screaming and fever and sweat and swelling, her water began flowing and the wood gatherer said: "Relief has come." When the newborn girl screamed, the milk from my breasts gushed forth. The twins came vying with each other and waving bunches of fresh flowers. They asked: "Girl or boy, girl or boy?" But they didn't get an answer.

I ripped my shirt and the milk flowed out like water, wetting my clothes and flooding the ground. The wood collector immediately took a knife and cut the cord connecting the newborn with her mother. The mother said her breasts were dry, with no milk in them for years. I sat and took the girl and put her between my hands and made her take my breast. The twins were watching the milk as it flowed onto the newborn's face and burst forth on my chest and her naked chest. Invigorating air played with my face. My body was relaxed now. It was devouring all the smells. The twins came near, wanting to drink from my milk. I told them to wait until their sister had her fill.

The mother asked me what name I'd give her.

I told her: "I still don't know."

I'm going back now to the station. Instead of the walk tiring me, it strengthens me. My breathing is even. I try to force my gait into a rhythm of slow breathing. She's wrapped up in a white cloth through which only her small red face appears, with locks of her thick hair. She's sleeping.

20

Aziz

7 p.m.

THE SENSE OF COUNTING I'd honed over the years was coming back. The car was moving quickly as I counted. I didn't care about the passing views because I didn't see them. Like someone who was not sitting in a fast-moving car. Like someone who wasn't there. I like counting. As in the past, but with real numbers instead of dripping water or pulsations of a festering limb. If I hit this number in this number of hours today, then in the number of months, then the years I spent in the casbah . . . . There was a bandage on my eyes and glasses over them, then the hood of the djellaba. Three darknesses. This made the process of concentrating easier. What I felt now was what a long-distance runner feels at the end of the race. The two men sitting in the front of the car weren't talking. I imagined them as accessories to what I was doing.

The car slowed down, turned right, and stopped. The engine shut off. The car door opened and the two men got out. Maybe they moved away from the car and maybe they didn't. I heard the rustling of grass under their feet. Maybe they were moving to make the blood flow in their veins. I felt a hand remove the hood, then the glasses, and then the bandage. I closed my eyes, and didn't open them for a while. Little by little the evening light snuck into them. Like the prick of a needle. I began to see as if through a fog. The car was parked in open space, under an isolated tree. The two men were a meter from me. They were sending glances to me, all of them curious. As if they were waiting to give a speech. One of them came close and greeted me warmly and the other did the same. They said together and at the same time: "Welcome back. The king has pardoned you and we're very happy. May God bless our master."

They took a step back. The two men were wearing white smocks. I thought they might be nurses, but I wasn't certain. I saw under the smocks military shoes and khaki pants. I thought: These two men aren't nurses. They were smiling and each of them was paying attention to what I might say or do. I wasn't thinking about this at all. I was still busy counting.

A Bedouin appeared without me knowing where he came from. There wasn't any house nearby. As if he'd sprouted up from under the tree. He was carrying a tray with a glass of coffee with milk, a croissant, orange juice, cheese, and a boiled egg on it. One of the men pretending to be a nurse put the tray on the car seat and stepped back next to the Bedouin. Before I put my hand on the piece of bread, Faraj the bird settled on the edge of the window. His appearance didn't surprise me. I told him I was sorry, joking, somewhat embarrassed: "We're not in a position where we can eat whatever we want. Our situation's very unusual."

The bird came closer and moved his beak. I was thinking about eating and then I pulled back. I noticed the two men were watching my movements. I said I had to appear normal as I was eating and not like someone talking to a bird and confiding in him ideas they might think were about them. The more they show interest and understanding and sympathy to me, the more my concern to eat normally increases. When I finished, the Bedouin thanked the two men for accepting his modest gift, picked up his tray, and left. This time I saw he was moving between the fields of mature wheat and disappeared little by little. The car set out again, tearing up the road and trying to get ahead of the cement. Through the glass, I could only make out the darkness of the night. This time they didn't direct words at me, not for a while. Then one of them turned to me, the man who wasn't driving, and said what I faced had to stay a secret. The country was surrounded by enemies. I was busy counting. The car stopped again and one of them said: "No doubt you know this region."

I looked around, trying to remember. There was a river and village lights on the other side, and a bridge. Was it the road my uncle was digging toward the capital? My sister Khadija told me a man knocked on their door one day and told my uncle's wife: "Si Mbarek, may God have mercy on his soul, he died."

"How'd he die?"

"Digging."

"And the road?" she asked him.

"He told her the road went all the way to the capital."

She smiled.

"Now, before seeing your family, you'll see the security official from the region," said one of the men hiding under the smock.

The car stopped before an old building erected on the side of the road. It seemed residential. With a normal façade and a normal door and normal windows. A woman was even spreading clothes out to dry, and children were playing on the stairs leading to the door. The official came out in full military uniform, raising his hands up high, with a wide laugh on his face as if we were relatives, and he kissed me on my left cheek and then my right. He said: "Welcome back." He wished me good days to come without problems. "The king has pardoned you and we're very happy, may God bless our master. He's the one who decided to send you to us to recuperate."

He then asked me: "Did you know where you were?"

I moved my head in a mechanical way without indicating anything in particular.

"No? You didn't recognize it? That's better for all of us. We too don't have any idea. No one knows. We all wondered, how this happened in a country like ours? But our country is noble and our king is merciful and thank God for all this. Maybe you hate—"

But I'd reached an advanced level of counting. I wasn't surprised that I had made it past three million. In the final stage of counting, you feel you've become light, you've finally shed everything around you. You look down on people, as if from a high-moving balcony. All your past has come down with the sweat running off you while you're counting.

There were many workers at the headquarters. I didn't know any of them. They all said hello to me. They pressed my hands warmly. Welcome back. We're all happy for you. May God pardon all sins. The local governor asked for silence as he stood under the flags. He thanked the supreme authorities, at the head of them his majesty the king, who insisted his generous pardon include me. The workers were shaking their heads as they clapped. The local governor then leaned toward me and told everyone to listen: "Be careful not to talk to the press. These people are only waiting for the chance to incite foreigners against us. They envy us for our order. For the stability we enjoy. They exploit every little thing to insult our heroic people."

He said in the end I have to forget and talk about what happened as a passing accident. That's better for him, for me, and for everyone. I forget and I act as if I . . . And he said their eyes are always open, they don't sleep. They observe everything.

I told myself the number I'd reached might be wrong. So I continued, I went back to my old ways.

When I left the office, the workers behind me left as well, with the local governor at their head. There, on the other side, a lot of people stood under lamplight. A pigeon flew from the top of the light pole. It flapped its white wings as it fixed itself in its spot. I knew from the way it flapped its wings it was Faraj, who had followed me all the way here. He flapped his wings and this time, he raised up a little and then came down and landed on my shoulder. I asked him if the others could see him and he shook his shoulders mockingly. He said: "Why do you care about them? Do you want to go back to the desperate situation you were in before? Look up a little."

I raised my head. "And?"

"What do you see?"

"The sky's dark."

"Other than that?"

"I don't see anything."

"Look closely."

"The moon."

"Maybe you haven't heard man's reached the moon?" I kept looking at Faraj, breathless and happy, not knowing where his sarcasm would lead.

"Do you know why man's reached the moon? Because life's better there. And because the moon's the last place for those who want to flee with their skin. Do you know this? You're a professional pilot. So you know flying isn't something you forget like riding a bike or using a typewriter. Right? Like knowing Moroccan Arabic."

I hadn't thought about it before from that angle. I wasn't in the right place to think about it. We laughed, Faraj and I. To make fun of him, I told him a dream I had when I was at the casbah. I told him I dreamt I was strolling on the moon. Between forests and waterfalls. With animals and people around me. Music. The only difference was that the people and animals looked alike. No difference at all. All of us walking on all fours. Suspended on the moon. Our feet above and our heads below. Like flies hanging on a roof. Faraj immediately exploded in a high chuckle he'd kept in so the others didn't notice. Their number had increased. Among them was the one who scaled the roofs of the clay houses, and also the one who scaled the trees.

I told him: "I'm not so miserable that I'd want to make such a harsh journey."

He said: "Wasn't all the information you collected about flying, either in schools or on your own, useful? Don't forget the efforts the Americans made so you could find yourself here. They need someone to explore the other side of the moon for them. Give yourself one last drop of courage. You won't go farther than your courage in any case. You won't regret the exhaustion. Go up. The great wave will carry you to another place. They'll push you to embrace infinity.

"When you seem convinced of it, ready for the adventure, when you leave the earth, many factors will work to change your weight, you'll increase or decrease your speed. For example, the weight of the shadow that might accumulate on your djellaba while crossing toward space might make you come down instead of going up. Then you have to wait for the next moment. If you hurry and leave now, you'll find yourself tomorrow, at the right time, at the right level, when the sun's at its hottest, making the shadow evaporate with a terrifying speed."

I told Faraj I knew all this. I worked out I would need five days of navigation through space to reach the moon. Faraj said mockingly: "What are five days compared to the years you spent tortured, sick, humbled, and jailed?"

On the other side, the number of people watching doubled. This time I saw my father and my uncle, my father's brother, among them. Not far from the nurses, the local governor, and the king with his entourage and all his torturers around him. This final view was what sped me up. I hit the air with my hand like I saw Faraj do, the djellaba inflated like a balloon, and I began to rise. They started hurrying and yelling for me to come down.

"Aziz, come down!"

"Aziz, where are you going?"

I was rising up and whenever I went up, I felt my chest constrict. But I know this happens to anyone trying to leave the earth.

I looked at the earth. The others appeared very small beneath me. They were still yelling. My uncle was accusing and threatening: "Come down, come down, son of a bitch." But I was going up. My father threatened: "Come down, you son of a bitch." The local governor threatened, as did the pasha, the mayor, and the king, all of them ordering me to come down. But I was flying in the sky. The sky was close. I had come down once but I wouldn't come down again. . . . As I rose up, they became small and their yelling and excitement diminished and their chances of grabbing me diminished. Until they disappeared entirely.

I then began to make out, in bewildering clarity, the gravity of the surface of the lit-up star. . . .

21

Benghazi
8 p.m.

I'M SPEAKING FROM THE MORGUE. And I didn't say this is death
until I saw it with my eyes in the mirror. You came with the
truck, right into the barbershop. The shirt was new and the
pants too. When I sold the ring I bought these things and only
the barber, who was delighted to see the cash, was left. He
said: "Sit on this chair." The chair's leather and soft, and only
respected customers sit on it. It's opposite the door, and the
breeze reaches it. But it was the truck that came in, instead of
the breeze. I saw death in the mirror coming from outside the
shop, getting closer. I said: "This truck's coming. That might
be its reflection, but if it keeps going like that, it'll come all the
way inside the barbershop.

In my mouth there's foam. I speak now from the storeroom
under the ground. Where they put me a while ago. I don't
see what's around me but I hear every movement. The wall's
complaining because it's been standing for so long and says
it's decided it will collapse in two days. Its neighbor tightens
its upper arm since it has been fighting with the owner of the
building. Oh, there's a line of ants passing near my legs and
talking about the nice day they had. A rat says to its neighbor
its children haven't eaten anything today and they're getting
close to me and smelling my neck. The water at the bottom of
the storeroom is singing monotonous songs because it's only
good for that. The driver looks over at me and tells the barber
he knew the truck brakes would fail one day.

There's also glass from the mirror in my head. And a piece of razor. But nothing else that will allow them to identify me. No papers, no contracts, none of the things that allow people to identify each other. And until now, no one recognizes me. If my uncle was here, he'd recognize me. They lift the cover, then look over and put the cover back on my face and move away (and by the way, the stench of the cover is unbearable.) My head's split open and in it are mirror shards, soap, foam, a piece of the razor, crushed like worn-out flesh.

After the driver left the morgue, the barber took it on himself to put his hand in my jacket pocket to take out the paper with the horse numbers. Will they recognize my name and address from the horse numbers? The name, address, and profession, all this, at my uncle's. With the heat of this exceptional year, my body will decompose quickly if some-one doesn't come to identify me. Or my wife doesn't come to bury me. Or the other one, as they call her, Zina. Is she in the square now, watching the mobs and hearing the songs? And who married who on this happy night? Did our turn come? Did they leave us a place among them to play music to honor us? The square's hot now and the fires are lit. Every groom takes his new wife to the tent and for all the things that come after that.

For her, I bought a shirt and pants. For her, I went to the barber. Will she too come and raise the cover to identify me? By waiting for this or that woman to come, I'm left waiting. Even for my corpse to rot. None of those who looked at me recognized me. The barber, the carpenter, and the transient, all of them said: "This man? We haven't seen him before." When they left, the barber put his hand in my pocket and took out the cash and I heard it go into his pants pocket. My family has no news about it at all. Seven girls, maybe eight, with their mother and huge debts. I didn't leave them anything else. Horses, dogs, and girls. The debts and the debtors remain. They don't die. We earned this at least. The most beautiful thing in this world is to die without repaying your debts. I'll see their miserable faces when they look over me too. They'll identify me from the first glance, but after it's too late. They'll spit in my face. That's all they can do. Even though I have a split-open head, and am dead on top of this, I won't care even if they care about me. The money the barber took. I don't feel any pain. The pain is outside. I'm relaxed because I won't pay those wolves a thing. And until now, no one appeared, not even my wife, to take my corpse from this cold place. There are two big rats in the corner consulting with each other but I don't pay their consultations any mind.

22

Aziz

Later

MY AUNT KHATIMA DOESN'T WANT to take the medicine. And I, from the door of the room, see my mother bring the spoon to her lips while my aunt refuses it, saying the medicine's hot. I ask my mother if my aunt's sick and she shakes her head no. She pushes me to the door. I come back to tell her I want to tell my aunt something. My mother shuts the door this time and my aunt disappears from sight. My mother and I go down to the bar and I ask her if my aunt's going to die and she scolds me. I go to the man sitting at the table and I tell him my aunt Khatima's going to die. My mother follows me and I run, disappearing behind the door. I hear my mother talking with the man and then she goes back to the counter. I come out from behind the door and hide under the table so she doesn't see me. I hear her tell me to come out. I'm under the table and I know she can't quite see me.

In the evening, when the men who drink come, there are a lot of feet so my mother doesn't see me at all. It's like that with my aunt. But my aunt's sick. She'll die because she doesn't want to take the medicine. I move on my knees to another table and I don't see my mother anymore. I see the man's two feet as they move around. As do his fingers. Is his face moving too? I move under another table. The man's face is turning to the bar. My mother's always sitting behind the bar, waiting for the sun to come in from the window and settle on her face. My mother likes the sun as it comes down on her face. She's looking at the man sitting at the table. From under the table, I see his feet. His shoes are old. I go over to his shoes and touch them. He moves his feet and my mother yells: "Leave the man alone."

I look at him and laugh. The man laughs with his old face. His face is like his shoes. I tug on his pants and tell him about my aunt Khatima. My mother scolds me but I tug on his pants again and run away. I wait for him to follow me. He doesn't. I hide behind the door, waiting for my mother to follow me. My mother asks me not to bother the man. My aunt, instead of the medicine, loves to drink sparkling mineral water because it relieves her pains. My mother is looking closely at the man. I tell her I want to tell him something. I wait to see what my mother will do.

She leaves the counter and goes over to him. She asks him if he wants a drink. I come out from under the table and tell the man I want a soda. She hits me on the shoulder and says, "Shame on you."

I laugh and run from her because she wants to grab me. The man says he doesn't want anything right now. Maybe later. My mother looks at him for a long time. She tells him his face is familiar. He tells her face is familiar. I laugh at their words. My mother takes a step back, rubs her nose, bites her lip, and gets close to him. She then goes behind the counter and looks for the satchel and comes back with a piece of old paper and puts it in front of him on the table. Part of a pack of cigarettes, like what I see on the tables of the men who come to the bar. The man looks at the paper breathlessly. Then he laughs. When she sits on the chair next to him, he says he has spent the past few years wandering. He moved between cafés and faces and forests and cities and bridges and alleys and villages. Hospitals and islands and skies. Especially hospitals. He remembered Stork Bar without remembering the address but the storks finally showed him the way. My mother says, "Storks come back to the nests they know."

The man says: "Yes, they know their nests. Before leaving, they put their scent on their nest so they recognize it when they come back."

"Did you follow them?"

"Yes, and I've arrived."

Their words are funny from start to finish. Storks are beautiful but their beaks are huge. When one of them hits its beak with the other, it becomes annoying. I leave them and stand at the door. There's less light than before, because the sun has started disappearing behind the mountain. I see the street is empty. Then it is full of people. My mother asks me what's happening. I tell her people are running around in the street. She comes and stands next to me. People in the street are running, not looking at us as we are looking at them. I go back inside without hiding under the table. I go to the counter and open the fridge and take out a bottle of soda. My mother doesn't scold me because she's standing at the door. I close the fridge. I come out from behind the counter and take a long sip. The man asks me: "Why are they running?"

I take another sip and shrug. My mother comes back in and stands next to me. I ask her: "Why are they running, Mama?"

"The king is dead."

"Like Aunt Khatima?"

"You aunt isn't going to die."

"Who's the king?"

'When you get bigger, you'll know who he is."

"I'm big."

The man turns to me and tells Mama: "It's true, she's big."

He touches my cheeks and I hit his hand. Mama says: "Shame on you."

I disappear under the table. I start looking at the men running in the street. My mother goes and lowers the blinds and locks the iron door on both sides so I don't see the men anymore. The noise and yelling and running continues in the street. This time, I see from under the table four feet instead

233

of two. I see that the man's feet have calmed down. I hear him ask her about my aunt Khatima and she replies: "It's the usual pain." I expect them to keep talking until I know why they're sitting next to each other. This time, I hear him tell Mama: "I owe you something." He isn't looking at her either.

My mother says: "What do you owe me?"

She takes my hands and brings me out from under the table and returns to her seat next to the man. He is looking at her but she, instead of looking at him, is playing with my hair. She puts me in her lap and keeps playing with my hair.

The man turns to me and asks her: "Who's this?"

My mother says, playing with my hair: "She's our girl."

"What's her name?"

"Aziz."

The man leans over me, wanting to kiss my cheek. His face doesn't look like mine. It doesn't look like my mother's. I wipe my cheek. She puts me on the ground. She keeps looking at the ground. And playing with her fingers. The man is looking at the ground too.

"How old is she?"

"Eight years old."

I say they know each other and I wonder why they're not talking.

"I owe you something." He is looking at her this time.

My mother says: "You don't remember what you owe me?"

She laughs loudly and puts her hand over her mouth.

Again he says: "I owe you something."

My mother's the one who bends her head this time. She tells me go play over there.

I tell her I'm going to see my aunt.

She says: "No."

I say I want to tell her something.

I go back under the table so my mother doesn't see me anymore. My aunt Khatima doesn't see me anymore. I hear the man say: "I owe you something." I look over at her. Her face grows red. I disappear again. I don't hear what they're saying anymore. I don't see their faces anymore. I see the man's hand moving and touching my mother's hand. I cast a glance at them between the table legs. The man's face is leaning over hers. His mouth is on hers and I think: This man knows my mother. He owes her a kiss. I laugh because he came from far away to get his kiss. I laugh because she gave him his kiss. I laugh because I am happy.

SELECTED HOOPOE TITLES

The Televangelist
by Ibrahim Essa, translated by Jonathan Wright

Whitefly
by Abdelilah Hamdouchi, translated by Jonathan Smolin

Time of White Horses
by Ibrahim Nasrallah, translated by Nancy Roberts

*

hoopoe is an imprint for engaged, open-minded readers hungry for outstanding fiction that challenges headlines, re-imagines histories, and celebrates original storytelling. Through elegant paperback and digital editions, **hoopoe** champions bold, contemporary writers from across the Middle East alongside some of the finest, groundbreaking authors of earlier generations.

At hoopoefiction.com, curious and adventurous readers from around the world will find new writing, interviews, and criticism from our authors, translators, and editors.